# THE CLAIM

Elisabeth Link, M.D

The Claim

# The Claim

*

## A Medical Mystery

Elisabeth Link, M.D.

ISBNs
Paperback 978-1-958277-05-8
Hardback 978-1-958277-07-2
eBook 978-1-958277-06-5

Library of Congress Control Number (LCCN)
2023947148

*M*onasteria Press LLC

# DEDICATION

*For the children with cancer and their families*
*I have served as a pediatric radiologist.*

# Acclaim for Elisabeth Link

*"A thought-provoking and suspenseful story by a talented writer."*

*"Captivating storyline with strong female role models."*

*"A timely and gripping reflection on the profit-driven healthcare industry."*

*"Lovers of mystery novels won't get enough of Elisabeth Links' intriguing plot."*

*"Elizabeth Link manages to entertain, engage, and provoke thought, creating a reading experience that lingers long after the final page."*

*"Truth, like gold, is to be obtained not by its growth,*
*but by washing away from it all that is not gold."*

Leo Tolstoy

CONTENTS

# The Claim

*

## A Medical Mystery

Elisabeth Link, M.D.

# PROLOGUE

Silicon Valley University of Evolutionary Computation (SUEC) was established in 2025 in the hills above Redwood City, California. SUEC realized a new model of collaboration between major tech companies and the state of California to develop cutting-edge technologies within the framework of a research-intensive university. Many innovations developed and explored at SUEC were years ahead of what was available anywhere else. SUEC owned a hospital in Redwood City, California, which was open to the public and provided cutting-edge medical care for adult and pediatric patients.

As the center of technological innovation in the world, generating billions of dollars in donations and revenue, SUEC was a constant target for spies, thieves, and other criminals. Therefore, the university had a large security team and sophisticated surveillance systems to protect its innovations, workers, and work products. In addition, the US government deployed undercover FBI and CIA agents to protect SUEC's assets of national interest and to identify any activities that might impair national security.

Over the past two years, FBI special agents Angus Weber and Terrel Wright collaborated with CIA undercover agent Dr. Annya Segond and SUEC radiologist Dr. Lili Pham to identify and eliminate security threats at SUEC University. Thanks to their outstanding collaboration, life at SUEC was currently calm and idyllic. SUEC researchers and clinician-scientists were focusing on their work and creating their next groundbreaking discoveries amid the beautiful scenery of the sunny California redwood hills. This was about to change as new crimes unfolded.

# - 1 -

# ANGUS

The Abduction
Saturday, October 8, 2033, 6:30 p.m.

Was it fate or chance? Wherever he went, he walked into a crime scene. Through sheer repetition and experience, he had learned how to deal with it and wrestle it down—most of the time.

FBI director Angus Weber steered his gray metallic Ford Mustang Mach-E up the rutted concrete ramp of the Sutton-Stockton garage in downtown San Francisco. The toll box in his car signaled with a beep that his car was registered at the entrance. The restaurant was just a few blocks away. Angus never parked directly in front of his destination. He certainly didn't want to endanger Annya, although she clearly could take care of herself. That was what he liked about her.

Angus drove to the second floor of the garage, backed into a parking spot close to the exit, and turned the engine off. By habit, he checked the surroundings. Densely parked cars and few open spots. Nobody in the Mercedes next to him. Another car leaving via the ramp. A mother dragging a crying child to a Fiat nearby. Two young people, hand-in-hand, waiting for the elevator. Nothing unusual.

Angus checked himself in the rear mirror and straightened his grayish hair. It had been a busy day. His stomach growled. Time for dinner. He stepped out of the car and followed the pedestrian ramp to the sidewalk.

The twilight of the early evening and the cool-wet gust coming off the bay saluted him. The San Francisco fog rolled into the city, whipping his face and tousling his hair. Angus closed his blazer and buried his hands in his pockets. Beneath his jacket, the Glock's cold steel pressed against his skin. He hoped he wouldn't need it tonight.

He had asked everyone at the Bureau not to disturb him for the next two hours. Unfortunately, he was never *really* off-duty.

Angus crossed the street in front of the Notre Dame Des Victoires Church, a stone building with a barrel-shaped bay and cross-topped masonry towers on each side. The stained-glass windows were illuminated from the inside, exuding singing voices into a cool evening breeze. He walked up Bush Street, passing by tall, heavily ornamented Beaux Arts apartment buildings and crossing the intersection with Stockton Street. A line of cars waited for traffic lights. A few pedestrians headed in his direction. A homeless man on the sidewalk held up a piece of cardboard—*Seeking Human Kindness*. Angus dropped a five-dollar bill in the tray in front of the man, who flashed him a toothless grin and thanked him with a blessing.

It was awkward to go to a high-end restaurant in downtown San Francisco. The contrast between the rich and the poor couldn't be more profound. Angus felt uncomfortable on many levels. But he had worked at the FBI headquarters in downtown San Francisco today, and this restaurant was close enough to minimize his downtime.

It had been a very long time since he had gone on a date. Twenty-five years, to be exact. He and Odette had been too young to create a family. A few dates, marriage, a son, divorce. She had thought she married into a *Criminal Minds* adventure, flaunting her special agent husband at dinner parties. Instead, he received a call, had to drop what he was doing, and went to work. *That's* what they both had signed up for. It had been a big misunderstanding.

Today would be different. Annya had a full life as an emergency room physician and undercover CIA operations officer at SUEC University. The CIA had recruited Annya at twenty-nine to help spot intellectual property theft by foreign entities at SUEC. Under the cover of her physician's job, she had uncovered several critical threats to SUEC, including a bomb attack. She was self-sufficient, independent, and *very* attractive.

Angus smiled when he thought of her confident look when she pushed her long red hair over her shoulder. Her molten copper hair cascaded down her shoulders in waves that danced like flames. Shaggy, untamed bangs framed her soulful emerald eyes, adding to her allure. Her athletic yet feminine figure was a sight to behold. She was the kind of woman who could make a man lose his breath. But it wasn't just her physical beauty that captivated him. It was also her aura of confidence and mystery. Annya seemed to know exactly who she was and what she wanted. She was a force to be reckoned with.

It took Angus a lot of persistence to get onto her schedule. They had to inform both the FBI and the CIA. No pressure. Annya was worth it. She liked him even though she'd hesitated to accept his invitation. She was weary of close attachments—too much risk. Just like him.

Angus turned right on Dashiell Hammett Street, a narrow, steep one-way street that connected Bush and Pine Streets. It was less busy here. On his left side, a line of cars parked along the sidewalk. A black cat trotted down the dimly lit path on the other side of the street, briefly gazed at him, and then disappeared in a small gap between the two buildings. A single van slowly drove down the steep street. A woman in a short blue coat walked up the sideway in front of him. Her long, wavy blonde hair and the briefcase in her hand bounced with every step.

To Angus' right, a red brick building emerged with a sign *Dashiell Hammett Place*. San Francisco writer Dashiell Hammett had lived here. Angus looked at the beautiful, illuminated foyer. Annya had planned to park close by as well. Perhaps they could walk back through this street, and he could tell her about his favorite crime writer.

A piercing cry filled the air. Angus looked around to locate it—the woman in front of him. The van had stopped. In a split second, a man with a black beanie and face mask jumped out and grabbed her. She dropped the briefcase and attempted to fight him off. The man pulled her into the van.

Angus tried to jump to her rescue, but the door slammed shut with a loud bang. He attempted to remember as much detail about the abductor as possible: stocky build, jeans, dark jacket, surgical face mask, half-covered mustache, wide-set eyes with bushy eyebrows, brown curly hair. It was too dark to make out more detail. The woman screamed again, then went silent.

Angus pulled his gun and jumped in front of the van. He aimed at the driver, who wore a black beanie and face mask.

"Stop! FBI!" he shouted.

The driver looked briefly at Angus. Angus didn't move. Was there a glimpse of hesitation in the man's gaze? Not for long. The van lurched forward. Angus jumped to the side and shot at the side window. The driver bent down, and the van tumbled to the right.

A woman at the corner of Bush Street screamed, "Shooter! Shooter!"

Several other people started screaming as well. Footsteps pounded on the pavement, people ran for their lives. He kept his eyes on the man. The driver corrected the course, and the van raced toward Bush Street. More people screamed and ran for shelter. Angus focused on the van and aimed for the wheels. He got one. Perhaps. The van raced around the corner with squeaking wheels. Angus ran after it. He heard honking cars in the distance. But when he reached the corner to Bush Street, the van had already disappeared.

Angus called his friend, Chief Police Officer Kendis Awololo, in charge of the downtown area.

Kendis immediately answered the phone. "Hey Angus, what's up?"

Angus shouted into the phone. "Adult victim kidnapped at Dashiell Hammett Street. Dark blue coat, blonde woman. Pulled into a silver Chrysler van. Tinted side windows. Two men with black beanies and facemasks."

"There are lots of silver vans out there," she said calmly. "Any identifiers?"

"The license plate was covered with a Mercedes paper sign— probably a decoy. I shot at the wheels and might have gotten one."

"If that's the case, they won't get very far. We have drones and cameras all over the downtown area. We'll find all the silver vans and check them out. Are you still in Dashiell Hammett? That street is only one block long."

"Yes, correct."

"I'm just a few blocks away. I will be there in three minutes."

A screaming police siren fired up in the distance. It was rapidly coming closer. Several people had opened the windows of the apartment buildings above him, watching or filming him with their phones. A few people peeked around the corners of adjacent streets. Angus slowly put his gun in his holster under an open leather jacket so that everyone could see it, keeping spectators at a distance. He ran back up the sidewalk to where the woman had been captured. The briefcase was lying on the sidewalk. He had to secure it.

"Are you really an FBI agent?" A man in an apartment building above him called down.

"I believe Universal Studios is filming here this week," a woman in a window next to him answered.

"I don't see a camera team," the man countered.

"Be careful. He has a gun," someone else called from the other side of the street.

Angus pulled vinyl gloves from his pocket, pulled them on, and explored the briefcase. A purse, no driver's license. A credit card. He read the name. *Dr. Frida Ending.* That was a start. There was an ID badge from "Pleonexia Health Insurance" with the same name. A cell phone in a pink case. A lipstick. A comb. THC gummies. Tissue paper. Several prints of medical imaging studies from SUEC. That was concerning. Angus took photos of all the items using his iPhone. He then put the briefcase back on the sidewalk.

The approaching siren stopped, and a police car with a rotating beacon emerged on the upper end of the street, slowly driving down the steep slope and stopping beside him. Spectators assembled in the distance. Kendis Awololo stepped out. A tall woman in a police uniform with four stars and four stripes. She greeted Angus with a brief nod and addressed the spectators.

"SFPD. If you saw a woman in a blue coat or a silver van here a few minutes ago, please come forward," she called with a loud, resolute voice and pointed at a police officer at her side. "My colleague here will also come around and interview everyone." She turned to Angus and lowered her voice. "Was this bad luck for these guys to kidnap someone in front of the FBI? Or is this a matter of national security?"

Angus shook his head. "It was pure coincidence. Although in downtown San Francisco, I might be more likely to walk down the street and witness a crime than *not* seeing a crime."

"I know what you mean," Kendis said. "We would need many more officers to get ahead of this problem. However, we have made progress in this regard in recent times. We have significantly reduced the number of aggravated assaults in San Francisco. In part, thanks to our collaboration with the Bureau."

Angus nodded. "Thank you for responding so quickly to my call. You know that time is of the essence in cases such as this."

Kendis adjusted her police cap. "Thank *you* for being in the wrong place at the wrong time. You are the best bet this woman's got. I'm surprised by this *coincidence*. Did you know any of the people involved?"

"No, I didn't. I don't think that this incident was related to national security. However, I will double-check that and let you know. There is a name badge in the briefcase and some medical files." He pointed to the briefcase on the pavement.

Kendis picked it up. "I will check this out. And my team will hunt down that van."

Angus nodded. "There is also a cell phone inside. Please check her latest messages, postings, photographs, and internet searches."

Kendis smiled. "Of course, Angus. This is not my first rodeo. I will inform you if we find anything that qualifies for an FBI collaboration. We could use your help."

"Sure, we can touch base in a few hours. As you know, the chance is slim that we will get her out of this alive, even if the kidnappers are after a ransom."

"I know. Our team will track the van down as quickly as possible. Can I call you around 10 p.m.? If we've got her by then, I could wish you a good night's sleep. If not, you can let me know if the FBI will assist."

"Sounds good." Angus put his gun back into his holster. "Meanwhile, I will check if this case might fall in our area of responsibility."

They shook hands, and Angus turned around, walking back to the Sutter garage. He didn't mention that the medical files in the briefcase were from the SUEC Hospital. SUEC was the flagship of healthcare innovations in the United States. SUEC filed the most exciting discoveries and new patents. Why were the SUEC medical files in the briefcase of the victim? Perhaps it was also a coincidence? If they were important to them, the kidnappers would have fetched the briefcase. Or were they unable to secure it because Angus had unexpectedly stepped in? He would find that out.

Angus checked his watch. 6:55 p.m. He had to call Annya and cancel the dinner. He couldn't sit on a plush seat, eat asparagus, and do small talk while it was unclear whether national security was at stake. He sighed. The worst part of disappointing her was the anticipation of disappointing her. He had plenty of experience in that department from the debates with his ex-wife. Angus braced himself for a flood of accusations as he dialed Annya's number. He knew that he was inconsiderate and unaccountable to let her down in the last minute. This was the end of the beginning. His heart sank as he heard her melodic voice.

"Hello?"

"Hello, Annya." He cleared his throat. "I'm terribly sorry, but I have to cancel our dinner tonight."

"Oh? What happened?"

"I witnessed a woman being kidnapped just three blocks away from the restaurant."

"Are you okay? Any injuries?"

*It was different dating an ER physician.* Angus brushed the sweat from his forehead. "Yes, I'm fine. The woman was dragged into a van. The police are chasing it."

"And you need to help with the case?"

"Actually, the victim dropped a briefcase that contained medical imaging files from SUEC Hospital. I assume it's unrelated. But I want to check it. I'm very sorry. I guess I could do it after dinner, but I just cannot sit at a table while this is going on. I would never forgive myself if this woman died in the meantime."

"Of course. Do you need my help checking the files?"

"If you don't mind?"

"Sure. See you at SUEC Hospital in about thirty minutes. We can meet in the radiology reading room. Lili is on call. I got a text from her that she is there to take care of a VIP patient."

"Great. See you there!"

Angus exhaled. That talk had unexpectedly made him feel better. He would never have a work–life balance, but he didn't have to be alone either. He didn't have to juggle two worlds. There was one world, and Annya would be in it. Change could happen.

# - 2 -

# ANNYA

The Apprentice
Saturday, October 8, 2033, 7:30 p.m.

Annya made a U-turn and drove back to Redwood City. She had been late for the dinner and was relieved when Angus called her. No need for excuses. *He* had called it off.

Annya had debated with herself whether she should go until about twenty minutes ago. She liked the FBI Director. He was smart, funny, and handsome. A man worth her time. However, she was not sure of her feelings for him. Did she like him as a colleague, friend, or more if chemistry was right? He was probably ten years her senior. This was a significant difference in terms of age, not to mention the power difference and administrative issues mingling between the CIA and FBI. Annya's life was sufficiently complicated. Adding an FBI director as a love interest didn't seem like a smart thing to do. Annya was financially independent, and she felt more than fulfilled with her responsibilities as an ER physician and undercover CIA operative. She had vowed that she would never again get fooled by romantic emotions.

But she couldn't stop thinking about Angus. He had hit a nerve when he told her about the incident. Who did he think he was? James Bond? He had too much courage for his own good. She worried about him. But was she ready for a romance? Not really.

She had survived domestic violence. Her ex-husband shot her in the head a few years ago. When she married him, she had no idea that he was a Russian assassin. Her marriage to Boris was not something she could forget and move on from. Annya palpated the big scar on her forehead. It was well concealed under her bangs. Feeling the groove under her fingertips made her shiver. She still suffered from flashbacks and post-traumatic stress disorder. Her defense reflexes kicked in whenever someone came too close too quickly. What if she punched the FBI director unconscious in the middle of the night? Well, he could probably defend himself. Hopefully.

Annya reached the parking lot in front of the ER. She felt much more at ease about the prospect of seeing Angus here than in a restaurant. The ER was her comfort zone. She was literally in charge here. She got out of the car and walked toward the modern, white-box-shaped building.

The ER entrance buzzed with activity. A patient on a stretcher was wheeled up the ramp by two paramedics. An electric vertical take-off and landing vehicle was landing on the roof, probably bringing another patient.

Annya greeted the security guard at the entrance and stepped through the sliding glass door into the long, sterile hallway. Fortunately, she had not chosen the black dress for the dinner tonight. Her tight pantsuit was sufficiently professional for the hospital and didn't raise any eyebrows. But then, her colleagues were so busy that they would probably not have noticed if she had walked into the ER naked. Her outfit was fine. If she was asked to check on a patient, she would add a white coat. The smell of chlorine disinfectants and alcohol-based hand sanitizers greeted her. An x-ray technician approached from the other end of the hallway, pushing a portable x-ray machine past her. He nodded briefly as the mechanical sound of the electric wheels passed by.

Annya entered the dimly lit radiology reading room, a windowless room with approximately ten computer workstations along the walls. Dr. Lili Pham, her long-time friend, was sitting in front of the workstation, discussing a case with Annya's junior colleague, Dr. Julius Philopator Zhang, assistant professor in the ER. Lili's pageboy haircut was getting out of shape. Annya had recommended her personal stylist to her about three weeks ago. But Lili had clearly not found the time to visit her. Always busy, like herself. Julius' appearance, on the other hand, was impeccable. The neckline of his crewcut looked razor-sharp, as if it had been cut yesterday. The content *in* this head was a different matter. Lili explained something to him, pointing at the monitor in front of them, while Julius looked at her with those lost eyes that Annya had seen too many times. Whatever Lili was trying to explain, he had no clue what she was talking about. Annya sighed. The young man was a piece of work. A walking lack of medical knowledge on the loose in the hospital, perpetuated by extraordinary confidence. If she could, she would fire him. But her department chair had asked her to be patient. Julius was the son of the CEO of OrchidBio, the largest biotech company in California, and an important donor for SUEC Hospital. Annya's chair explained that he didn't believe that Julius had plans to work long-term in clinical medicine. The young man had graduated at the bottom of his class and secured an ER residency through his father's connections. At his job interview at SUEC, he stated that he wanted to get clinical exposure to develop ideas for a start-up company. That shouldn't take too long. They only had to survive for a few months. His father would thank them generously.

Julius turned around and greeted Annya, his hands on his hips. "Hello, Annya. This is perfect timing. We have a teenager in the ER with a bone tumor. I requested an MRI, but insurance denied it. Pleonexia Health Insurance. We had a lot of issues with them recently. They deny every request for children with cancer at SUEC."

Lili rolled her eyes.

"Why would you say that, Julius?" Annya asked calmly. "You don't usually treat children with cancer?"

"Well, Rogério Queirós Trento does, the Pediatric Oncologist. I met him at the Tonga Bar last weekend, and he told me everything about how Pleonexia treats their customers—or I should say, how they don't treat their customers." He chuckled.

"And now you think you found such a case in the ER?"

He nodded. "Yes, I did! The insurance agent denied my request for an MRI because of Lili's report for the x-ray."

Annya turned to Lili. "What did the report say?"

Lili sighed. "It's a UBC, a unicameral bone cyst."

Annya gave her a knowing look. "Can we see it?" she asked.

"Of course." Lili brought up the images on the workstation.

"There is a large cyst in the right proximal humerus." She pointed at the abnormality. "There is a fracture through the lateral aspect of the lesion with a bone fragment in the lesion below the fracture, a so-called fallen fragment. This is a typical unicameral bone cyst, a benign lesion."

Annya turned to Julius. "And you would like to order an MRI because…"

He looked at her with a jutted chin. "You told me that a bone tumor always requires an MRI."

Was this young man teachable? She had to try. "Well, I said that about bone *sarcomas*, malignant tumors of the bone," she said calmly. "This here is a cyst. A benign lesion."

"And this does not require further imaging?"

"Usually not. But, the patients should be referred to orthopedic surgery. Can you please call them? They will take care of the lesion and the insurance authorization."

Julius' face brightened. "Sure, I'll call them. They can deal with the insurance. I'll be happy to get that off my plate. Will the orthopedic surgeons do surgery?"

Annya nodded. "They will likely inject calcitonin and methylprednisolone into the lesion to stimulate healing. Since there is a fracture, they might also decide to add bone chips to stabilize it."

"May I observe the procedure?"

"Feel free to ask the surgeon who will be performing it."

Julius left the room. This time, Annya sighed.

"That guy is impossible," Lili commented.

Annya shrugged. "Tell me more."

"He behaves like a medical student. He is an attending physician. He's not here to observe; he's here to work."

"Well, it might actually be less work if we don't have to undo his mistakes for a few hours."

Lili looked at her with pity in her eyes. "Is it that bad?"

Annya shrugged. "He comes in late and leaves early. He needs help with every case, and he takes a break after every case. I often don't know where he is. He is wandering around in the hospital doing who knows what. I don't think he fully understands the concept of working in a hospital. He told me he worked for a full month at his father's company to earn his Lamborghini himself."

Lili laughed. "Wow, I'm impressed."

Annya nodded. "He still lives with his father in a mansion in Atherton, with an army of staff."

"That explains why he was sitting in the hospital cafeteria, waiting for somebody to take his order. The ER team is still joking about it. I'm sorry you have to deal with that guy."

Annya shrugged. "I guess it could be worse. He is neither arrogant nor mean. He can be quite charming and patients like him. He's simply clueless about how ninety percent of the world around him works."

"So, he's here to get an idea for a company?" Lili asked. "Any leads yet?"

"I don't know," Annya responded. "Two weeks ago, he asked me what I thought about an Uber for the hospital, an app where anyone in the hospital could volunteer to bring a patient from one location to another for some extra cash. I explained to him that strangers cannot drive a patient around and most staff members cannot just drop their work. Most of us don't find time to go to the bathroom. Except Julius, of course. Many of us have eight, nine, or ten-hour shifts without any break."

"What did he say when you told him that an H-Uber was not a good idea?"

"To his credit, he is responsive to critique. He just shrugged and said that he would come up with another idea. Last week, he donated toy robots to children in the pediatric ward. The robots had an integrated GPS and should direct patients from one point to another. I don't know who should fund a toy robot for every child. But at least this invention does not occupy our staff and is a nice distraction for the children."

Lili looked at the x-ray in front of her. "So, he's not stupid. He's quite creative. But his lack of medical knowledge is terrifying. Did he really pass his medical exams?"

"Apparently, he was thoroughly vetted," Annya said. "But we definitely need to keep an eye on him. I guess he is just not into studying."

Lili nodded. "I think I can help a little. Most new patients get an imaging exam as part of their initial workup. I can help correct any issues with initial imaging diagnoses."

Someone knocked on the door. Annya and Lili both looked at the door. Most staff just walked in. Was this a patient who got lost? A tall man in a gray suit slowly opened the door. He looked apprehensively around the corner and stepped in. Annya's heart leaped. It was him.

# - 3 -

# ANNYA

The Files
Saturday, October 8, 2033, 8:00 p.m.

Angus strode into the radiology reading room with an air of confidence. "Hello, ladies. Am I interrupting anything?"

Annya didn't like the antiquated tone. Standing tall, she met his gaze squarely and replied: "Hello, my lord. Great to see you here!" Her voice carried a mix of humor and veiled challenge. *Would he take offense?*

Angus looked at her with an amused smile. "Touché," he said with a graceful wave.

His gaze momentarily unsettled her. Was it genuine appreciation? She maintained her poise, looking at him with determination and self-assurance, refusing to yield an inch.

"Oh, you didn't come in for Julius. You came in for *Angus*." Lili smirked at Annya. *Was it that obvious?*

Angus gave Lili a probing look. "Who is Julius?" he asked with raised eyebrows.

"Her ex-husband," Lili responded with a grin.

Angus shook his head with a smile. "That cannot be. Her ex-husband passed away."

Annya appreciated that he didn't mention that she had shot her ex-husband dead. Lili knew. But the door was open, and most of her colleagues would probably be uncomfortable with that piece of information—and the fact that she carried a gun at all times. Another detail she had in common with Angus, besides being workaholics employed by law enforcement.

"Dr. Julius Philopator Zhang is a young physician in the ER,"

Lili explained. "We have to help him out once in a while. Quite a lot, actually."

Angus stepped calmly toward Annya and locked eyes with her again. "Great to see you, Annya," he said calmly. His stern blue eyes sent unspoken messages to her brain, a silent understanding passing between kindred spirits. *I'm glad you're here.*

The shared sensation of unity and comfort caught her off-guard. Her heart exploded. She tried to contain a shiver running down her spine. *This is ridiculous. I'm not a teenager,* she told her deranged self. *I'm the Medical Director of the ER. Don't blush in the reading room.* She looked down.

Lili cleared her throat, and the magical moment evaporated.

Angus smiled at her. "Lili, you didn't lose your wit."

"Great to see you too, Agent Weber," Lili responded politely. "What brings you here today? I hope it's not a new crime."

Annya looked up. "Can we tell her?"

Lili looked from Angus to Annya. "Whatever it is, please confess. I will be a more effective ally if I know what this is about."

Angus nodded. "Well, unfortunately, a woman was kidnapped tonight, a health insurance agent. She carried copies of medical images from SUEC patients in her briefcase."

"Oh, you wanted to consult Radiology?" Lili said with a hint of surprise in her voice. "Did you bring the images? Do you have a warrant to search the patients' files?"

Angus shook his head. "I don't. But I don't need to know any of the patients' names. I just wanted to ask you to look at the images. If there is any indication that these cases impact our national security, then the FBI has the authority to access the information of these patients, and we can work from there."

"Okay, what should I look up?" Lili asked.

Angus pulled up his phone and showed the medical file numbers to Lili. She typed the first one into the computer workstation. An x-ray and several other medical imaging studies appeared on the screen.

"This is a patient with Hodgkin lymphoma," she explained. "The chest x-ray shows a widened upper mediastinum. This led to the PET/MRI exam here which confirms the presence of a malignant tumor in the chest and abdomen."

Angus came closer to review the images. "What is PET/MRI?" he asked.

"Positron emission tomography and magnetic resonance imaging, an imaging technique that can simultaneously detect a radiotracer and image the body with high resolution. The best imaging technique we can offer our patients to find their tumors. And quite expensive," Lili explained.

"I understand. Is there any connection to Pleonexia Health Insurance?" he asked.

Annya tried to remember why this name sounded familiar. *Hadn't Julius just complained about that insurance?*

Lili flipped through the patient's file. "Yes, the patient had that insurance. There's quite some paperwork going back and forth between the insurance company and SUEC. The insurance states that SUEC is out of network. SUEC argues that the patient lives close by, and care here would be most efficient for them. Nevertheless, the insurance denied coverage, and the patient was ultimately treated elsewhere."

"So, Julius did have a point today," Annya concluded. "He said that this insurance was causing a lot of issues for our patients."

Angus raised his eyebrows. "What kind of issues?"

Annya shrugged. "Julius mentioned that multiple pediatric oncology patients had issues with health insurance authorizations."

Angus made a note on his iPhone. "That could be important. Let's check if this is a common theme." He turned back to Lili. "Can you look up the next patient number?"

Lili brought up the next patient and reviewed the images.

"This is a CT scan which shows a soft tissue mass that has destructed the seventh right rib." She pointed to the abnormality. "An MRI scan was done as well and shows the mass in greater detail."

"What was the diagnosis?" Annya asked.

Lili checked the file. "Based on the images, I would have thought that it was a bone sarcoma. But it turned out to be a primary bone lymphoma."

"And let me guess, this patient was also covered by Pleonexia

Health Insurance?" Angus asked.

"Correct," Lili answered. "Covered and not covered. There was another dispute about insurance coverage and who would treat the patient."

"We are getting somewhere," Angus concluded. "There might be a pattern of issues with the insurance. There are two more patient numbers listed here. Can you check those as well?"

"Sure," Lili said. She brought up the next imaging study. "This is a patient with Langerhans cell histiocytosis," she explained.

"What is that?" Angus asked.

"This is a condition where bone marrow cells cause tumors throughout the body. The radiograph here shows multiple tumor lesions in the calvarium."

"Does the patient have Pleonexia Health Insurance?" Angus asked.

"Yes, they do," Lili responded. "And there was another dispute." She flipped through the file. "In this case, there was disagreement whether the child could receive a whole-body MRI scan."

"Why would the patient need a whole-body scan?" Angus asked.

"The result can affect the treatment of the patient, Lili explained. If there are multiple lesions in different body areas, then more aggressive therapy might be needed."

"How was the dispute resolved?" Annya asked.

"The patient received x-rays of the entire body. That is much less expensive but provides fewer details and exposes the child to radiation. The whole-body MRI would have been radiation-free, but it was denied," Lili read from the file.

"Pleonexia Health Insurance again?" Angus asked.

"Yes, the exchange is signed by Pleonexia claim office."

"How can an office be a correspondent?" Angus asked. "It should be a person?"

"This happens more and more frequently," Annya explained. "An approach to avoid responsibility. People don't sign anymore with their names but with so-and-so office."

"That is terrible!" Angus said. "Offices don't write letters, people do."

"Welcome to our world," Annya responded with a wry smile.

Lili nodded and brought up the next case. "This is another child with Langerhans cell histiocytosis." She pointed at the images. "These x-rays show a lesion in the right femur. In this case, an MRI was done and it shows an underlying mass in the bone marrow."

"This patient was covered by Pleonexia Health Insurance as well," Annya read from the file. "And there was another dispute. This carrier seems to be quite a pain when it comes to covering care."

Angus looked at the images. "I found these cases in the briefcase of the woman who was kidnapped today. There was also a badge from Pleonexia Health Insurance with her name on it. So, presumably, she worked for the insurance."

"Do you think she was kidnapped because of these insurance claims?" asked Lili.

"Perhaps she planned to expose the insurance in a negative way," Annya suggested.

"But then, the insurance could have fired her or politically destroyed her," Lili weighed in. "Isn't that how powerful companies handle whistleblowers?

Angus nodded. "Let's gather more information before drawing any conclusions."

"Whoever took her didn't kill her. They needed her alive," Annya thought out loud. "For what?"

"To extract more information from her?" Lili said.

"Then they would not leave a briefcase behind," Annya countered. "Or kidnap a woman in front of witnesses—in downtown San Francisco."

Angus nodded. "I don't think these were professional kidnappers, which makes the situation more dangerous. They might be overwhelmed and act erratically."

Lili said, "What if this insurance business was completely unrelated? Kidnapping for extortion. Perhaps she has a wealthy spouse, and these files have nothing to do with it?"

Annya typed on her iPhone. "I googled her name, and there isn't much coming up," she said. "Doesn't look like a celebrity."

"The SFPD would have informed us by now if there was a risk

for extortion based on personage," Angus said. "We certainly need to talk with her family members. Whatever the reason for this abduction is, they might know something."

Annya scrolled through her phone. "She is one of many insurance claim agents at Pleonexia Health Insurance. Her specialty was pediatric oncology. That's why all of the cases here were tumor cases."

Lili added, "And the denied insurance claims probably made a lot of people very unhappy—providers, patients, parents, extended family members."

Annya looked at Angus. "If this is revenge for something she did at the insurance company, then her life is in grave danger."

Angus nodded and pulled out his phone. "I think we have enough evidence to get the FBI involved. I will let the SFPD and Terrel know. We will start interviewing Frida's family members and check out everyone whose claim this woman denied. The first forty-eight hours are critical."

Annya sent him a probing gaze. "You want to call your colleague, FBI agent Terrel Wright?"

Angus nodded.

Annya hesitated for a moment. Then, she said. "You might want to check your emails first."

He looked at her in surprise. "Why?"

"I'm not at liberty to say. Just check it."

Angus reached for his phone and checked his inbox. "There is a note from Terrel", he said. "He needs to take a few days off from work. He's with Niles at SUEC Hospital. Niles has a kidney tumor and needs surgery." He looked at Annya in disbelief. "Terrel is here in the hospital? With his son? You knew this?"

She shrugged. "Patient privacy."

Angus looked at Lili. "You knew this as well?"

Lili nodded. "I came in just for him."

Angus stared at them. "Is it serious? His son Niles means everything to him."

Annya put her hand on his shoulder with an urge to protect him. "I'm sorry, Angus," she said. "We are only allowed to discuss a patient with close family members. But you can ask him yourself. Since he already sent you a note that he's here, you could stop by the patient room. He is in the pediatric surgery ward upstairs."

"I will surely do that, and then, I will talk with the family members of Dr. Frida Ending, the insurance agent. I guess I'm on my own with that."

"If her abduction has anything to do with the insurance claims of cancer patients here, perhaps there might be an opportunity," Annya said softly. "If he agrees, we could move Terrel and his son to the oncology ward. His son will be in a single room anyway, so it might not make a big difference to him. But Terrel could investigate patients and staff there undercover. If he is open to do that, of course. I know it's a big ask."

Angus looked at her with admiration. "You are brilliant!"

She smiled. "I know."

"Thank you!" He embraced her with both arms. And then he whispered into her ear. "How about lunch at Donato Enoteca tomorrow?"

Annya looked over his shoulder at Lili, who had discretely turned around and scrolled through the next imaging study on her worklist, pretending not to notice.

*Whatever. Tomorrow is Sunday.*

"Sure, sounds good," she whispered back. "I have the morning shift. We could meet at 2 p.m. at the ER backdoor? If you can make it."

He gave her a broad smile. "I will do my best."

Annya was not sure if she was happy or mad with herself. Well, she could always change her mind.

# - 4 -

# FRIDA

### Trapped
### Saturday, October 8, 2033, 8:30 p.m.

Frida's head hurt, and her eyelids felt swollen. It took immense effort to open them. Her vision felt blurry. Above her was a bright neon light. It hurt to look at it. She was in a hospital bed with the blanket tugged around her up to her chin. The pillow under her head felt eerily cold and coarse as if somebody had put an ice cap on her head. It smelled of sanitary soap and disinfectant. Frida tried to sit up, but there was something around her body that held her down. She palpated her body with her hands. Somebody had stripped off her clothes. She wore a hospital gown. A broad elastic strap strangulated her loins and her stomach. Her brain was slow to decipher what it was—a restraining belt. She tried to pull on it, but her hands were too weak. She felt dizzy and nauseated.

Frida took a breath, and then she concentrated on turning her head to take a look around. Her skull felt like it weighed a thousand pounds. But she did manage to move it. A small rectangular room with no furniture except her bed and a small overbed table to her right. Blank white walls around her. A closed, plain white door to her left. Frida's eyes hurt. Everything was too bright under the bleak neon light above her.

She closed her eyes and tried to remember. A man had pulled her into a van, held her down, and injected something into her thigh through her clothes. Perhaps ketamine. She screamed and tried to fight him off while the van raced down the street. There were gunshots outside of the van. She tried to kick and jump for the door. But the man was strong. He encircled her throat with his right hand and watched her as she lost consciousness. Frida remembered the hateful glare of two brown eyes above a surgical face mask. Terrifying. Then he did something else. What was it? A low-pitched, buzzing sound of an electric motor. She had gasped for air as her mind went blank. Not much to build on. Why was she abducted? Who was the man? Why was she here? She had no idea. Frida's mind clouded again. She doze off.

Little sparks of thoughts meandered through her cataleptic mind, whispering, *There's something else you need to remember. Something important.* She tried to recall the situation in the van again. The man choked her with his right hand, his left reaching out for something. Something moved over her head, again and again. Her mind faded away. The van stopped. The door opened. The loud voice of a man shouting, "What did you do?"

"Nobody will recognize her now," the other man responded. Frida's eyes opened widely. She remembered. The man in the van had shaved her head. She cried out in horror and reached for her head. Bald. Her beautiful blonde hair. Gone. That's why her head felt so cold. The man in the back of the van had shaved her head. The other man was upset when he saw her. That was not planned. The two men had started arguing. Frieda had tried to get out of the van while they were yelling at each other, but she could hardly move. Then, one of the men turned around and grabbed her, dragged her to another car, and threw her onto the back seat. She had felt another needle injection in her thigh, and her drugged mind had drifted away again.

Frida woke up to the sound of approaching footsteps. A key was turned, and the door opened. A man in a white coat and a woman in blue scrubs entered. *A physician and a nurse?* What would they do with her? Would they hurt her? Frida felt sweat running down her temples. It was the man from the van. Same eyes, same face mask. She wanted to yell at him. *What did you do to me?* But her tongue was so heavy. It only produced gibberish.

The woman walked toward her and put her hand on her forehead. "Please calm down," she said to Frida. "You are safe now."

"Whaaat?" Frida managed to say.

"I know you wanted to kill yourself," the woman said softly. "You were so lucky that our doctor came by and caught you before you could throw yourself in front of the Cal Train."

"No, fshchrrlarchrochr." Frida tried to protest but the words would not come out. She felt dizzy. This was a big misunderstanding. She had to explain it to the nurse. But her tongue was paralyzed. Frieda's heart raced. The man and woman's faces started to rotate around her in circles.

"Just get some sleep," the woman said softly. "We will do a tox screen to find out what drugs you're on. If there is an antidote, we will give it to you. Otherwise, we will wait until it is out of your system, and then you can tell me everything."

Frida nodded. The woman was a nurse, and she didn't know about the abduction. Perhaps that was good news. She was not with the kidnappers. And one of the men had scruples. Perhaps he had gotten her here. A hospital bed was probably safer than a garage or basement where the lunatic could just strangle her to death. But the doubtful one had not released her either. What did these men want from her? And which of the two was standing in front of her?

"Remember, she tried to kill herself," the man said. "She might tell you fabulous stories to get away. Make sure she stays safe here."

The nurse nodded eagerly. "Of course," she said. "We have a lot of experience with that here. I'm so glad you saved her, doctor. You *are* a guardian angel!"

"That's my vocation, indeed." The man chuckled and put his arm around her shoulders.

They turned around and left the room. The door shut. Their voices faded away.

Frida's mind raced. Was this worse than a basement? How would she get out of here?

# - 5 -

# ANGUS

## Priorities
### Saturday, October 8, 2033, 8:30 p.m.

Angus stepped calmly into the patient room. Terrel's four-year-old son, Niles, was lying in a hospital bed, sleeping. His chocolate brown cheeks were slightly flushed. He didn't look sick at all, which made the situation even more heartbreaking. Terrel's wife, Imani, was sitting on a chair beside her son, holding his hand. Terrel sat on the other side, engaged in a whispered conversation with a young man in a starched white coat, presumably a physician. The man looked familiar. Angus had seen him earlier today in the hallway in front of the Radiology reading room. Terrel, Imani, and the man looked up as Angus entered.

"Hello, Angus. Thanks for coming by," Imani said with tears in her eyes. She wore a tracksuit, and her hair was in disarray—very different from her usual appearance. She got up from her chair. Angus stepped toward her and hugged her softly. The second hug today. He was not a touchy guy, but this was an extraordinary day.

"How is Niles doing?" he asked.

"He went through a number of exams today," Imani explained in a low voice. "First an ultrasound, then an MRI under anesthesia. We first tried without, but the long tube was too scary for him. He couldn't lie still. And so, he got a sedation. He's sleeping it off."

Angus nodded. "I'm so sorry you have to go through this. What a nightmare." He looked at Terrel. "How are *you* doing?"

Terrel had deep dark circles under his eyes. "Thanks for asking," he responded. "To be honest, I'm exhausted. I took some photos of the MR images." He handed his iPhone to Angus.

Angus looked at the glaring screen. "What am I looking at?" he asked.

"There is a large mass in the right kidney," the man in the white coat explained. "Likely a Wilm's tumor, a malignant tumor of the kidney. At least that's what radiologist Dr. Pham said."

Angus looked at the images on the screen. He had been trained at the FBI in recognizing human anatomy on medical images, but he was not a physician.

"The tumor looks quite big?" he said. "It occupies nearly the whole abdomen." Perhaps he should have kept that to himself. Imani's eyes filled with tears.

"Yes, indeed," Terrel responded with a trembling voice. "Imani and I were terrified when we saw it at first. It is a very large tumor. Lili said that Niles is really lucky that there are no metastases and that the tumor hasn't ruptured yet. If that happened, then Niles' chance to be cured would decrease significantly. SUEC has the best pediatric surgeons in the world. They'll remove the right kidney with the tumor on Monday. They want to keep Niles here tomorrow to prepare him for the surgery and do another ultrasound to make sure all vessels are patent. And they'll do a genetic test."

"A genetic test?" Angus asked.

The man in the white coat nodded. "Patients with Wilm's tumors can have specific genes that predispose them to malignant tumors. This is important to know for the treatment of this tumor and future evaluations for other tumors. Unfortunately, African-American patients with Wilm's tumors have the worst outcomes of all patients. If Niles has a genetic predisposition, then he will be enrolled in a screening program to catch other tumors early."

Tears ran down Imani's face. She gently stroked Niles' cheek.

Terrel added, "The tumor will be resected as soon as possible. Dr. Julius Zhang here just explained this to us."

*Julius Zhang?* Angus looked at the man. Annya had not mentioned that he was *that* handsome. A physically fit young man in his early thirties with high cheekbones, broad shoulders, and expensive looking clothes. He looked as if he had just stepped out of a fashion magazine.

"Nice to meet you, Agent Weber," the man said cheerfully and extended his hand.

*Was there a hint of apprehension in his sparkling eyes?* Angus shook his hand with a wry smile. *Did I mention my name?* he thought.

"Mr. Wright told us that you were coming," Julius explained as if he had read his mind.

"I see." Angus looked at the young physician. He didn't know him, and he didn't trust him. He had to talk with Terrel. Alone.

"I just came through the ER, and I believe your colleagues were looking for you there," he said coldly.

"Of course," Julius responded with a broad smile. "If Annya needs me, I will join her right away."

*Do all staff address each other by their first name?* Angus looked him up and down. He couldn't suppress the feeling that the man looked suspicious.

Julius waved, turned around, and left.

Terrel waited until the door had shut. Then, he asked. "Hey Angus, did this guy commit a crime? You looked at him as if you wanted to arrest him?"

"No, not at all," Angus lied. "He seemed to be very nice."

"I appreciate your concern, but I was surprised that you came by in person," Terrel said. "It is quite late. You could have called."

Angus looked at his colleague. Terrel was clearly going through an awful time. But crimes didn't stop in times of family emergencies. A woman's life was on the line, and Terrel was his best man. He needed a good moment to ask for his help.

"Can we talk outside?" he asked.

Imani looked alarmed. She would likely not approve.

"I just don't want to wake him up." Angus pointed at Niles.

She nodded hesitantly.

"Of course," Terrel responded.

They stepped out of the room. Several nurses and children with their parents walked up and down the hospital hallway. It was too busy.

"I saw a quiet place when I came here," Angus said.

He led Terrel down the hallway and down the stairs. The children's hospital was a modern U-shaped building with a fenced garden and playground in the center. Angus had noted the door to the garden when he went to the pediatric ward. There was nobody at this late time of the day. They stepped into the garden. A few solar torches illuminated a gravel path in front of them with flickering lights. The air was crisp and cool. The light evening breeze was less harsh than in the city. It smelled of pine trees and rose bushes. Angus took a deep breath. He pointed to a park bench in front of a well-manicured lawn area.

"Should we sit down here?" he asked.

"Sure."

They both settled on the bench. Angus adjusted the gun in his holster. It had been a stressful day for him as well. He described the incidents of the past few hours as succinctly as possible. Terrel listened intently. Then, he asked his question.

"So, you want Niles to move from the pediatric surgery ward to a patient room in the oncology ward so that I can check out families and staff there?" Terrel summarized.

"I know it's a lot to ask," Angus said. "You have to focus on your family right now. I get that. But ultimately, you do need to move to oncology anyway, right? If you can keep your eyes and ears open there, that could be incredibly helpful."

Terrel shook his head. "I'm not sure, Angus. For now, Niles needs the surgery. Once the tumor is out, he will recover and then be transferred to oncology. A premature move might negatively affect Nile's care."

Angus had prepared for that question. "Annya assured me that the nurses on both wards are trained to care for children after surgery. The surgeon will check on you as they would in the other ward. You will have a private room for your family, so Niles and Imani should hardly notice any difference."

"I don't know how Imani would feel about moving. She just got to know the staff."

Angus nodded. "I understand. Please talk with her. A woman's life is in danger. An important clue to her rescue could be in that ward."

"Niles' life is in danger as well. He's my only son," Terrel exclaimed, his voice quivering with emotion. "I'm not sure I have the energy to talk to anyone else right now. My son has a huge tumor in his belly. I'm on a family leave." His exhaustion was palpable.

"Of course. I don't ask you to do anything extra. Just stay vigilant, keep your senses alert," Angus implored, trying to steady his voice. "Interactions with the staff will naturally unfold."

Terrel looked doubtful.

Angus tried to think of an argument that could convince him. *Why did his son get sick at exactly this time? It was a most unfortunate coincidence. But they could leverage it to obtain information from the inside.*

"You're my best man, Terrel," he tried again. "We are literally tapping in the dark right now. As you know, time is of the essence in cases such as this. If there is anything on that ward that could lead us to the kidnappers, I'm sure you will find it."

"Why can Annya not help with this? She is a professional spy?" Terrel asked, his shoulders slumping under the burden of his worries.

Angus shook his head. "I'm afraid this is not a matter of foreign intelligence, as far as we know," he said, choosing his words carefully. "So, this is not official business for the company. But she will also keep her eyes open—as a friend."

Terrel's gaze shifted downward to his feet. "I will keep my eyes open as well. But my son cannot move to a different ward at the moment. He needs surgery, so he's on the surgical ward right now. And I'm pretty sure Imani would not approve the move either. We are worrying about the surgery and trying to keep our act together in front of Niles. He trusts us. What will he think when he wakes up after the surgery, in pain, unable to move, with drains coming out of his belly? I cannot think about anything other than my son right now. You must understand that."

Angus sighed. "Of course. I respect that. Just think about it and let me know if you change your mind."

# - 6 -

# TERREL

The Rejection
Saturday, October 8, 2033, 9:00 p.m.

Terrel walked back to the pediatric surgery ward. He felt bad that he led his partner down. Angus always put the job first. He was available twenty-four seven and never left a call or text unanswered. Terrel remembered how Angus had called him back during his honeymoon when Terrel had faced difficulties with a case. He had helped him on numerous occasions, no matter what day or time it was. Angus' birthday, Thanksgiving, Christmas, New Year, Angus was always available. Always. Now, it was time for Terrel to pay him back. And he couldn't. He was different. His family was his top priority. It always had been. His heart ached every time he imagined his little son undergoing a big surgery—a big scalpel would cut Niles' little belly open, the huge ugly tumor would be removed, and the right kidney. Would his son be okay with one remaining kidney? Why did he have two if one was enough? Would it bleed a lot? What if he bled too much? How would he handle the pain after the surgery? Imani was losing her mind over all these questions. She could hardly hold herself together over worries that something could go wrong. How should Terrel explain to her that they should move from one ward to another because of a case? Impossible. He had to look after his family now. There were other colleagues at the FBI who could look for an abducted woman.

Terrel stepped back into the patient room. Niles was sitting in his bed, spooning cereal into his mouth. He had not lost his appetite. Niles beamed at him as he entered the room. "Hi, Daddy. I got a robot!" He held a multicolored toy robot in the air with his left hand.

Imani was still sitting beside her son. She wiped away a tear with the back of her hand and sent Terrel a faint smile. "A gift from the hospital," she explained. "The robot was in the gift box that Dr. Zhang brought to us. Too bad he was not here when Niles opened the box. He was so excited!"

"I called him Chip," Niles added.

"Wow, let me see it!" Terrel came closer to inspect it.

It was a small humanoid android with a square head, big dark eyes, a silvery cylindrical body, and flexible limbs. The robot's eyes turned red when Terrel touched it. "Hello, Terrel," it said with a metallic voice.

Niles laughed.

"How does it know me?" Terrel asked.

"We uploaded your photo," Imani explained. "It has an integrated photo app and camera."

Niles dropped his spoon and reached for the toy. "You can press here." He pointed to a button on the body. "Then it takes a photo."

"And there is a small trackpad and screen on the back where you can add a name," Imani added.

"Wow, impressive!" Terrel smiled. "Does it know all of us?"

"Yes, see here." Niles turned the toy around so that it faced him.

"Hello, Niles," the toy said. He turned the toy to his mother. "Hello, Imani!"

They all laughed.

"What else can it do?" Terrel asked.

"It has an integrated GPS," Imani said. "It can tell you where you are and guide you to any location in the hospital."

Terrel looked at the toy. "Interesting."

"I knew you would love it." Imani smiled. "You have to start your questions with 'Hello, Chip.'" She turned to the robot. "Hello, Chip. Where are we?"

"Hello, Imani, you're in room 22 on the pediatric surgery ward at SUEC Hospital."

"Hello, Chip. How do I get to the bathroom?" Terrel asked.

"Walk toward the window, take the door on your right," the robot responded. Niles laughed.

"How do I get to the playground?" he asked.

"Exit the room," the robot responded. Niles pushed his plate and blanket away.

"No, sweetie, you need to stay in your bed," Imani intervened, holding him back. "It is very late already."

Niles grunted in disapproval.

Terrel took the toy. "I can try it for you," he said. He went to the door, opened it, and stepped out.

"Turn left," the robot said. Niles clapped his hands.

"Wow. It would guide me all the way?" Terrel asked.

"Yes," Imani responded. "This is such a great invention! Fun for Niles, and we will never get lost here."

Terrel inspected the toy in his hand. There was an ethernet port. He walked back into the patient room. With a few deft maneuvers, he connected the toy with his iPhone. "See here," he said with a blend of enthusiasm and satisfaction as he turned to his son in the hospital bed. He carefully positioned the toy so that the screen on its back faced his son. "If you want to contact me," he explained, "you just push my photo on the screen."

Niles' gaze locked onto Terrel, his eyes shimmering with gratitude and relief. With a satisfied smile, he extended a finger and pressed Terrel's photo on the back of the toy robot.

Terrel's phone made a short, high-pitched sound, and a text message with Niles' photo appeared on the screen. He showed it to his son.

Niles laughed, and their eyes met in a shared moment of understanding.

Terrel's chest swelled with a mixture of protective instinct and deep love. The toy, with its newfound purpose, would ease Niles' anxiety and make their time in the hospital a little more bearable.

A young woman in blue scrubs came down the hospital corridor. "Hello, Mr. Wright. I see you got a SUEC robot, a new invention from Dr. Zhang. How do you like it?"

"I think it is a great idea. Niles loves it. We have to try it some more before we can tell how well it works," Terrel responded.

The woman pointed at an ID badge, which was tugged at the front pocket of her scrub. "I'm Sally, Niles' nurse practitioner for the night shift. Can I come in?"

"Of course!"

Terrel went back into the patient room, and the nurse followed him. "Hello, Niles. How are you doing?" she asked.

"Fine, thanks," Niles answered politely.

"Do you have any questions for the night?" the nurse asked Imani.

"Thank you. We are fine for now," Imani responded. "The couch here can be turned into a sleeping bed?"

"Yes, correct," the nurse responded. "There's also a pillow and blanket in the cabinet on the right. One parent to stay here. The other can go home."

"I will stay today," Imani responded. "My husband will stay tomorrow."

"Sounds like a plan," the nurse said with a smile.

"When will he have his blood draw and ultrasound tomorrow? Can he eat breakfast?" Terrell asked.

The nurse hesitated for a moment. "Well, I'm afraid we didn't get insurance authorization for the blood test yet," she said.

"But Dr. Zhang said that he had ordered it."

"Well, I'm afraid the blood test for the genetic test was rejected."

"Rejected?" Imani asked in a high-pitched voice. "Dr. Zhang explained to us that our son needs this test to find out if he is at risk for developing other tumors. Who in the world would say that this is not necessary?"

"Don't worry," the nurse responded. "A rejection is usually just a matter of form, not substance. It is possible that Dr. Zhang made a mistake when filling out the insurance authorization request form. We will fill out the form again and hopefully solve *that* issue."

Imani sighed. "Okay, so you think this can be resolved?"

The nurse nodded. "I'm pretty sure we can handle it," she said.

"When will the new ultrasound be done?" Terrel asked again.

The nurse looked at him. "Well, the ultrasound is another story. It was denied for lack of medical necessity. A denial means that the insurance believes that the test is not needed at all."

Tears welled in Imani's eyes. "What on earth does that mean?"

The nurse adjusted a strand of hair behind her ear. "Well, they don't want to authorize the test. Niles already had an ultrasound and an MRI today. The insurance agent thought that another ultrasound would not be necessary. But the images thus far didn't show us the abdominal vessels well enough. The surgeons requested another look. So, we will appeal to the insurance with a peer-to-peer discussion. Your doctor here at SUEC will call up a physician at the insurance. We don't know how that discussion will turn out. Unfortunately, the insurance claim agent we had to deal with over the last several months was really difficult and rarely gave in."

Terrel looked at his son playing with his robot. "I cannot believe that the insurance makes it so difficult for us at a time when our kid is sick."

"Please don't take it personally," the nurse said. "We deal with this all the time. It's ridiculous that we have to beg for permission from insurance personnel who may not fully understand the underlying disease."

Imani shook her head. "Why would *anyone* deny medical treatment for a child? What horrible people make such decisions?"

"I have never met any of these insurance agents, so I can only guess," the nurse said. "The less money an insurance company pays for you, the more profit it makes. The CEO of Pleonexia made ninety million dollars last year. The insurance agent might deny coverage because bigger profits will get them a bigger bonus. They don't know you or any of the patients personally. So, to them, it's just a business transaction."

"Well, it is an attack on my family," Imani said, clenching her fist. "If the physician here says that Niles needs another ultrasound to see the vessels before surgery, then he needs another ultrasound scan. Who has the audacity to say otherwise?"

The nurse nodded. "Believe me, I feel your pain. As a nurse, I want to take care of my patients. But I waste so much time on authorization processes that could be better spent with these kids. The entire system needs a reboot."

Niles looked up. "Chip does not respond," he said. "He needs a reboot, too!"

Imani leaned toward her son, stroking his head. "Let me have a look," she said softly. She took the toy, turned it around, and hit the button on the back for a few seconds. The toy moved the extended arms into a neutral position, stayed still, and then made a few beeping sounds. Imani gave it back to her son. "There you go."

"Hello, Niles," the robot said.

"Thank you!" Niles said with a broad smile.

Imani looked back at the nurse. "He loves this toy!"

"These robots were a great invention indeed," she said. "Dr. Zhang created them. Or he paid someone to create them. Either way, since we hand these robots out to our patients, we don't need to explain the labyrinth of the hospital anymore. And if we miss anyone, we can find them with the find-the-robot app."

"That is really good to know," Imani said. "What a genius this Dr. Zhang is!"

Terrel cleared his throat. "Well, since you mentioned that there are authorization issues for the blood test and the ultrasound scan, what about the surgery?"

The nurse looked at him. "I didn't want to bring it up because your wife was already so upset about the imaging scan. We have not received authorization for the surgery either. However, the surgery is only planned for Monday, so we have some time to work this out."

"On a Sunday?" Imani asked with raised eyebrows. Her cheeks flushed. "Which insurance administrator will work on a Sunday?"

"I know this is tight," the nurse said softly. "But our pediatric oncologist Dr. Queirós Trento was pretty optimistic that he could get this done. Our surgeons trust him. They agreed to put Niles on the schedule for Monday. They can always postpone the surgery to Tuesday if the authorization does not come through in time."

Tears welled up again in Imani's eyes. "These uncertainties make me completely mad."

Terrel reached for her hand. "We will get through this together," he said in a soft voice.

"Can we talk with the pediatric oncologist?" Imani asked.

"Usually, the oncologist is on site until about 6 p.m. in the evening on the weekends," the nurse responded, "unless we need him for an emergency, of course. He will stop by tomorrow when he finds the time. He already convinced the surgeons to schedule your son's surgery, so you're definitely on his mind."

"The staff here is really doing everything they can," Imani said with a hoarse voice. She reached for a paper towel and blew her nose.

"Yeah, we are all here for you," the nurse patted Imani's shoulder. She looked at Imani and Terrel. "There is one more thing. You could stay in the oncology ward until the surgery if you want. We are completely full here and will have difficulties admitting another child if another surgical emergency comes up tomorrow. There are two vacant rooms in the oncology ward."

"But we need to talk with the surgeon as well tomorrow?" Imani asked.

"Of course," the nurse responded. "The surgeons do their rounds much earlier than the oncologists. You could stay here for the rounds with the surgeon early in the morning. After that, I could help you with the room change and bring you over before the oncology rounds. That way, you could speak with both the surgeon and the oncologist. Niles is so full of energy, and the pediatric oncology team has many more activities for the kids than we have here. A playroom, a clown, a playground, and a parrot in the garden outside."

Niles had explored his robot while the adults were talking. But now, he looked up and exclaimed, "I want to see the parrot!"

Terrel smiled. His son had an amazing ability to play with his toys and follow the conversations of adults around him at the same time.

"And you will definitely see Dr. Queirós Trento tomorrow," the nurse said to Imani. "He is our human weapon for the insurance authorizations."

"Maybe that's a good idea," Imani said, eyeing her husband for reassurance. "What do you think, Terrel?"

Terrel looked from his wife to the nurse, who glanced back at him with an innocent smile. *Did she manipulate them?*

"What will happen after the surgery?" he asked.

"You could come back here or go back to the oncology ward," the nurse said. "We work very closely together. The nurses on both wards are experienced with post-surgical care. The surgeon and oncologist will come to see Niles wherever he is. You could decide tomorrow after you have seen both wards."

"If you think that it will be good for Niles, then I don't have any objection," Terrel said slowly.

"I wouldn't offer it if I didn't think that it would be a good idea," the nurse said firmly.

"Okay. Then it's settled," Imani said with a resolute voice. "We will move to the oncology ward tomorrow."

"Yeah, I want to see the clown and the parrot!" Niles cheered.

"We will go see them tomorrow, sweetie." Imani embraced her son, new tears dwelling in her eyes. "But now you need to sleep. It is very late already." She gently pushed him back into his pillow and tucked the white blanket around him.

Niles eyes were small. His eyelids drooped, partially veiling his gaze. He held his robot tightly.

"I will let the oncology team know and help you with the move after the surgery rounds. Have a good night," the nurse said. She waved at the family, turned around, and left.

Imani adjusted the robot in his arm so that the toy would not pinch on his belly. She gently stroked Niles cheeks, whispering words of comfort.

Terrell was captured by Imani's unyielding love. Yet he couldn't help wondering if the nurse had arranged their move.

He texted to Angus. *We are moving to the oncology ward after all. It was Imani's decision.*

Angus answered right away. *Excellent. Please just keep your eyes open.*

Terrel responded. *I won't investigate anything. But I will let you know if I see anything suspicious.*

*Of course, that's all we need,* Angus texted back. *Thanks, and all the best to your family!*

Terrel felt a little better. It was good to have a pal like Angus.

He didn't see Angus' text to Annya. *It worked. I'm glad you have so many friends in the hospital. Thank you for your help.*

# - 7 -

# ANNYA

The Suspect
Saturday, October 8, 2033, 9:00 p.m.

Annya walked out of the hospital. She checked the time on her iPhone: 9 p.m. Time had flown by. One thing had led to another, and here she was, finally, on her way out of the hospital with a growling stomach. It was dark outside, and there were only a few cars in the dimly lit parking lot. Most of the outpatients and staff had left. A few Eucalyptus trees were swinging in the wind. Her car was standing alone under one of the trees. Annya thought about the woman who had been kidnapped. Hopefully, she was still alive. She had been working on insurance claims for SUEC Hospital. Had anyone at SUEC abducted her? Someone Annya might know? Her thoughts were interrupted by the tapping sound of footsteps behind her. *Tap, tap, tap.* The sound came closer quickly, definitely toward her. A threat? Annya's reflex system instantly switched to alert mode. Sometimes, a few seconds decided between life and death. The footsteps were now directly behind her. Too close. Annya stopped quickly and jerked her head backward as hard as she could.

"Ouch!" a familiar male voice cried.

She turned around and saw Julius holding his chin. Good for him that he was so tall; otherwise, she would have hit his nose.

"Julius, what on earth are you doing here?" she said calmly.

"You hurt me!" he exclaimed.

She looked at his face. There was a bruise on his chin but no blood. She had not hit his teeth. He was lucky.

"You cannot follow a woman in the dark in a parking lot like that," she said. "If the woman is trained in self-defense, you may get

51

hurt."

"I'm sorry if I scared you," he said apologetically. "I called you from the hallway when you exited the building, but you didn't hear me."

She really wanted to go home. "What's the matter?" she asked.

Julius was still holding his chin. "We got another child with a new tumor diagnosis, and I wanted to consult with you on what to do with him."

"What tumor?"

"A mass in the chest."

"Did you get imaging?"

"Yes, we got a chest x-ray, CT scans, and an ultrasound. Lili is still in the reading room and can explain the images to you."

"And you cannot do this by yourself? You are on service tonight, I'm not," she said sharply.

"I'm sorry. I only started working in the ER recently and have not seen that many children with cancer. See, I risked my life by asking you for help." He pointed at his chin.

Annya sighed. That was a bad bruise, indeed. She did feel sorry for him. "Okay, let's have a look."

"Thank you!"

They walked back to the hospital and the radiology reading room. Lili was sitting at her workstation, scrolling through some medical images, and talking with a short, plumpish young man in a dark blue suit to her right. He turned around. A round face with hazel eyes and a mustache outlined by curly brown hair. Annya recognized him. It was the pediatric oncologist, Dr. Rogério Queirós Trento. His gaze went from Annya to Julius.

"Hello, Julius," he said. "Thanks for texting me about this patient."

"No problem," Julius said with a broad grin. His eyes sparkled as if on the cusp of revealing a well-kept secret.

The oncologist evaded his gaze, focusing on the case on the screen.

Annya and Lili exchanged a look. Julius' strategy to disguise his own inexperience was to inform as many colleagues as possible, who would then initiate the needed steps. At least his inexperience had not led to any major patient care issues with this approach.

"Nice to see you, Dr. Queirós Trento," Annya said politely. "Are you on call?"

"Yes, I am," the oncologist responded.

"I was not sure if you would get my text," Julius said. "I'm really glad you came."

"I'm sorry you were called so late," Annya said to the oncologist.

"No problem at all," Dr. Queirós Trento responded. "I had to come in for a child with leukemia and rising fever, so I was already here."

"Rogério is the best. We met at the recent SUEC summer party," Julius explained with a chuckle. "Rogério's parents are from Brazil. That's how he got this long name: Rogério Gabriel Queirós Trento. A given name, a second name which is a saint's name, his mother's last name, and his father's last name."

Annya nodded. It was funny that a younger colleague was mansplaining international relations to her. Of course, he didn't know that she had a secret life as a CIA agent in addition to her day job.

She pointed at the medical images that Lili reviewed at the workstation. "And we are all here to review this patient's scan?" she asked. "It looks like a very large mediastinal mass."

"Yes, indeed," Lili responded. "The CT scan shows a large mass in the mediastinum, extending from the right lower neck to the base of the diaphragm. The mass appears very inhomogeneous, with contrast-enhancing soft tissue, cystic areas, and calcifications."

"The patient has an elevated Alpha Fetoprotein, AFP," Rogério added.

"So, this is most likely a Germ Cell Tumor," Annya concluded. It was great working with an expert team. Together, they could tackle any diagnosis—except Julius was clueless.

"What do we do with it?" he asked. "The tumor seems to compress the heart and the airways."

"I will admit the patient," Rogério said calmly. "He needs a CT or MRI of the abdomen to check for any additional lymph nodes there, and an ultrasound of the testes to exclude a primary tumor in the gonads. In addition, we will need a biopsy in order to determine which type of germ cell tumor this is."

"This is usually done by the Interventional Radiology (IR) team," Annya added. "Although the surgery team can help if IR cannot do it for some reason."

"I will call IR right away," Lili said.

Annya sighed. This tumor was not that rare. With some basic clinical knowledge, Julius could have really managed this on his own. She wondered if she should talk with him about it. But then she dismissed that thought. It was better if he reached out to others when he was unsure about a case. The patient would be properly taken care off. That was most important. Annya thoughts meandered to Angus. How he had locked eyes with her right here, where she was standing now. She admired his focus and intelligence.

"What health care insurance does the patient have?" she asked.

Lili checked the files. "Pleonexia Health Insurance."

"Any issues with authorization?" Annya asked.

"None mentioned in the notes," Lili responded.

Rogério's gaze furrowed. "We had major issues with Pleonexia recently. I often have to call them personally to negotiate coverage for a patient. They are extremely difficult to work with. They reject and deny everything they can. We have to constantly fight with them. So much wasted time for our nurses and physicians, which would be better spent with our patients. But tonight, they have been extremely accommodating. I didn't have to call anyone at all."

"Perhaps a new insurance agent," Julius chuckled again, his broad smiling face fixed on the oncologist. Rogério remained impassive, his expression stoic.

Annya looked at her junior colleague. *Why did he conduct himself in such an inexplicably foolish manner? Did he know about the abduction? Or had he anything to do with it?*

# - 8 -

# ANGUS

The Husband
Saturday, October 8, 2033, 9:30 p.m.


Angus walked up the long, white, ornate staircase of a beautiful Victorian house in the marina district of San Francisco. He rang the doorbell of Kuruk Ending, Dr. Frida Ending's husband. A young man with fair skin, light-colored hair, and hazel eyes opened the door. His shirt loosened from his worn-out jeans; his sleeves were pulled back. Angus estimated that he was probably in his late thirties.

"Hello, are you from the FBI?" the man asked. Angus had called him to announce his arrival.

"Yes, I'm FBI Special Agent Angus Weber," he confirmed and showed his badge to the man. "And you're Kuruk Ending?"

"Correct." The man nodded. "Please come in."

Frida's husband led Angus through a narrow hallway with shiny parquet and white-painted ornamental wood panels on each side. They entered a large living room with floral-patterned wallpaper, long French windows, and heavy brocade curtains. Angus marveled at the intricate detailing on the walls, the crown moldings on the ceiling, and the big chandelier, a complex glass structure that sent countless light reflections on a large, polished mahogany coffee table in the center of the room, like little dancing stars in a fairy tale. The room was filled with antique furniture upholstered in rich fabrics.

Mr. Tessay pointed to a large coral velvet sofa. "Please have a seat."

That was too much plush for him. Angus sat down in a matching chair opposite the coffee table, and Frida's husband settled on the couch.

"You have a very beautiful home," Angus marveled.

"Thank you," the man said. "I have some mixed feelings about it."

"Why is that?"

"I inherited the house from my mother, who descended from an old aristocratic family in San Francisco. My father was Native American, and the Victorian era was not exactly beneficial to our community. It was an era of broken treaties and forced removal of native tribes to reservations. My father never liked the house, and if I had the resources, I would live elsewhere. But I could never afford another home in San Francisco."

Angus looked around. The room, with its ornate details and opulent furnishings, was a stark reminder of the bygone era. He sympathized with Kuruk's sense of unease about the resources poured into such extravagance during a time when Native Americans were oppressed, exploited, and slaughtered.

"I understand the dissonance," he said calmly. "And yet, you're lucky. Few people make enough money to own a house in the Bay Area these days, and yours is exceptionally beautiful."

Kuruk nodded. "I chose to stay here to reclaim the space and reshape its narrative. It should represent my tribe's values of kindness and compassion. I regularly organize community events here. We gather with like-minded neighbors to share our stories and build connections." He gave Angus a probing look. "But you're not here to ask me about my community events, are you?"

Angus adjusted his glasses. Now, he felt uneasy. Decades of experience in his job had taught him many things, but delivering bad news remained a challenging task. He took a deep breath, aware of the weight of the words he was about to share.

"Indeed, I'm here because of a different matter," he said calmly. "It's about your wife. I assume she didn't come home today?"

Kuruk looked at him with widened eyes. "Why are you asking that? Is Frida in danger? We separated about a year ago. Frida moved into an apartment in downtown San Francisco, closer to her workplace. I could call her if you like?"

Angus shook his head. "That won't be necessary. I'm afraid she cannot be reached right now. I have more information to share if you're her registered domestic partner. Or are you divorced?"

"We have chosen to give each other some space for a while. But we are not legally separated. We are still married, just living apart for some time to reflect on our relationship. But why are you asking? Did Frida commit a crime? Is she okay?"

Angus prepared for the impact his words could have. "I'm afraid she was abducted this evening."

"What?" Kuruk clasped his hands over his mouth, his face draining of color. "Who kidnapped her? Is she injured?"

Angus carefully observed the man in front of him. He seemed to be in true distress. "We don't know that yet," he said calmly.

"Why would anyone kidnap her?" Kuruk cried.

"I was hoping you could help me out with that question. Is it possible that someone wants to extract a ransom?"

Tears glistened in Kuruk's eyes. "I don't think so. And if they do, they got the wrong hostage. Frida's family is from San Pablo in the San Francisco East Bay. Frida's father was a truck driver, and her mother was a homemaker with occasional jobs as a supermarket cashier. They both passed away a few years ago. Her older brother works at Ikea in Los Angeles. There's no ransom to get from that family—or me for that matter. My only wealth is this house. Do you think her life is in danger?"

Sometimes, there was no easy way to deliver bad news. The truth was the truth. "We have to assume the worst until we find out what the kidnappers want," Angus explained. "Does she have any enemies?"

Frida's husband struggled to contain his emotions. "Too many to count. This was part of the reason why we separated. People were leaving angry messages on her phone, and someone spilled tomato sauce over her car on our driveway so that it looked like it was covered in blood. It was awful—the opposite of everything I believe in. I couldn't bear it anymore."

Angus pulled his iPhone from his pocket to take notes. "Who were these people? And why were they so angry?"

Kuruk shrugged. "I didn't know any of them. Frida is a claim agent at Pleonexia Health Insurances. Her job is to review insurance claims and reject as many as possible. And she is *very* good at that. Perhaps the best. She got big bonuses for exceeding cancellation goals for her unit. She wanted to celebrate those with me, but I couldn't stomach it. I work as a nurse at SUEC Children's Hospital and I see the daily struggles of the children in our clinic. I'm horrified that some of them might not get their treatment because of Frida's objections."

"But you married her? Was this not always a problem?"

"No, she was a very different person when we first met at SUEC Hospital. She was a junior physician in the department of pediatrics, then an assistant professor. She was so full of energy and enthusiasm. She literally worked around the clock for that department, taking care of patients, teaching students, and publishing important research. Her parents were so proud of her. She was the only family member to go to college and become a physician."

"And then she switched to the insurance company? Burnout?"

Kuruk shook his head. "Anger and bitterness. The director of the pediatric oncology ward retired. The job was advertised, and she applied. She had seven years of job experience and 150 publications at that time. The search committee selected a male applicant who had two years of experience and five publications—a fraction of hers."

"Interesting." Angus took more notes on his notepad. "So, why was the other candidate chosen over her?"

Kuruk shrugged. "Office politics, I guess. She contacted the department chair and demanded an explanation. The chair told her that the search process was confidential and that the committee had come to a well-vetted conclusion. Frida complained to the Dean's Office, providing her CV with multiple objective skills and work products, all of which far exceeded that of the other candidate. Yet again, the Dean's Office sent her a note that, unfortunately, her application couldn't be considered and the reasons were *confidential.*"

"I'm sorry. Sounds like misogyny."

Kuruk nodded. "You bet. But the worst part was that people started gossiping behind her back. There must've been a reason why she was overstepped. Something had to be wrong with her. Everyone felt entitled to criticize her. Before this incident, everyone had complimented her experience and productivity. Now, she was too pushy, too aggressive, too emotional."

"Typical stereotypes?"

"Yes and no. When we met, Frida was the nicest, happiest person in the world. But all this mistreatment created a deep anger in her. These people *made her* pushy, aggressive, and emotional."

"I'm sorry to hear that. Sounds like a toxic environment."

Kuruk nodded. "It was a disgrace. Imagine the potential lost to our community. Frida is the smartest and most brilliant physician I've ever met. She was the best in her class in her medical school and residency program. She exceeded all expectations wherever she worked. If given a chance at SUEC, she would have produced ground-breaking medical innovations. But she was actively demoted. I was glad when she finally decided to quit and join the insurance company. I was hoping that that would make things better, that she could start over. But her resentment remained unresolved. Now, she rejects *their* applications every day. She was mistreated by assholes, and out of revenge, she became an asshole herself. Sorry for my strong language." He looked down.

"It seems that her resignation hurt her patients twofold," Angus summarized. "The patients whom she does not treat anymore as a skilled physician and the patients whose insurance claims she rejects now as an insurance claim agent."

"Correct. The poor patients suffer the consequences of the mistreatment of a physician by an abusive, corrupt system. Frida was so *angry*. I felt so sorry for her. She was clearly traumatized. We couldn't even discuss the matter with her without her exploding. That's when we decided to separate for a while. I still love her dearly, but I didn't know how to help her. I was hoping that time would heal her wounds and that she would eventually move on."

Angus nodded. "I understand the situation much better now. Thank you for providing this information. Do you have any idea who might have kidnapped her? And what the kidnappers might want?"

Kuruk shook his head. "I'm sorry. I have no idea. A parent of a patient? If a child is sick and someone makes them suffer more, they might seek justice. Or someone who is working on the pediatric oncology ward and is fed up with the constant insurance denials?"

"Do you have any specific suspects in mind?" Angus asked.

Kuruk shook his head. "Sorry, I don't. But regardless, you have to find Frida as quickly as possible."

"Of course, the first forty-eight hours are the most important."

"That's not what I meant. Frida has type 1 diabetes. She has to get her insulin."

*Type 1 diabetes.* Angus tried to remember. "What happens if she does not get her insulin?" he asked.

Kuruk's eyes dwelled again with tears. "She will get a diabetic ketoacidosis. Without insulin, her body cannot use the glucose in her blood as fuel and uses fat instead. The fat will be broken down to ketones, which make the blood acidic. When dangerous levels of ketones accumulate, she will become severely dehydrated and lose consciousness. If the problem is not addressed, she could die."

Angus took more notes. "How fast will that happen?" he asked.

Kuruk shrugged. "Not sure. Perhaps two to three days. Sooner if she consumes high amounts of sugar."

Angus got up from his seat. "Thank you very much, Mr. Ending. You helped a lot today!"

"Of course. Please bring her back safely! You can call me anytime if I can be of any assistance."

Angus nodded. "I will do what I can."

***

Angus checked his watch as he walked back to his car parked two blocks down from the Ending's home. 9:58 p.m. Fog had settled over the city. Angus stepped over some trash on the sidewalk. There was a man in a raincoat on the other side of the street, watching his dog sniffing at a large oak tree. A few cars drove by. Angus' car welcomed him with a double blip as he opened the door with the remote. He took a seat and dialed Kendis Awololo's number. She answered right away.

"Hey, Angus, any leads?"

"Not yet, unfortunately." He provided a brief summary of his encounters of the evening.

"Great work," Kendis said. "At least we have an idea about the motive."

"Did you find the van?"

"Yes, we found a silver van with a flat tire in the Yerba Buena parking garage about seven blocks down from Dashiell Hammett Street. Good shot! It didn't have a license plate."

"Did anybody report a stolen car?"

"No, not yet. I assume the kidnappers escaped with another car in the garage. The owner probably parked there for the night and will only notice tomorrow."

"So, we are completely in the dark about where they might have gone."

"I'm afraid we've lost them. We analyzed the surveillance cameras in the garage, identified all cars that exited around the time of the abduction and are in the process of locating them. No luck thus far."

"Did you check the van?"

"Of course. Our team has checked for fingerprints or DNA. We found plenty from the woman but nothing else. The kidnappers did a thorough job. They probably wore gloves and wiped everything before they switched cars."

"Who is the owner of the silver van?"

"An eighty-two-year-old retired plumber from Twin Peaks. It was stolen as well."

"And your team found nothing?"

"Nothing that would lead us to the kidnappers or the victim."

Kendis was an outstanding police officer. But Angus only trusted his own eyes. "If you don't mind, I'd like to have a look as well."

"Of course, be my guest. The surveillance team is still there collecting evidence."

"Okay, I'm on my way."

# - 9 -

# FRIDA

The Breakout
Saturday, October 8, 2033, 10:00 p.m.

Frida woke up again. She looked around. Someone had turned off the light. It was dark. There were no clocks anywhere. She had no idea how long she had been out, but she felt more lucent and could see more clearly than earlier. The drugs in her system must have weaned off.

The full moon sent soft rays of light into the hospital room. She could outline the hospital bed, the bedside table, and the shadow of her fingers in front of her, including the wedding ring. Strange that they had left it on. Kidnappers who didn't care about diamonds. Her limbs also felt less heavy. She reached for her head and felt the bare skin of her scalp. She had hoped that it had been a nightmare, but it was real. All of her hair was gone. Frida clenched her fists. Her strength was back.

And there was another change. The belt around her waist hurt less. Frida carefully palpated it. It was less tight than before. She could slip her flat hand under it. Perhaps the nurse took pity on her and loosened it while she was sleeping. Frida suddenly felt energized. She moved upwards in her bed. The belt hit her pelvic bones. She pushed it downward with both hands, summoning all of her strength. It moved a little. Good. She put her feet on the mattress and pushed her body up. The belt moved an inch down. She pushed again from above. One more inch. And pushing the body upwards again. The belt was getting closer to her hips. This was the tightest part. It hurt. A lot.

Frida heard footsteps approaching. She pulled the blanket up to her chest and closed her eyes. The door opened, and the light went on. Frida didn't move and kept her eyes shut. The footsteps came closer. Frida focused on her breathing: *in and out, in and out*, as evenly as possible. The person was right in front of her. She could see their shadow through her closed eyes. Was it the nurse or the physician? Frida smelled a hint of roses. Hopefully, the woman. They grabbed the blanket. *God, please let her not see the belt on my hips*, Frida prayed. *I won't get a second chance like this.* The person pulled Frida's arm out from under the blanket and felt her pulse. Frida tried to quiet her panicking mind. *Stay calm, stay calm, stay calm*, she chanted to herself. The nurse moved the blanket down a few inches and placed something cold on her chest. A stethoscope. Frida lay perfectly still, careful not to move her eyes behind her eyelids. *Breathe in, breathe out*, she reminded herself. The cold instrument disappeared. The person tugged the blanket around her and turned the light off. The door shut.

Frida lay still for a moment, listening to the receding footsteps until they were gone. Then, with all her strength, she pushed the belt on her hips down. It was stuck. She exhaled to decrease the circumference of her lower belly and make more space. She pushed again. The belt slipped down. Her body was free! Frida could have cried for joy. She sat up and looked around.

Now, the next part. She had to get out of there. Behind her was a small window. It had no handle and could probably not be opened. But the transom above it was adjustable. Could she fit through it?

Frida got up. The world started spinning around her. She sat back on the bed and waited for a moment. Her body adjusted a bit. The spinning stopped. She was still very weak. She went to the window and inspected it. It might work.

Fortunately, she had been doing a lot of yoga lately, and her body was very agile. She stepped onto the windowsill. She still felt dizzy and placed her right arm through the windowsill to hold her body in place. Then she moved her right leg up. The lower frame was too sharp.

She went down, got a towel, and placed it over the lower window frame. That was better. Her right arm and leg were through the windowsill. Then, she pushed herself up with her left leg. Her body moved up. She steadied herself with one arm on each side of the window and pushed her pelvis through the narrow opening. The towel got lost, and the skin on her left thigh was scratched open. She bit her tongue. She had to get through. She turned her body so that both arms were now inside and her lower body was outside. There was no balcony, only a small windowsill. Her bare feet fumbled to locate it. There it was. She steadied herself. Her shaking hands began to loose their grip.

Were there approaching footsteps again? Frida panicked. She moved her head through the window and looked around. She was on the second floor of a large building. Below her was a small garden and a playground. To her right was a water pipe. She tiptoed over and grabbed it.

The door in her room flung open, and the light was turned on. A man in a white coat stepped into the room. That same man again. He stared at the empty bed, then looked around. Frida let herself down onto the water pipe, her hands becoming weaker and weaker with every movement. They had to hold her entire body, but they were not strong enough. Frida could hardly find support for her front toes along the way. She got a few meters down. The water pipe was slippery there. Frida tried to tighten her grip, but her hands gave in. She fell backward into the darkness. *This is where I die*, she thought. She landed with a crash on a tall container.

"Help, help!" someone inside screamed. "We are under attack! We are under attack!" She heard the sound of gunshots below her. Coming from inside the container? Directed at her? Her right shoulder hurt. She was not sure if it was from the impact or if she had been hit by a bullet. Then, she lost consciousness.

# - 10 -

# TERREL

The Parrot
Saturday, October 8, 2033, 10:30 p.m.

Niles had fallen asleep. Terrel kissed Imani goodbye and left for the night. They would take turns sleeping at the hospital or at home so that they would not lose their strength during these difficult times.

Terrel walked down the stairs to the first floor of the hospital, thinking about his little family. He had grown up in East Oakland and knew threats from the outside by heart—poverty, crime, theft, gun fights, protection rackets, and corrupt police officers. His father had been a primary school teacher, and his mother a homemaker, taking care of him and his brother. A devoted Christian, his mother had raised her sons with strict rules and kept them away from drugs and alcohol. Terrel had completed his bachelor's degree at Saint Mary's College in Moraga, California, funded by a scholarship. He met his wife Imani when he was twenty years old. They had married when he was twenty-two, and Niles was on the way a year later. He couldn't afford to continue studying, and so he decided to join the FBI when he was twenty-three years old, the minimum age for joining the Bureau. Since then, both he and Imani had worked hard to get their little family into a nice, safe neighborhood. They got a loan to buy a house in San Mateo when Niles was three years old.

Terrel thought that he'd created a safe little harbor for their family. He had never anticipated that the threat could come from within. A tumor was eating Niles from the inside. Unthinkable. The emergency physician had told them that they were still lucky that the tumor had not metastasized. Niles would get surgery and would then be fine. Hopefully. Terrel vowed that he would spend more time with his son. His family had always been his priority, but he had missed Nile's kindergarten events and sports games because of his job. No more. Niles and Imani would always come first, no matter what. Life was so fragile. It could be taken away at any moment.

Terrel walked down the hallway on the first floor of the hospital when he heard a loud crash and gunshots. The noise came from the garden, where he and Angus had their discussion earlier that day. He saw two security guards with flashlights running toward the rear end of the garden. Terrel pushed through the exit door to the garden and followed the guards. At the end of a well-manicured lawn was a large octagonal aviary cage with a beautifully carved wooden frame, stainless steel mesh, and a pointed aluminum roof. The roof was largely deformed. Inside the aviary was a large, colorful parrot, mostly red with a big splash of yellow and blue on its wings and tail. A macaw. He was jumping up and down on a large tree branch, swearing at a man in a white coat who held a young woman in a hospital gown in his arms. Her bald head and limbs were hanging down lifelessly. A nurse came running toward him.

"My goodness, doctor. How did that happen?" she exclaimed. "Is she dead?"

"She's just unconscious," the man said calmly. "Apparently, she climbed out of the window and down the pipe. She must have fallen down, or she jumped. I don't know. The aviary saved her life."

A security officer stepped forward and palpated the neck of the woman. "There is a pulse," he said. He held his hand in front of the woman's mouth. "And she's breathing."

Terrel had reached them along with several spectators.

"I'm sorry about this incident," the man in the white coat addressed the small crowd. "This is a patient from the psychiatry ward. She is fine. We will bring her back up."

"There were gunshots!" one of the spectators called.

"This was the parrot. Not sure where he learned that," the man said, pointing at the bird.

"Caramba!" the bird yelled at the crowd.

"That's his name," the security guard explained.

The spectators laughed. Terrel exhaled. A psychiatry incident. No need to get involved. He had other concerns right now. The crowd dissipated. The physician walked toward the building entrance with the patient in his arms, the nurse following closely.

The parrot continued to scream at the humans walking away from him. The white skin around his eyes was flushed. Terrel stood still and looked at the bird.

"I'm sorry. This must have been very disturbing. A human body falling on your roof," he said calmly.

The colorful parrot stood still and eyed Terrel through the mesh. Terrel's iPhone rang. He picked it up. There was no call. He looked around, but there was nobody else. He put his phone back in his pocket when it rang again, and again, there was no call. The third time, he realized that the tone was coming from the cage. The bird mimicked the phone faultlessly.

"You did this!" he said to the bird, pointing at him with his index finger. "That was a nice little trick. You can do that again for Niles tomorrow."

The parrot looked at him with a tilted head. "You can do that again tomorrow," he echoed. "Caramba."

Terrel nodded. What was he doing here? His son was sick. He suddenly felt tired. He was not up for games tonight. It would be another difficult day tomorrow. Time to go home. All the other people had left already. He turned around.

"We will kidnap her and get her to approve the claim," a male voice said behind him. Terrel jerked back. Was there someone after all? He walked around the aviary and checked his surroundings. There was nobody else, as far as he could tell. Was it the bird again?

"What did you just say?" he asked the feathered animal.

The bird blinked. "We will kidnap her and get her to approve the claim," he repeated.

Terrel pulled his cell phone again and started the recording mode.

"Caramba, repeat that," he said.

The bird looked at him again with a tilted head. He imitated the cell phone ring again.

"No, what did you just say?" Terrel asked.

The parrot made the sound of a smoke alarm.

"Sir, you need to step away from the parrot, please." A security officer approached them. Terrel had not noticed him.

"Did you hear what the bird just said?" Terrel asked.

"I heard that he is making siren sounds, which will disturb our patients. These parrots need to sleep at night, just like humans," the guard said firmly. "The garden is closed for the night. Please come back tomorrow."

"Of course." Terrel looked back at the bird, who drowned his beak in his chest feathers. "I will come back tomorrow."

He walked back to the atrium of the hospital. He sat down on a seat at the entrance area and sent Angus a text message. *I think I found a witness.*

Angus responded right away. *Great! I knew you would find something.*

Terrel responded, *It's a parrot.*

Angus sent a triple question mark. *???*

Terrel typed. *He imitated a voice that threatens to abduct a woman who should approve a claim.*

*Interesting,* Angus responded. *The bird could just have picked up something on the radio or from a different incident.*

*Agreed,* Terrel typed. *We need to know more. He needs to be interrogated.*

Angus sent a smiley face. *How do you interrogate a parrot?*

*I won't. Remember, I have to take care of Niles,* Terrel typed. *Perhaps you can send someone to figure this out?*

*Sure, I will look into this,* Angus responded. *Thanks for keeping your eyes and ears open!*

# - 11 -

# ANGUS

The Van
Saturday, October 8, 2033, 10:30 p.m.

Angus put the phone back into his pocket as he crossed Market Street in downtown San Francisco. A group of homeless men watched him from the corner at Ellis Street. One of them yelled some profanities after him. Angus put his head down. He had no time for a confrontation. He increased his pace and continued down 4th Street, passing by old Victorian mansions with crumbling facades, which had clearly seen better times. The four-lane street was busy. Cars raced by above the speed limit.

At the corner to Mission Street, a homeless woman in a ragged coat leaned against the pole of the traffic light, holding her hand out, mumbling something incomprehensible. The expression on her face was clear—misery and despair. He gave her two dollar bills. They were the last he had.

Angus crossed the street and stepped into the Yerba Buena Gardens parking garage, a large multi-story concrete building. A few people were standing in line at the cash register. The last looked over his shoulder with an anxious gaze. Likely tourists. Locals had toll boxes in their cars, which were recognized at the entrance and exit.

Angus walked up the dirty concrete stairs, stepping over dropped coffee paper cups, cigarette buds, beer cans, a used shirt, and various unidentifiable litter. It smelled of urine and cannabis.

At the entrance to the second floor, a policeman greeted him and checked his badge. The majority of the second floor had been sealed off with barricade tape. Several police officers patrolled along the perimeter of the sealed area, holding back spectators. Others were taking photos or sketches of the scene. Angus spotted Chief of Police Kendis in the center of the scene, inspecting the silver van. The sliding door stood wide open, and the right back tire was flat. It was surprising that the kidnappers had gotten this far.

Kendis greeted Angus as he came closer. "Hi, Angus. Do you recognize the van?"

"Yes, this is it," Angus confirmed. "You can see the holes in the front and driver side window—and the flat tire. If you find any bullets, they should fit to my gun."

Kendis nodded. "We secured three of them and will send them to forensics."

"Did you find anything else?" Angus asked.

"We looked for fingerprints. But we only found prints from the woman. The men likely used gloves. We found hair from the victim but none from the men."

"Did you find any clues in the videos from the parking garage?"

"We got more details from the videos, but not enough to track them down. The van arrived here shortly after 7 p.m. Two men in dark pants and jackets got out. They wore face masks and beanies, just as you described. We didn't get a good photo of their eyes, so we couldn't try an iris identification. They seemed to argue about something. The woman tried to exit the car. One of the men grabbed her and carried her to a red Fiat. The other smashed the window of the back door and opened it. They placed the woman on the back seat, got into the front seats, started the car, and drove away."

A sense of disappointment washed over Angus. "Did you identify the Fiat?" he asked.

Kendis nodded. "Yes, we did. It exited onto Minna Street and drove to Bayview and Hunters Point. We lost them there. There are only a few cameras in that area, and many of the existing ones have been smashed or are non-functional. We found the Fiat close to Hilltop Park. They probably stole another car."

"Can you find it by checking police reports?"

"Yes, we are in the process of doing that," Kendis said, her voice carrying a mix of determination and resolve. "But it will take time.

There are about seventy reports of stolen cars in San Francisco every day. We are checking them all, starting with those that have been stolen in the Bayview district around 7 p.m. But it is also possible that the kidnappers stole a car elsewhere and just parked it there. Or the theft has not even been reported yet. So, I'm not sure if we will get a lead that way."

"Can I see the van?" Angus asked.

"Of course," Kendis said with an inviting gesture toward the car. "Be my guest." Time was of the essence, and they both knew it.

Angus walked around the van. There were multiple scratches and small dents, but nothing too helpful for a suspect identification. The driver's door and the sliding door toward the back cabin were open. Angus inspected the driver's seat and dashboard first. They were shiny and dust-free. Somebody had wiped them down. Angus had previously thought the kidnappers were amateurs. But this looked like the work of a professional. The passenger seat was perfectly cleaned as well. No crumps, no hair, no dirt on the floor. Nothing in the glove compartment. Angus got out and looked into the back cabin.

"We found a few blonde hair strands and some blue fibers on the back seat, probably from the woman and her coat," Kendis said. "I sent it to forensics as well. There are plenty of fingerprints from her. We have secured those as well."

"Nothing from the kidnappers?" Angus looked under the seat.

"No."

Angus went to the back of the van and opened the trunk. It seemed to be empty as well. He turned on the flashlight of his iPhone and looked around. There was something in the right back corner. Angus got closer to inspect it. A colored feather? He pulled it out of a chink behind the back seat. A large red feather.

"What did you get there?" Kendis asked and came closer to inspect the feather in Angus' hand.

"Perhaps the feather of a parrot," Angus said.

"What does that have to do with anything?" Kendis asked.

"Well, I learned earlier today, that a parrot at SUEC talked about a kidnapping event."

"And you think that is related?" Kendis shook her head. "The bird could just have picked up something from a TV show. Or it could be a kid's prank?"

Angus held up the feather. "If this feather is from the same parrot, then the bird may be talking about our kidnapping event here."

"Or it could be unrelated, and this is just a random pigeon feather painted red?" Kendis countered, her voice laced with a hint of skepticism.

Angus met her gaze with a confident smile, his mind already connecting the dots. "That will be easy to check. Parrots synthesize their own red pigments, named psittacofulvins. Those pigments are found nowhere else. Not in other birds, other animals, or even plants."

"Wow, how do you know that? Is that part of the FBI training?"

"I helped uncover a parrot trafficking ring a few years ago."

Kendis shook her head. "Bird trafficking? Is that a thing?"

"A very lucrative business," Angus responded.

Kendis probed further. "So, if the feather is from the same parrot, you think you have a lead?"

Angus produced a Ziplock bag from his pocket and carefully placed the feather in it. "Yes, exactly. It's about observing the patterns, the subtle threads that tie seemingly unrelated events together. I will ask my team to get a feather from the parrot at SUEC and send it to our forensic lab for a DNA match analysis. If this feather belongs to the parrot that talked about a kidnapping event, then the owner either is the kidnapper or knows the kidnappers."

Kendis leaned forward, inspecting the feather in the bag. "This is crazy. How much does the parrot know?"

Angus shrugged. "I will ask him tomorrow."

"How will you interrogate a parrot?" Kendis asked.

Angus smiled. He had asked that same question earlier today.

"I don't know that yet," he said. "But I will figure it out."

# - 12 -

# FRIDA

The Demand
Saturday, October 8, 2033, 11:00 p.m.

Frida found herself tied up in the same hospital room and same bed as before, with the same restraining belt, except it was now tighter than ever before. She could hardly take a breath. It had been cold outside, and she realized that her body was still cold as well. She shivered under the thick blanket. She hadn't eaten for hours. She was thirsty and hungry. She looked around. The room was dark, with naked walls around her. There was an outline of a glass of water on the table beside her bed. She wanted to reach for it, but she felt dull pain around her wrists. Her hands were now tied to the restraining belt as well. She used all of her strength and twisted and pulled her hands under the cuffs, but she only tore her skin. Her capturers had been more thorough this time around. Frida felt pearls of sweat running down her temples. Her tongue was dry and stuck to her palate. She tried to lean her upper body toward the table. Perhaps she could reach the glass with her mouth. But the belt was tight. She couldn't move an inch. Frida leaned back and tried to think. The nurse had been told a suicide story about her. She didn't seem to know that Frida was abducted. If this was a hospital, there had to be a bell so that she could call her. She palpated the area around her hands. Nothing. She screamed.

The key in the door turned almost immediately. The man in the white coat stepped in. Her capturer. He turned the neon light on. Frida felt a reflex to cover her eyes from the piercing light, but her hands were tied. The man stepped toward her with long strides, his face contorted with anger. He carried a laptop under his arm and placed it on the table beside the water glass. He leaned over her and looked at her with cold, dark eyes.

"Hello, Frida," he said with a low voice. "I told the nurse that I would keep an eye on you. She has to attend to the entire ward and cannot sit at your bed all night long."

He leaned forward and raised his hand, fingers outstretched until it hovered just inches away from her. Frida could feel his hot breath on her skin, a chilling reminder of lurking danger. She spit in his face and screamed again as loud as she could. She needed the nurse. She was her only chance of rescue. With a quick move, the man put his hands over her mouth. It felt raw and callused, smelling of dirt. A rush of panic surged through her veins, her instincts urging her to fight back. But the weight of his palm pressed firmly against her lips silenced her, trapping her terror within. Frida grasped for air.

"If you scream again, I will kill you," the man said coldly, his gaze devoid of mercy. "It will be my gift to the world. One more word out of this ugly mouth, and you're dead. Do you understand?"

Frida felt dizzy. Her body trembled. She nodded. The man removed his hand slowly. Frida took a deep breath.

"I need some water," she said.

He slapped her face. "You're not here to make demands," he said with an angry voice. "You only think about yourself. You, you, you. I'm not concerned about *you*."

"What do you want from me?" Frida cried.

"You will answer *my* questions. *Only* my questions." He reached for his laptop, opened it, and placed it on her lap.

Frida's cheek burned, and her heart raced. She was scared to make another noise. The man looked at her as if he was only waiting for a reason to slap her again.

He brought up a photo, a headshot, of a young girl. Perhaps five years old. Stunning wide amber eyes framed by long brown curly hair. A real beauty. She smiled into the camera. Her lips widened as if she said something while the photo had been taken.

"Do you know her?" he asked.

Frida shook her head.

The man slapped her again. "Think harder. Her name is Maya. This photo was taken before she started her chemotherapy."

"I have never seen this girl in my life," Frida cried. "Perhaps this is a big misunderstanding."

The man brought up a set of medical imaging studies. "Do you recognize this?" he asked with a hateful gaze.

Frida looked at the medical images. They looked faintly familiar. The CT scan demonstrated a large soft tissue mass in the abdomen, which extended upwards through the chest all the way up to the lower neck. The mass was centered in the area of the left adrenal gland, contained small calcifications and encircled the abdominal vessels. A metaiodobenzylguanidine, MIBG, radiotracer scan confirmed the very large primary tumor and multiple metastases.

Frida looked at the man, scared to ask him if this was his child. It dawned on her that this was about her insurance work.

"Do you recognize *these* images?" he repeated.

"I believe this is a neuroblastoma," Frida mumbled.

"Well, you seem to recognize something after all," the man said with a bitter tone. "Let me help you out. Maya lives in Las Vegas, Nevada. She was diagnosed with neuroblastoma about three years ago and received her first treatment there. She endured three years of chemotherapy, surgery, and radiation therapy. She lost all of her beautiful hair and got thinner and thinner. But the worst was the pain. The surgeries, bone biopsies, lumbar punctures, needle sticks, anesthesia, chemotherapy. And after all that, her tumor came back. We were told that she would qualify for MIBG therapy. Do you know what that is?"

Frida swallowed.

"Do you know what that is?" the man asked again, holding his fist in front of her face.

"Metaiodobenzylguanidine (MIBG) is a compound that can be combined with radioactive iodine (I-131) to deliver radiation therapy to the tumor tissue," Frida said softly.

"That's right," the man exclaimed. "MIBG therapy is supposed to be more effective, less painful, and requires less time in the hospital than other treatments. But this therapy is only available in certain hospitals. To get it, Maya had to move out of state to a hospital in California. And this is where you came in, you little shit."

He held a piece of paper in front of her. "This is *your* letter, informing Maya's mother that her treatment was not covered. Attached is a pamphlet that states that Pleonexia Nevada only covers medical expenses in Nevada. This limitation is not disclosed on the Pleonexia website or on the ten-page "Summary of Benefits" provided by the insurance, even though Pleonexia also has offices in California. Such a major limitation should be listed in bold letters at the top of the first page! But it wasn't."

"That is insurance policy, not much I can do about it," Frida said. Her tongue felt heavy. She was so thirsty.

The man's gaze furrowed. "*You* should have recognized a network deficiency. If the needed care cannot be provided within the network, then the insurance can authorize out-of-network treatment. For rare pediatric cancers such as neuroblastoma, getting the best care often means going out of state. *You* could have authorized out-of-network treatment, but *you* chose not to do that. *You* prevented Maya from getting potentially life-saving treatments."

"I'm really sorry," Frida said with a hoarse voice.

The man patted her shoulder. "I have good news for you, Frida. You will set this right tonight. Maya has just been admitted to SUEC Hospital. And you will approve her treatment now."

He pushed a button on the browser on the laptop computer. The Pleonexia website opened. He clicked the link to the intranet. Then, he produced a magnet key from his pocket and released Frida's hands.

"There you go." He elevated the upper part of her bed.

"This is not me alone. It is a procedure that involves downstream administrative approval," she said.

"Just be yourself and don't worry about others," the man grunted. "Do your part."

Frida looked at the man. What would he do after she had completed his request? Kill her? The hate in his eyes made her shiver.

He produced a Taser from his pocket and held it in front of her. "Do you need more persuasion?" he asked.

"No." Her primal instinct to survive kicked in. With trembling fingers, Frida typed the password and logged into the internal network. "I need my phone for dual authentication," she said.

The man produced a brand-new phone from his other pocket. "Here you go," he said. "I duplicated your account."

*How did he do that?* Frida didn't dare ask another question. She logged into the claim authorization system. "What is her last name?" she asked.

"I have the medical record number for you," the man answered. He dictated the number, and Frida found the claim request. Maya Trento Esposito. Frida tried to concentrate, but she felt so thirsty. Her entire body started to tremble, and her vision got blurry. She went through the claim request. She had to add a justification for out-of-network coverage. Then, she hit the approve button.

"As I said, it requires additional sign-off," she explained.

"Let me worry about that," the man said. He snatched the laptop from her.

Frida watched the man as he turned around. Was he Maya's father? She felt pity for him. But a sick child didn't justify a crime. She needed water—and insulin. Should she tell him about her diabetes? Her cheek burned. No, better wait for the nurse. She would come by to check on her eventually.

The thirst was unbearable. Frida reached for the water glass. Fortunately, the man hadn't tied her hands again.

He jumped around. "Still thinking all about yourself? Didn't I tell you not to move? This will teach you a lesson!" He held the Taser at her neck.

Frida's body started to convulse in an uncontrolled full-body muscle contraction. It was more painful than anything she had ever experienced. The glass toppled over and fell to the ground, the precious liquid spreading over the tiled floor. After a hellish few seconds, the cramps stopped.

"That's for all the pain you caused my little girl," the man said. He sent her a last hateful gaze, turned around, and left.

# - 13 -

# ANNYA

## The Link
### Saturday, October 8, 2033, 11:00 p.m.

Annya checked her watch. 11:00 p.m. already, and she was still in the ER. She had chatted with Lili for a while to find out if Julius had been present for his entire shift. Lili confirmed that her colleague had been busy with his patients since 2 p.m., consulting her about her opinion for every single patient. Due to his critical comments about the insurance claim rejections, Annya had wondered if Julius had anything to do with the abduction of the insurance agent. But he had an alibi. He was working in the ER when the woman had been kidnapped. Of course, considering his wealth, he could've easily hired somebody to do the job. But why? There was no clear motive either.

Annya went to see Julius in the ER to see if she could spot anything else that was suspicious. He happily consulted her on another case. And another. He had his usual positive, cheerful attitude, no signs that this day was anything out of the ordinary for him. His chin was still swollen from the encounter in the parking lot, but he didn't seem to have any negative feelings about it either. He thanked Annya for her help at the end of the shift and left.

And here she was, walking down the hospital hallway again, her stomach growling like an angry lion. She had covered the morning ER shift earlier today, only munched a granola bar for lunch, then Angus had canceled their dinner. Annya realized that she was starving. She didn't have much food in the refrigerator in her apartment, and who knew if another clinical emergency would come up until she got there.

Better to eat something now. Fortunately, the SUEC Hospital cafeteria was open 24/7.

Annya took a right turn in the hospital atrium and followed the signs to the cafeteria. Few people were walking in this direction at such a late time. After a busy day, Annya relished the silence, listening to the soothing echo of her own footsteps in the empty corridor.

She reached a large hall with high ceilings and large windows that overlooked an outdoor garden. She scanned her ID at the entrance gate and went to the server-less food serving area. She grabbed a tray and an iced tea, then went to the salad bar and from there to the heated kitchen tops. Various cooked food items had been doled out into appropriate servings, covered in recyclable plastic domes, and placed onto trays on self-serving racks. Annya chose a few slices of pizza and went to the exit, where her card was automatically charged. She grabbed some cutlery on her way out and went to the dining area, a beautiful hall with a green wooden parquet floor, large indoor palm trees, and a variety of wooden booths and benches, barstools, and chairs with integrated power units that allowed patients, visitors, and staff to charge their electronic devices.

There were a few people scattered around. Annya was surprised to see the pediatric oncologist on one of the highchairs. He had spotted her as well and waved. Annya walked toward him.

"Hi, Dr. Queirós Trento. Can I join you?" she asked awkwardly. She didn't usually eat in the cafeteria, and she didn't know the oncologist very well.

"Of course," he said with an inviting gesture toward the high table on which he was sitting. "I hate to eat alone. Call me Rogério if you like."

"Thanks, Rogério. You can call me Annya." Annya took a seat opposite of him and arranged her food items around her. She opened her iced tea and started to eat a slice of pizza. It tasted fantastic, slightly salty dough with a flavor of tomato, basil, and mozzarella cheese. She gulped down the whole slice and flushed it with a large swig of iced tea. A warm sensation expanded in her belly. She felt much better.

The man in front of her spooned a thick soup. It smelled deliciously of beans, bacon, onions, and garlic.

"What are you eating?" she asked.

"Feijoada," he answered, licking his lips.

"What is that?"

"It is a slow-cooked black bean stew with beef and pork, a national dish of Brazil. I was surprised they had it here."

"Is that where you come from? Brazil?" Annya asked, reaching for another pizza slice. She remembered Julius' comments, but this was a great starter for a conversation.

Rogério nodded. "My parents immigrated from São Paulo to New York when I was eight years old. My father started a restaurant, and the entire family helped build it up. For me, the immigration to the US was a gift. I was good at school, I met a great mentor, I won a research contest, got a scholarship, and went to Stanford for both undergraduate and graduate school."

"That is impressive," Annya said. "A true American story."

Rogério had finished his soup and wiped his mouth with a napkin. "Yes, indeed. I feel incredibly fortunate for the opportunities provided to me. But it wasn't easy," he said. "I came to Stanford with a single suitcase. Inside was all I had. I survived on ten dollars a day, planning all expenses to the penny on an Excel sheet. With so many rich kids around me, I was ashamed to share my situation with anyone. I had odd jobs, and I studied around the clock to build a better future."

"What kept you going?" Annya asked.

"Don't get me wrong. I wasn't unhappy," he said. "I was proud to be at Stanford—and so was my family. I gave them a sense of honor. I didn't know about office politics or greedy companies at that time. There was an innocence and purity about those days. I was just a kid chasing his dreams."

"And you're not anymore?" Annya asked. As a CIA field operative, she was trained in undercover interrogations. The information provided by her new colleague could be important. And it would allow her to predict how he would react in other situations. She ate her salad slowly now to encourage him to speak while she was eating.

"Well, the world is more complicated than we think when we are young."

"What do you mean?" Annya asked. "You seem to do very well as faculty at SUEC?"

Rogério looked down. "Yes, I was always the lucky one. I'm sorry, I really don't want to waste your time with drama."

"Are you on call tonight?" Annya asked.

Rogério nodded.

"Then, we have plenty of time." She smiled at him. "If something bothers you, it often helps to share it with a friend."

Rogério sighed. "I didn't know we were friends. We just met. And there's not much to tell. I fell head over heels in love with the prettiest girl in my class at medical school. Her name was Destiny, *nomen est omen*. She came from Puerto Rico to New York as a young girl. We connected over the many things that felt strange to us at an elite college, the invisible rules and expectations of rich people. Her smile was like a sun that lifted me above my desolate existence. She was full of optimism, always seeing the good in people. I wanted to marry her. But she died. That's it. That's the story."

"I'm sorry.  That is very tragic indeed," Annya said. "What happened?"

"Destiny got sick," Rogério explained. "She developed excruciating bone pain along her back, hips, and thighs. I still have her photo and her MR images. She inspired me to become an oncologist." He opened a file on his iPhone and showed it to Annya.

Annya looked at the images. A photo of a teenage girl with hazel eyes and long silky black hair smiling into the camera. Annya flipped through the MRI images, which were very small on the iPhone display. But Annya could see that the entire bone was abnormal. "Leukemia?" she asked.

"Yes, indeed," he said. "The problem was Destiny's high deductible insurance plan. To save money, she went to the doctor as infrequently as possible and tried to economize everywhere. She waited too long for the pain to just go away. When it didn't, she signed up for a research MRI, which she could get for free. She didn't know that the images were only reviewed by an expert once a month. So, after many weeks of pain, it was finally determined that her bone marrow was very abnormal. She was referred to an oncologist, who initiated the necessary blood and bone marrow analyses. Destiny was diagnosed with acute lymphocytic leukemia when the disease was already far advanced."

"I'm very sorry to hear that," Annya said. "And from your earlier comments, I assume that she didn't recover?"

"She died a few months later," Rogério said. "Her family was fighting with the insurance company about coverage every day along the way." Tears filled his eyes.

*Perhaps his first love,* Anny thought. *Sharing this still upsets him to the core, even after such a long time.* She gave him a probing gaze. But he had recovered already. Excellent self-control.

"Julius said that you're very good in negotiations with the insurance companies. Is this where that comes from?" she asked.

"Yes, I was very much influenced by this experience." Rogério took a sip from his diet Coke can.

"Did you find a new love?" Annya asked.

Rogério shook his head. "Destiny was the love of my life. I never married after she died."

Rogério's cell phone went off. He looked at the display, then Annya. "I'm sorry I told you my whole life and didn't get a chance to learn anything about you," he said. "This is the oncology ward."

"Don't worry. There isn't much to share on my end," Annya responded. "I'm an undercover police officer."

Rogério smiled with a nervous look. *Eye-mouth disconnection.*

"Just kidding." Annya smiled back.

They both laughed. He took the call.

Annya put the two trays and empty plates together. "I can return those," she said.

"Thank you!" Rogério nodded with a grateful look, then turned around and walked toward the hospital corridor with long strides.

Annya took out her phone and sent a text to Angus: *Check out Dr. Rogério Gabriel Queirós Trento. Personal issues with health insurance. Could be revenge.*

He answered right away. *Thanks. Will do.*

# - 14 -

# FRIDA

The Exigency
Saturday, October 8, 2033, 11:30 p.m.

Frida was not sure how much time had gone by since the man had left the hospital room. She felt dizzy and nauseated. The moon crept through the hospital window and faintly illuminated the sterile room. The ceiling above her started to spin around. Had someone drugged her again or was her diabetes getting out of control? Frida tried to sit up, but the restraining belt held her back. She was thirsty. Her tongue felt swollen, parched, and glued to the roof of her mouth. A single drop of moisture would help. She reached for the glass on the floor. Her fingertips could touch it, but she couldn't grab it. It was just beyond her reach, teasing her weakened resolve. Frida fixed her eyes upon it. *Think*, she reminded herself. *You can solve this.* Fortunately, the glass was made out of some plastic material. It had not burst into shards. She stretched her arm and could touch it with her fingertips. She rotated the glass around, and there—she got it at the rim. Frida brought it up to her mouth. A little fluid was left in it. She licked it out. It didn't help much. Time crawled forward, every minute amplifying her unquenched thirst. Frida's vision blurred as her body weakened. Her diabetes had never been a choice. It was an unyielding companion, a constant reminder of her body's fragility.

Frida stared at the bare walls around her. Was there something crawling down the wall on her right? An insect? She squinted her eyes, trying to make out what it was. A big dark spider with long, hairy legs! It was coming toward her. There was another one and another one. A whole army of spiders crawled toward her. Frida screamed as loud as she could.

She heard footsteps approaching. *Please, the nurse,* she prayed. The key was turned, and the door flung open. No, it was the man again. He turned on the neon light, which hit her like a whip. Her eyes hurt. But the spiders were gone. The man walked toward her, inspecting her intently. Sweat was running down her temples, and she had difficulties focusing her gaze on him. She lay still in her hospital bed, her weakened body a vessel of vulnerability, unable to escape. The man's silhouette appeared fuzzy. He extended his hand toward her. *Not another hit.* Frida held her arm in front of her face. He gently put his hand on her forehead. It felt cool and much softer than before, not calloused at all. *How did his hand change like that? Strange.* His face looked worried. *Was she dreaming?* The silhouette of the man was duplicated. Now, there were two of him, standing in front of her.

"She has fever and a flushed face," the man said. "Perhaps she caught something while running around outside in her nightgown."

"I couldn't care less," his shadow beside him said. "We can kill her. Just push a cushion on her face."

Frida screamed again. The nurse had to hear her. She was her only chance of rescue from this nightmare.

The shadow slapped her face. There was the calloused hand again. "If you scream one more time, I will kill you. Do you understand?"

Frida swallowed. She stopped screaming. Fear encircled her throat.

The man turned to his shadow. "You are not a murderer," he said calmly. "You wanted to get care for your little girl. You got it."

"And now what?" the shadow said. "Do you want to let her go? She will continue to hurt innocent children and try to send us to jail."

"No, she won't," the man said. "She will understand. I need one more day with her. She is a good person. She experienced her own hardships and made wrong choices. Just like you."

"Are you on her side now?" the shadow cried. "She needs to be punished!"

Frida understood the gravity of their debate, and her heart pounded with a mixture of fear and disbelief. She strained to decipher their intentions, her mind caught in a maelstrom of dread and desperation.

"Look at her," the man said. "She has been punished enough already. Don't you remember? 'Darkness cannot drive out darkness. Only light can do that.' Martin Luther King. You cherished his quotes when you were young. You got the revenge you wanted. And your girl is getting her treatment now."

Frida looked from the man to his shadow. The realization that her life hung in the balance hit her with a force that eclipsed her thirst. Waves of terror crashed over her. Was this debate real or was she fantasizing? The man and the shadow looked identical. She remembered the old story about the two wolves in every person, one good, the other evil. They were constantly fighting with each other to gain control. The wolf whom you feed will be the wolf you become. Could she sway the wolves to do good?

"I have diabetes," she whispered with a hoarse voice. "I need my insulin." Frida's body trembled, her senses heightened to the point of impeding collapse.

The man palpated her pulse and held his face close to Frida's.

"She has an increased heart rate and respiration rate. And she is perspirating. I will call the nurse," he said calmly.

"Thank you," Frida whispered.

"What a sweet new friendship!" the shadow exclaimed with a hateful expression on his face. "Did you already forget what she did?"

"No, of course, I didn't," the man said calmly. "But I do believe that she can learn. If you kill her, she will just be replaced by another claim agent. If she *decides* to help us, she could be a powerful ally."

"Why don't you ask her now?" the shadow said, pointing at Frida with a hateful gaze. "Will she suddenly turn a switch and be a good person? No, she is far too greedy for that. She is getting paid to deny *children* life-saving care. How much more evil can a person be?"

"She needs to get better first, then I will talk with her. If she truly has type 1 diabetes and experienced all this stress and didn't get her insulin, there is a high risk that she develops a ketoacidosis."

"Why would I care?" the shadow asked.

"In the absence of insulin, the body starts burning off fat tissue to create ketone bodies, which can act as a poison. This can be life-threatening."

"Great!" the shadow responded. "We just leave her to that, and the problem solves itself. We never touched her, and tomorrow, we have one less problem. I want her to *pay* for what she did!"

"We are here to do good, not to murder anyone," the man said firmly. "Give me one day. I can turn her around."

"No way," the shadow countered. "She is evil."

"Give me one day," the man insisted. "If I'm not successful by tomorrow evening, then I will step back and deny that I was ever involved. You can take over and solve the problem your way."

Frida's mind raced, scrambling to comprehend the magnitude of the situation. Her life hung on a mere debate as if she were nothing more than a chess piece to be sacrificed.

The shadow looked at the man, contemplating the situation. "Deal," he grunted. "Either she's a new person by tomorrow night, or we say goodbye to her once and for all. I can't wait for that to happen."

Frida looked at them with wide-open eyes. How could anyone contemplate such a heinous bargain? What did the man want from her? She had to play along with him to save her life. A surge of determination coursed through her veins. She would find a way out of this nightmare.

The shadow followed her neckline with his extended index finger. "I cannot wait to make you pay for all the pain you caused my little girl," he said coldly. "I *swear* I will make you pay!"

A shiver ran down Frida's spine. She didn't say anything.

"I know how you feel," the man said softly. "But you need to focus on your daughter now. This woman is just stealing your time. Let's go." The man and his shadow left, closing the door behind them.

A few minutes later, the nurse rushed into the room.

# - 15 -

# TERREL

The Parents
Sunday, October 9, 2033, 7:00 a.m.

Niles was holding his robot in the air as the nurse led his wheelchair down the hospital hallway to the pediatric oncology ward. It was hospital policy to transport patients in a bed or wheelchair rather than letting them walk on their own.

"Turn right," Chip the robot said. Niles giggled. The nurse took a right turn and continued down the hallway. Imani and Terrel followed them. Terrel was filled with anxiety. Was it the right decision to move to the oncology ward? Niles was scheduled for surgery. The chemotherapy would come later. Of course, they needed to develop a relationship with the pediatric oncologists. But was it good to do this now, before the surgery? Would Niles get scared when he saw other kids suffering, bald and pale? Terrel watched his son, who was completely absorbed by his robot toy. How would he take all this? His heart contracted.

They reached a closed double door with a sign for Pediatric Oncology. The nurse pushed a button at the entrance, and the doors opened automatically.

"You have arrived!" Chip the robot said in his metallic voice.

Another hallway stretched out in front of them. It was more colorful than the one with framed children's paintings on both sides of the wall. They heard guitar music in the distance. A teenager with an amputated leg crossed the hallway on crutches. Imani sent Terrel an alarmed gaze. He saw a mixture of apprehension and fear in her watery eyes.

They passed a row of doors on each side of the hallway, which were adorned with whimsical designs. One door showed friendly woodland creatures frolicking amidst fluttering leaves, and another depicted smiling dolphins and an octopus dancing through coral reefs. Sally explained that these were the patient rooms. Some of them were closed, and others were open. Terrel peaked into one of the rooms and saw a family having an early morning picnic on their prayer mats. Niles waved at them, and a young girl waved back.

They continued down the hallway until they reached a nursing station, a large, semicircular desk adorned with an array of monitors and a variety of medical equipment. Nurses in scrubs of various colors walked in and out of the station, interacted with holographic computer screens or gathered in huddled conversations. The sound of ringing telephones, clattering keyboards, and the soft murmurs of conversations filled the air. Sally approached a male nurse behind the desk. He got up and walked to the family.

"Welcome! My name is Aziel," he said. "I will take care of you during your stay here." He leaned over to Niles. "Hello, Niles. It is great to meet you!"

"Hello," Niles said. "Will you show me where the clown is?"

Aziel nodded. "Of course! The clown comes to our playroom every morning at 10 a.m. Until then, you can check out the playroom if you like?"

Niles nodded eagerly. Aziel extended his hand. Niles slipped off his chair and grabbed it, his robot tucked under the other arm.

Aziel looked at the parents. "Perhaps one of you can come with us, and the other can help Sally getting Niles belonging's organized in his new room? His room number will be thirty-three. Please put any valuables in the lockers there."

Imani looked at Terrel. "Do you want to go with them?" she asked.

"Sure," Terrel said.

"There is a small kitchen at the end of the hallway." Aziel pointed ahead. "You can get coffee and snacks there if you like."

"That sounds great," Imani sighed. Terrel saw the first smile on her face this morning. Perhaps it was good that they had come here after all. The team here was experienced in taking care of all the small things that a parent with a sick child couldn't think about. Imani followed Sally down the hallway while Aziel showed Niles and Terrel the children's playroom, a large bright room with painted walls in a jungle theme and beautifully crafted arched windows.

Niles stopped at the entrance for a moment, deciding what to do. To their left, two children were playing with a model train. In the middle, a guitar player was surrounded by a group of kids. To their right was a table with painting materials, where a little girl and a woman in a hijab were working together on a watercolor project. Niles walked toward the guitar player and sat down on a multi-colored seating cube between a young boy in pajamas and a bald little girl in a pretty blue and white dotted dress. She was perhaps five years old. They smiled at each other. Niles didn't seem to notice her bald head.

"You can find me at the nurse station if you need anything," Aziel said in a low voice to Terrel. "Dr. Queirós Trento will do his rounds around 8 a.m. Please be in your room then if you want to talk with him."

Terrel nodded. The nurse left, and Terrel took a seat on a bench in the back of the room beside a few other adults who were watching their kids or checking their phones.

The guitar player was telling a story between his songs. The kids listened intently. When he played the guitar again, they clapped and sang along.

The woman beside him leaned toward him. "Which kid is yours?" she asked.

Terrel pointed at Niles.

"Oh, what a cute little boy! You must be very proud," she said. "My Maya is sitting right next to him." She pointed at the girl with the bald head. "She is here for MIBG therapy. I really hope it will get her tumor under control."

"Were you content with the treatment here at SUEC?" Terrel asked.

The woman nodded. "The team here is outstanding. They go above and beyond to help these kids. Especially Rogério. He is an angel," she said with admiration in her voice. "I don't know how I would have pulled through without him. He reminds me a lot of my ex-husband, the good parts of him anyway."

"You're divorced?" asked Terrel.

The woman's gaze dropped. She nodded slowly, her lips forming a thin line. "Yes. My husband, the man I thought I'd spend my life with, he...he cheated on me. Not just once but multiple times." Her fingers slightly trembled as they clutched the edge of the bench. "He shattered my heart into pieces, and I couldn't bear it any longer. I had to throw him out to find some semblance of strength left in me."

Terrel's heart ached for the pain he could see radiating from her.

"And then," she paused, a pained expression crossing her face, "then, Maya became ill." Her voice dropped to a hushed, almost reverent tone. "My daughter. My sweet Maya." Tears shimmered in her eyes. "I've always wondered," she continued, her voice tinged with a mixture of guilt and regret, "if the stress of our separation was somehow responsible for her developing that tumor."

Terrel's heart softened as he gazed at her. He spoke gently, "I don't think there's always a reason for why these things happen to our loved ones. We often search for answers, trying to make sense of the pain, but sometimes life just hands us an unlucky fate."

The woman's eyes met Terrel's, a glimmer of gratitude shining through the lingering sadness.

"It must be difficult to manage this all by yourself," Terrel added.

The woman's lips slightly quivered as she nodded once more. "You bet. I was so grateful that Rogério offered to help me deal with the insurance. Greedy monsters. Never expect your insurance carrier to do the right thing! I had to fight for our daughter's life and for healthcare coverage by Pleonexia."

"Pleonexia?" Terrel said. "We have the same insurance carrier. Are they difficult?"

The woman looked at him with pity. "I'm afraid Pleonexia is the worst," she said. "They deny everything they can. Every week, I get new bills and don't know which of these are covered or not. I lost our entire life's savings to Maya's care. But the worst part is that I have to deal with all this while Maya is getting through her therapy."

A man in a black shirt and blue jeans leaned forward and chimed in. "We faced the same issues with our son, Grant. Pleonexia denied coverage for his MRI scan at SUEC because he already had a CT scan from our local clinic. But Grant's tumor was more complicated than the average tumor. His physicians needed more information to plan his therapy properly. Did you know that Pleonexia denied 40 million insurance claims last year? 40 million! The staff here are too busy to appeal because they are saving our children's lives. Most parents don't appeal because they are overwhelmed and don't understand how the system works."

The man with the guitar started singing "Old MacDonald Had A Farm." The kids sang along. A nurse walked toward the parents with clapping hands, inviting them to join in. They did.

Terrel tried to process the information about the health insurance. Hopefully, he would not encounter similar issues.

After the song, the guitar man started to tell another story. Niles, along with several other kids, hung on his words.

Terrel leaned toward the woman beside him and asked in a low voice, "Is there a particular person at Pleonexia who is responsible for the insurance problems? Someone who can be contacted?"

She shook her head. "I only get letters from the Pleonexia Claims Office. If there were a single person who is responsible, I would kill them," she said firmly, looking at Terrel with a serious gaze.

She meant it.

"And I would help her!" the man said.

The woman and the man laughed, a brief release of tension in the face of overwhelming challenges.

Terrel looked at them in surprise. The parents here were ordinary people, thrust into extraordinary circumstances by the cruel hand of fate. They bonded over their shared frustrations and determination to fight against an uncaring system. And their anger could probably get out of control quite easily.

"Thanks for sharing your experience," he said politely. "Our family just arrived, and I appreciate your insights. My name is Terrel Wright." He extended his hand.

The woman shook it. "Damitra Trento Esposito," she said.

"Nice to meet you, Terrel," the man said. "I'm Jabari Smith."

Terrel made a mental note. He would write down their names as soon as he found a private moment.

# - 16 -

# FRIDA

The First Lesson
Sunday, October 9, 2033, 7:00 a.m.

Frida woke up renewed and energized. The nurse had administered insulin, intravenous fluid, and electrolytes last night. And a sleeping pill which had sent her into a deep sleep. When she woke up, the thirst, dizziness, and nausea had resolved. The nurse brought her a healthy breakfast and introduced her to the daytime nurse. Frida explained to both that she had been brought to the hospital against her will and that she wanted to leave. They only gave her a knowing smile, patted her shoulder, and told her that she had to stay for a few more days until she was better. They clearly believed the suicide story from the man in the white coat more than hers.

One good thing had come out of Frida's attempted escape. She now knew where she was. She had recognized the hospital garden immediately. She was at SUEC Hospital. The hospital where she had worked for years. She knew the building by heart—and the people who worked there. Unfortunately, as a pediatrician, Frida had had limited interactions with the adult psychiatry department. But if she could get out of this ward, she could run down the backstairs and secret corridors that only the insiders knew—and other physicians, of course, like the man who got her here. She asked for the name of the man in the white coat, and the nurses responded that he was her rescuer and wanted to stay anonymous. He had to be a physician in this hospital. Otherwise, the nurses would not accept his orders. But he was not her treating psychiatrist. Otherwise, they would have revealed his name. Frida requested to see the responsible physician and was told that the psychiatrist on call would do remote rounds on the weekend and come by in person on Monday. She asked for a telephone, and the nurse politely told her that phone calls or visits were not allowed at this time. Frida remained tied to her bed. At least she got a button that allowed her to call the nurse any time. When Frida told the nurse that she had to go to the bathroom, the nurse brought a bedpan. She explained that considering Frida's night escapades, they couldn't risk letting her loose again. She squeezed Frida's hand, told her that she would check on her later again, and left. Frida clenched her fists. She had to get out of there as quickly as possible.

Frida tried to calm down her anxious mind and think. She couldn't leave unless and until she got out of the restraining belt. Fortunately, the nurse had released her hands. She explored the belt with her fingers. It was much tighter now than ever before, no way to squeeze herself out of it. The ring finger of her left hand got stuck under the belt. When she pulled it out, she noticed a small tear in the belt. *My god. That was it.* The diamond ring could cut the belt. It was a piece of work, but she could make it. Frida got to work right away. She took the ring off and rubbed the diamond against the belt. A few more strings cut, and a few more, and so on. Her cheeks flushed in excitement as she noticed her progress.

She heard footsteps approaching. She quickly slipped the ring back on and pulled the blanket up to her chest. The door opened, and the man in the white coat stepped in. It had dawned outside, but he switched on the light regardless. White rays of light embraced them.

"Good morning, Frida. Are you feeling better this morning?" He extended his hand.

Frida hated that he addressed her by her first name. But she nodded and shook his hand. It was soft. It had felt very different last night. Frida peeked at his left hand. It looked fleshy but no different than the right hand. Perhaps he had worn gloves yesterday. That was the best explanation she could think of. She looked for an ID on his coat and couldn't find any.

"Who are you?" she asked.

"I'm your guardian angel," he said.

"Well, I don't believe in angels, and I haven't heard of ones that drive vans and abduct innocent women," she snapped back.

"Me neither," the man answered. "You were not abducted. Perhaps you're imagining something. You were in a state of ketosis when you arrived."

"I know very well what happened," Frida snapped.

"Is that right?" the man answered. "Do you remember how you tried to throw yourself in front of a train?"

Frida looked at the man. She started to doubt her own senses. The man looked dignified and trustworthy in his starched white coat. "No," she said. "Why would I do that? Perhaps *you* confuse me with somebody else."

"You felt remorse for how you treated innocent children," the man said. "Can I help you remember?"

A spark of doubt rose in her mind. What was he talking about? Did she do something while she was sedated? She remembered the Taser and decided to play along.

"Sure," Frida said. "Please help me remember." She was the master of debates. If this man wanted to tell her some fairytales, she would talk him into the ground.

The man handed an iPad to her. He opened it and clicked on a file. "This is what you saw," he said.

Frida looked at the file. There was a medical record number and history on the top: twelve-year-old male with a malignant germ cell tumor. There were medical images attached. She recognized the format of the file. This was how she received insurance claims at Pleonexia. She didn't recognize the case. She received too many of those. She looked at the man in front of her. Was this his son, perhaps?

"Open the medical file," he asked.

Frida opened it.

"What does it show?" the man asked her.

"I assume that is this boy's tumor," she responded. "I usually don't look at the images. I rely on the radiologist report."

"Okay, let me help you out here," the man said. "The ultrasound shows a mass in the left testis, suggestive of a malignant germ cell tumor. The CT scan of the abdomen shows large lymph node metastases in the abdomen at the level of the hilum of the left kidney.

This is a typical area of metastases from testicular tumors."

"I know that," Frida said. "And your point is?"

"My point is that you don't know the patient behind these images," the man said softly. He clicked on another file on the iPad, a video file. It showed a young male teenager lying in a fetal position in a hospital bed, sobbing. A woman with short, layered red hair was sitting on a chair beside his bed.

"Should I ask the nurse to bring you some more pain medication?" she asked. She was in her late thirties. Her straight, long nose and thin lips resembled those of the boy, perhaps the mother.

"I don't need anything!" the boy cried, turning around and pulling the blanket up to his neck.

"He just had surgery," the physician explained to Frida. "An orchiectomy, a resection of the left testis. Can you imagine how traumatizing this is for a young teenager?"

Frida shrugged. She felt uncomfortable.

The woman in the video patted the boy's shoulder. "I'm here with you, Carl," she said softly. "We will fight this together!"

"I wish I was dead," the boy cried.

"Please don't say that, sweetie," the women whispered, tears streaming down her face. She tried to embrace the boy, but he turned away from her.

The man stopped the video.

"The pediatric oncologist who took care of this patient prescribed anti-depressants. But guess what happened?" He stared at Frida with a furrowed gaze.

"I don't know," she said. Although, she had a feeling what he was hinting at.

"Well, the insurance agent sent this poor mother a letter that the costs for the anti-depressant would not be covered because they were not deemed medically necessary. *You* sent her this letter!"

"I'm sorry I didn't know this background story," Frida said.

"Well, it didn't stop there, didn't it, Frida?" His voice rose.

"I don't remember," she whispered, fidgeting in her bed. Hopefully, he would not hit her again. She had just been doing her job.

"Well, the poor mother decided to pay for the anti-depressant out-of-pocket. The physician recommended that Carl should also see a psychologist to process his traumatic experiences. His mother struggled for days to convince her son to agree. He finally summoned the courage to accept help. And Pleonexia—*you*—informed them that visits with a psychologist were not medically necessary. Do you have any idea how his mother felt? Or the boy?"

Frida looked at the man, silent.

"Carl started seeing a therapist anyway, thrice a week for $350 per visit. While helping him cope with his cancer treatment, his mother had to deal with the insurance—or, more precisely, with *you*! *You* denied the request, arguing that it was not demonstrated that Carl's mental health condition was interfering with his overall functioning on a *daily* basis in a *'clinically significant'* manner. What on earth is that supposed to mean?"

"I'm sorry," Frida whispered.

"Is that so?" the man asked. "Then I have good news for you! You can tell that to his mother."

The man left the room. Frida felt nauseated. What did he mean? Would he call the boy's mother? Did he want to force her to process his claim as well?

A few minutes later, the door opened again, and the man stepped into the room with a woman at his side. Frida looked at her with wide-open eyes. How embarrassing. It was the mother from the video. She wore jeans and a light-yellow sweater with coffee stains on it. Her short, layered red hair was out of shape and her face pale.

Frida swallowed. She pulled at the restraining belt around her waist. But it was as tight as ever. There was no escape. What would they do to her? Would they take revenge?

"Hello, I'm honored to meet you," the woman said with a soft voice.

"Pardon me?" Frida was confused. She looked at the man in the white coat for an explanation.

He stared at Frida with an intense, cold gaze, like he would slap her again at any moment. He seemed to have changed, like he was a different man. A minute ago, he seemed to be an intellectual. Soft, understanding, trying to explain a problem, trying to convince her on an intellectual level. Now, a predator was standing in front of her. Ready to kill.

A shiver ran down Frida's spine. Was he the one with a psychiatric problem here? Perhaps he was schizophrenic? Split personalities?

The woman reached for Frida's hand and squeezed it tenderly. "Thank you for approving our pending claims—all of them! The medications, the unauthorized blood tests, the psychology consult. I cannot tell you how much this means to me and my son! Now he can focus on getting better."

Frida looked confusedly from the woman to the man. She had not approved anything. What was going on? "I'm not—" She wanted to clarify, but the woman continued talking.

"Thank you from the bottom of my heart! I will never forget what you did for us. I'm forever grateful!" The woman squeezed her hand again.

Perhaps best to play along. "You're welcome," Frida said, looking down at her hand, intertwined with that of the woman.

"I heard that you tried to kill yourself because you were caught between the pressure from the insurance company and the well-being of the patients whose claims you processed. I want to reassure you that you did the right thing. I'm so grateful that you helped my son. Thank you for *all* the patients that you supported. *You* made all the difference. *You* helped our kids to get the treatment they needed."

Tears streamed down the woman's cheeks. She wiped them away with the back of her hand.

Frida looked at her and back down at the bed sheet in front of her. She didn't know what to say.

She saw from the corner of her eyes that the man's big hand was coming toward her. She winced. The man patted the woman's shoulder. "Our patient is still weak," he said. "We have to leave now."

"Of course," the woman said. She leaned toward Frida and kissed her cheek. "Please get better. We need people like you. People who fight for us from the inside. Please continue fighting!" She embraced Frida, squeezing her tightly. Then she turned around and left through the door.

The man also leaned down to Frida. His cold eyes conveyed hate and disgust. He whispered into her ear, "Do you see what you did? They suffer because of *you*. I will come back and make you pay." He pulled his white coat sideways. Frieda saw the Taser in the pocket of his suit underneath. She shivered.

The woman at the door turned around. "Are you coming?" she asked the man.

"Of course." He turned around and followed her.

The door shut behind them.

Frida frantically pulled at the restraining belt around her waist. This man was crazy—some kind of lunatic or psychopath. She had to get out of there before he would come back. She took her diamond ring in her right hand again and continued to cut the belt. It would take some time. But she would get through it.

# - 17 -

# TERREL

Revelations
Sunday, October 9, 2033, 7:30 a.m.

After the guitar player had finished his performance, Terrel and Niles stopped over in the kitchen to grab some morning drinks: a hot chocolate for Niles and a black coffee for Terrel. Jabari Smith, the father who had briefly talked with Terrel in the playroom, was in the kitchen as well, preparing a sandwich at the kitchen counter. It smelled of freshly roasted coffee and burned toast.

Jabari looked up. "Hi, Terrel. Would you like a sandwich as well?" He winked at Niles. "Is this your son?"

"Thanks, we had breakfast earlier," Terrel responded. "And yes, this is Niles."

"I would like a toast with peanut butter," Niles answered.

Jabari grinned. He fetched toast from the toaster, opened a peanut butter jar, added a generous serving on the toast, and handed it to Niles.

"Thank you, sir," Niles said politely. He turned to his father and asked, "Can I have my cocoa as well?"

Terrel smiled faintly. "Of course."

He got a cup from the kitchen counter, filled it with the hot liquid, and gave it to Niles as well. That breakfast combo was not exactly healthy. But Niles would get anything he wanted today, and he knew it. Niles smirked at his father, taking a big bite from his sandwich.

Terrel sighed. At least he had not lost his appetite. His heart wrenched as he saw his son stuffing his toast in his mouth with his delicate little fingers, peanut butter outlining his mouth. How would he handle a big surgery and the pain that would come with it? Niles had never been seriously sick in his young life. Terrel couldn't bear thinking about tomorrow. He felt lightheaded. He got himself a cup of coffee and took a big sip. A warm sensation expanded in his stomach. He felt a little better.

"What do you do for a living?" Jabari asked.

"I'm working for the government, administration," Terrel provided his standard answer. "And you?"

"I'm a journalist at the *New York Times.*"

"Wow, that's impressive," Terrel remarked, studying the man once more. He didn't quite fit the typical mold of a reporter. Yet, his inconspicuous demeanor could very well be intentional and help him to succeed with his investigations. Caution would be wise in his presence, but there was also potential to leverage his skills.

"What are you here for?" Jabari asked.

An open question by a seasoned investigator. Terrel placed his cup on the table. "Do you mean in the hospital? Niles has a tumor in his kidney," he explained. "A Wilm's tumor. It will be removed tomorrow."

Jabari looked at Niles. "Okay, superman. I wish you all the best for that."

Niles didn't react. He was completely focused on his sandwich. Did he not hear them or was this an evasive tactic? Terrel wasn't sure. He needed to turn the interrogation around. *He* had to ask the questions.

"You mentioned that you're here with your son?" Terrel asked.

Jabari nodded. "Yes, Grant had a Wilms tumor as well. The tumor was growing into the renal vein, which made it difficult to remove it. Most kids get surgery upfront. But Grant got chemotherapy first to shrink the tumor. He finally got his surgery last week, and the surgeons got everything out. My wife and I were so relieved. The clinical team here is top-notch. They work around the clock to help these kids."

Terrel nodded. "I can see that. How is your son doing now? He's not with you?"

Jabari eyed Terrel from the side. "He's meeting with the

physiotherapist. He had a rough few days after the surgery. It was a big operation. But now, he's slowly recovering. He can walk around, but still has quite some pain."

"I see." Terrel's heart wrenched. He looked at Niles. His son was too young for this. It was his job to protect him. But there was nothing he could do to save his son from the surgery and the pain and suffering that came with it.

Terrel tried to direct his thoughts to more rational territory. If they would talk one more minute about the surgery, he would go completely mad.

"You mentioned that you had issues with your insurance?" he asked Jabari.

"You bet," Jabari said with a grim smile. "Almost everyone here does. I'd literally be on the phone with Pleonexia Health, fighting with them, while my three-year-old son was getting chemo beside me. The system is completely broken. Greed everywhere."

"Yeah, agree!" a brittle female voice behind him echoed. "You're so right!"

Terrel turned around and saw a tall woman in a worn-out grayish tracksuit walking into the kitchen. Her eyes were swollen, and deep lines outlined her thin lips. She reached for the coffee can as well, pouring almost the entire contents into an oversized mug.

"Sorry to interrupt," she said, turning around and sitting down at a table in the back of the room.

"You said earlier that if you knew the responsible insurance person, you would kill them?" Terrel asked Jabari. "That seemed extreme to say, even if your kid is sick?"

Jabari patted his back. "You just arrived, Terrel. Let's wait two more weeks, and you will gladly shovel the grave for these insurance jerks."

The woman in the back clapped enthusiastically.

"I will loan you my gun," another woman in scrubs yelled from a couch to their right. Everyone laughed.

Niles giggled and clapped his little hands as well.

Terrel felt overwhelmed. All these people were so cynical and on edge. Could Jabari harm an insurance agent if she harmed his child?

Probably. And so would the other parents. Everyone in the whole ward seemed to be suspects.

"What have the insurance agents done to you?" he asked the woman with the brittle voice.

"They didn't help us when we needed them," she said. "Worse. They have obstructed necessary medical care. I guess that's what it comes down to for every single one of us."

"What did that mean for you?" Terrel asked.

The woman took a tiny sip from her coffee. The mug in her hand fumed. It was probably too hot. "My family is from Kansas City," she explained. "My son Willi has a very rare brain tumor, and the world experts for his condition are here at SUEC. I contacted Pleonexia, and they approved out-of-network care. We transferred here. Then, Pleonexia changed their mind and decided not to pay our bills."

"Can they just change their decision like that?" Terrel asked in surprise.

The woman shrugged. "Apparently, that's legal."

Jabari nodded. " You're not alone," he said. "Every week, we get an itemized list of charges, along with information from Pleonexia for which items they pay or not. We used all of our savings to cover the bills for our son."

"I'm so sorry," Terrel said.

"The atrocity is that we do have health insurance," Jabari said. "We paid our fees for Pleonexia for decades so that our bills would be covered when anyone in the family got sick. Now, my son is ill, and they are not doing their part. Health insurance that does not cover medical bills? There should be a law that they have to pay what the hospital charges. Or that the hospital can only charge as much as the insurance pays. Either way, the patient should not be crushed in the middle."

"We are in the same boat," an obese man in a washed-out SUEC sweater joined the conversation. He sat down beside Jabari. "My wife, our two daughters, and I will all go uninsured so that the family can save money to cover the bills for our six-year-old son," he said.

"This is terrible," Terrel responded. He looked at Niles, who licked his fingers. "I cannot even think about such things at the moment. I have to focus on my son."

"I have a doctoral degree and cannot figure this out," the woman in scrubs added. "I find it very unsettling that insurance employees have the power to decide who gets what care. It's very upsetting how often I have to explain the treatment of a pediatric tumor to the 'medical director' at the insurance company, who has never heard of it. Peer-to-peer reviews have taken at least two years off my life."

Terrel looked at her. She was sitting on a fake leather seat with her legs resting on an elephant ottoman. Blue scrubs, a SUEC ID on a string around her neck, and smart eyes. Who was she?

"I'm an instructor here," she said as if she had read his mind. "A junior oncologist and daily Pleonexia victim. Look at this letter that I received from them yesterday." She produced a crumbled piece of paper from her pocket and read out loud. "Dr. Li, compared to your peers, your oncology service bills are greater than the average billing behavior. This report is intended to be informative and does not question your medical judgment. If we continue to note high-level billing codes, Pleonexia may request medical records of your patients for the purpose of validation and education."

"What does that mean?" Jabari asked.

"I don't know exactly, but it does sound threatening to me," the young woman said. "I love messages that explicitly say they aren't questioning my judgment—followed by clearly questioning my judgment. It seems like they want to scare me into billing lower codes."

"Could you do that?" Terrel asked. "If they want to save money, perhaps that is a good thing?"

The woman shrugged. "There is a lower code if you take less time with the patient in the outpatient clinic and if you address fewer health issues at once. Should I cut off a conversation about the care of a child with cancer? Should I not discuss all health issues to save time? Should I assign my time based on insurance profit rather than the patient's needs?"

"Disgusting," Jabari exclaimed. "Greed everywhere! We need a reset. All major players, hospitals, insurance companies, pharmaceutical companies, and anyone else dealing with healthcare should be not-for-profit corporations."

The group clapped again.

"Oh, my god," the woman in scrubs exclaimed, checking her cell phone, which emitted blinking sounds. "I got a text that I missed the start of the morning rounds. Dr. Queirós Trento already saw half of the patients without me. How embarrassing!" she rushed out of the room. The obese man followed her, and the group disassembled.

Terrel watched them disappear in different rooms along the hallway. Perhaps it was good that he had moved to this ward. He was surprised about the other parents' brusque comments, but he also felt a deep sense of community with them. No child should have to go through what their kids had to endure. Sharing each other's heartbreaking stories instilled a sense of comradery and common humanity. The sort of collective pain and suffering that melds people together. Hearing Jabari's rant about the health insurance made the thick lump of anxiety in Terrel's chest feel a little lighter. He was not alone. He had accomplices.

He had learned a lot from the other parents in a very short time. They could help him navigate his own issues with Pleonexia—if he encountered some. And perhaps he could provide Angus with some insider info as well. A health insurance agent was kidnapped. *Were any of the people here involved?* Terrel would keep his eyes open. But for now, he had to focus on his son.

Niles had finished his cocoa and looked up at him with a content gaze. Terrel smiled and reached for his tiny hand. It was sticky and soiled. But the squeeze of Nile's little fingers stole his heart every time. Terrel squeezed back. A hand Morse code for union, love, and trust. *You and me. You and me.* They would hold on to each other, no matter what was coming their way. Niles and Terrel walked together in unison to their new room.

# - 18 -

# ANGUS

The Chase
Sunday, October 9, 2033, 7:30 a.m.

Angus drove down Highway 101 from San Francisco to SUEC Hospital in Redwood City. He had sent an FBI officer to SUEC Hospital last night who had secured a feather from the parrot and sent it to the FBI forensic lab. Angus had submitted the feather from the van as well for a DNA match analysis. The forensic team had sent him a note early this morning. Both feathers belonged to the same parrot. The parrot that had talked about a kidnapping event. Angus had to interview the bird as soon as possible. He was the best lead they had thus far. Angus would also check to see if the bird had a leg band. That would allow him to identify current and past owners.

It was not particularly busy on the highway on a Sunday morning. Angus used the transit time to call Elena Nurak, CEO of Pleonexia Health Insurances in San Francisco. He had sent her an email last night, informing her that he would call at this time. Apparently, she had received his message. She answered right away.

"Hello, Agent Weber, what can I do for you?" she asked with a low, resolute tone.

Angus had looked her up on the web this morning. A lady in her late fifties with gray hair, gray eyes, and a conservative feminine gray suit. Long list of accolades for her leadership and financial success. Twenty million dollar compensation last year. The Silicon Valley Post called her a rare example of a successful female leader in Silicon Valley.

"Hello, Mrs. Nurak, I'm calling because of your employee, Dr. Frida Ending," Angus said. "She has been missing since last night. I was wondering if you have any idea about her whereabouts or who might want to harm her."

"That is very strange," the CEO responded. "She is not missing at her workplace. She has been working all night last night."

"She has been working?" Angus asked in surprise. "Do you mean remotely? How do you know it was her?"

"She logged into our system with her dual authentication," the CEO explained. "This is pretty fool-proofed. It requires iris authentication for login and an additional authentication number sent to her phone."

"Well, hackers can do a lot these days," Angus said. "If she logged in when they were around, they could have hijacked her session and then had free access to your system."

"Hijacked her session? What does that mean?"

"An attacker can take over a target's internet session—for instance, Frida's insurance claim reviews. Were there any unusual claim-processing activities last night?"

"I'm glad you called. That sounds very unsettling. Now that you mention it. Yes, there were a few things. First, she does not usually work at the weekend, let alone at night. She's very efficient and hard-working. She processes more than a hundred claims a week. But she works pretty much eight to five. Last night, she approved claims from an entire ward. That was unusual because it involved all claims from one specific location, and she approved them all. Usually, she's very tough, with a high rate of rejections and denials."

"And the specific location was?"

"SUEC Hospital, pediatric oncology."

"Interesting. Did anyone on your end interfere?"

"No, there are only a few people working in our company on the weekend and rarely at night. I received an automated notification because she approved so many high-priced claims. But she's one of my best agents. I trust her judgment. She is high enough in the hierarchy that she does not need secondary approval."

"Is she in the system now?"

He heard typing sounds in the background.

"She is still logged in. I will cut her off now."

Angus almost missed the exit to Redwood City. "No, no," he said quickly. "Do not disconnect her. My team can track down her location—or that of her imposter. That will allow us to find them. If you just cut her off, then the criminals will find another way into your system and continue from a different line."

"I'm not sure. This could cost us a lot of money. If unusual approvals continue at the same rate, then I have to put an end to this. My security team can strengthen the firewall from our end. If they know that there's a security threat, they can keep intruders out."

"Give us two hours. Mrs. Ending's life could depend on it."

The CEO hesitated for a moment. Then, she said, "I will give you one hour. I will ask our IT team to track her activities carefully. In one hour, we will block her privileges. Will you pick up the bill that she creates in the meantime?"

"Sorry, the FBI does not have such resources. But I will bring back your employee safely."

"That is very noble of you. But I'm afraid I'm not the Red Cross. I have a business to run. I expect that the FBI will bring her back safely *without* ruining us in the process."

"Of course, I will do the best I can."

"My team will monitor the situation closely and call you if we need to end this sooner."

"Thank you, Mrs. Nurak."

Angus reached SUEC Hospital. He parked in the open parking lot behind the ER. Perhaps he could nudge fate to let him run into Annya. He sent a text to his team in San Francisco, asking them to track down the IP address and location that was used to log into the Pleonexia account under Frieda Ending's credentials. Then, he got out of the car and walked toward the back entrance of the hospital. He wanted to interview the parrot. How? He had no idea yet. One step at a time. His intuition would help him to figure this out. There was always a way. Even if the bird would keep his beak shut, he could get a photo of his leg band and track down previous owners.

Angus entered the hospital building and walked down the hallway toward the garden, where he had met with Terrel yesterday. It was busier today than last night. The hallway was full of patients, visitors, families, and healthcare workers, some heading in his direction, others the opposite way. An elderly lady with a hunchback stopped in front of him, her trembling hand clenched around a cone, asking him for the direction to the ER. He offered her his arm and led her to the reception. Then he continued to the door that led into the garden.

When he opened it, he almost ran into a man with a white coat on his way out. Sturdy build, curly brown hair, blue surgical face mask. Angus looked at him in surprise. This was the man from the van. Same furrowed brows, same eyes, same mustache, partly covered by the surgical mask. Angus was contemplating his own judgment when he noticed a spark of recognition in the man's eyes. In a split second, without saying a word, it was clear that the man had recognized him as well. He turned around on his heels and quickly walked back into the garden under the cover of a large, blooming rhododendron bush.

"Hey, wait!" Angus shouted and ran after him into the park and around the bushes. Angus saw the white coat a few meters in front of him. The man accelerated his speed and disappeared behind a climbing tower. Several kids were running around it on a playing ground. Angus had to slow down in order to make his way through them. On the other side of the climbing structure, the man started to run down a gravel path that led in a semicircle around a large green area where several teenagers were playing soccer. The man ran along the path toward another glass door at the rear end of the hospital building. Angus caught up quickly. The man cut the semicircle and ran across the lawn for the door. Angus raced after him. The man was probably younger but shorter and heavier than him. Several spectators screamed and pulled kids out of the way. A woman in scrubs called for security. The man in the white coat was breathing heavily, his boots making loud thuds on the grass. Angus could see sweat running down his neck, soaking his perfectly starched white coat. Angus came closer and closer, extending his right arm to reach for the man.

Suddenly, from the corner of his eyes, Angus noted a round object coming toward him fast. A blow hit his right ankle, smashing his right foot medially. He stumbled and fell forward, hitting the ground. The man in the white coat pulled the glass door wide open and disappeared into the building.

Angus pushed himself up onto his knees, his palms stinging from a mixture of dirt and oozing blood. The pain made him grit his teeth, but he didn't let it show. A soccer ball sat nonchalantly to his right. He glanced around, trying to steady his focus, when he noticed two slender teenagers cautiously approaching, their faces etched with guilt. They mumbled words of regret, explaining that they had been playing soccer on the greens nearby. The wayward ball had unintentionally veered off course and struck him with unexpected force. One of the kids produced a handkerchief and offered it to Angus. Angus cleaned his hands as best as possible. The bleeding subsided. There were only superficial scratches on his palms. His trousers were covered in dirt. He brushed it off and then examined his ankles. His ankle had fractured a year ago, and an orthopedic plate was still in his calf bone. Perhaps that protected the bone from a new fracture. His ankles seemed to be okay. Angus had been lucky, after all. The teenagers continued to apologize. Angus took a deep breath to regain his composure. Slowly, he nodded to the teenagers, silently assuring them that he understood it was an innocent mistake.

A security guard approached and asked him if he wanted to make a complaint. Angus refused. He handed the soccer ball to the kids, and they hurried back to the green area. Angus felt sore, but there was no major injury. With cautious steps, he walked slowly to the glass door and swung it open. Behind the door was another hospital hallway. Angus took a moment to glance around, observing the steady stream of doctors, nurses, and patients passing by. No sight of the man in the white coat. He got away.

# - 19 -

# TERREL

The Oncologist
Sunday, October 9, 2033, 7:45 a.m.

Terrel and Niles stepped into his son's new hospital room in the oncology ward. The room was bright and spacious, with large windows that let in the warm California sunshine. The view from the windows was breathtaking, with the forest-lined Redwood hills stretching out to the horizon. The room was sparsely furnished, with a solitary patient bed, a bedside table, and a chair. A vase of fresh jasmine and white roses sat on the table, their sweet scent filling the air. Imani was sitting on a couch underneath the window, reading something on her iPad. She looked up as they entered the room.

"There you are." Her gaze was more relaxed than earlier today.

Niles ran to her, jumped on the couch, and settled beside her, checking out her iPad. Terrel walked over and kissed her cheek.

"Wow. Did Niles get flowers?" he asked.

"These are for me!" Imani beamed. "A greeting from the medical team. How thoughtful!"

"I'm glad we moved here," Terrel whispered into her ear.

Imani sighed and looked at him with longing eyes. "I wished the coming week were already behind us," she said. "I'm so glad you took time off from work to be with us full-time. I couldn't do this without you by my side."

"We can do this together. All three of us." Terrel kissed her again. "We will make it through this!"

The door opened, and Nurse Sally, Aziel, the instructor, and a short, plumpish young man in a white coat stepped in.

"Hello, I'm Dr. Queirós Trento, your pediatric oncologist," he introduced himself with a resolute voice.

Terrel looked at the man in disbelief. This was the physician whom he had seen in the hospital garden last night. The physician who had carried the psychiatric patient into the hospital. The woman who had jumped out of a window. It had been dark, and he had only seen the man for a short moment. But he did have a very good memory, especially for faces.

"Did I see you in the hospital garden last night?" he asked.

Dr. Queirós Trento looked at him with raised eyebrows. "Hello. You must be Mr. Wright," he said calmly. "It is nice to meet you. And I'm not sure what you're referring to. I was on call last night. It was very busy, and I didn't have a chance to visit the hospital garden. Why are you asking?"

Terrel looked at the man. That mustache was quite unique. "I thought I saw you last night in the hospital garden," he insisted. "Carrying a young patient into the hospital."

"I believe this might be a misunderstanding, Mr. Wright," the nurse weighed in. "Dr. Queirós Trento came in for another patient last night. He was in the ER and on the ward all evening. You must have seen somebody else."

"Perhaps," Terrel responded. He started to question his own judgment.

"Honey, I believe they are all here to talk about Niles," Imani said with a curt voice.

"Yes, we are," the physician said softly, stepping toward Niles. "Hello, Niles. How are *you* doing today?"

"I'm doing fine. Thanks for asking," Niles answered politely, holding the robot toward the man and pressing the recording key.

Terrel smiled with pride. Niles was growing up quickly, and he had clearly inherited a detective gene from his father.

The physician squinted to look at the toy. "I can see that," he said. "Did you get one of our new robots?"

"Yes, I did. I called him Chip," Niles explained.

"And how does Chip feel this morning?" Dr. Queirós Trento asked.

"He's a little nervous," Niles said.

Dr. Queirós Trento leaned forward. "I see. You can tell him that everything looks good. The surgery will be tomorrow, and it will be done by a very experienced surgeon. There is a tumor in your belly, and it needs to be removed. You understand that, right?"

Niles nodded with a furrowed gaze. "Will it hurt?" he asked.

"The surgery will be done under anesthesia," Dr. Queirós Trento said. "You'll be asleep and won't feel anything when the tumor is removed. Don't worry. We'll take good care of you." Dr. Queirós Trento patted Niles head. "I know this is a lot to take in," he said. "But you're a brave boy, and I know you can do this."

Niles took a deep breath. "Okay," he said, his voice slightly quivering.

Imani took his hand. "I'm here with you," she said. "I'm not going anywhere."

Niles smiled weakly. "Thanks, Mom," he said.

Terrel's heart sank. He knew that Niles was scared, and he didn't know how to make him feel better.

Dr. Queirós Trento went back to the medical team and flipped through Niles' chart, nodding approvingly. Then, he addressed the parents.

"You already talked with the pediatric surgeon this morning. You are in good hands. She is outstanding. This afternoon, the anesthesiologist will come by to talk with you as well. And we ordered an ultrasound to make sure that the abdominal vessels don't contain any tumors. We don't really expect anything there. It is just a precaution."

Niles' eyes widened. "An ultrasound?"

The man smiled at him. "Don't worry, Niles. We will just take some pictures of your belly. No big deal. It only takes a few minutes. It does not hurt, and it does not require a needle stick."

Nick nodded. "I don't want any more needle sticks."

"I know," the oncologist said softly. "I'm afraid there will be one more needle prick tomorrow to get you ready for the surgery. But we will add a numbing cream to your arm so that you will hardly feel it."

Niles looked at him with a doubtful gaze.

"Niles should also get a genetic test?" Imani asked.

"You remember this very well, Mrs. Wright," the oncologist said. "We will get blood for the genetic test when Niles is sleeping during the surgery tomorrow."

"Sally told us that we are still waiting for the insurance authorizations?" Terrel asked.

The oncologist smiled broadly. "We got authorizations for everything. The genetic test, the ultrasound, and the surgery," the instructor said with a proud smile.

Terrel and Imani exchanged a relieved look. "That was easier than I thought," Imani said.

"Dr. Queirós Trento is a wizard when it comes to obtaining insurance authorizations," Nurse Sally beamed at the physician beside her. Their shoulders touched, and they locked eyes for a moment.

Terrel cleared his throat. This was a pediatric ward, not a hotel bar. "How do you make it through the red tape?" he asked.

The oncologist smirked. "Well, I learned a number of arguments over the years. When I have to dispute a certain test or treatment with a medical professional at the insurance company, I first ask for their name and whether they have malpractice insurance in California. I then let them know that I'm putting their name in the chart as a consultant. If they deny treatment that I feel is necessary, then I document that as well in the chart. That way, a family can sue them for malpractice, and most agents give in at that point. Nevertheless, some insurance agents are still resistant to our pleas. We have a few other arguments up our sleeves for such situations."

"We are so grateful for your efforts on our behalf," Imani said with admiration in her voice. "You are an angel."

Terrel looked at his wife from the corner of his eyes. The man was not particularly attractive. What made him so captivating? The doctor title?

"His second name is Gabriel," Sally said with an upward gaze toward the physician.

The instructor rolled her eyes.

"Well, it was very nice to meet you all," Dr. Queirós Trento said. "Please be here this afternoon. Aziel will take you to the ultrasound suite and anesthesia preparation. There's not much else going on this morning. So feel free to explore the ward or the hospital."

Terrel smiled at Niles. "I have an idea what we can do," he said. "I saw the parrot in the garden. We can go visit him."

"That sounds great!" Niles exclaimed. "Does he speak?"

"Yes, he does," Terrel said.

He noted a strange expression on the doctor's face. Was that apprehension or even fear? Or perhaps he was concerned about an infection risk? Terrel didn't have a chance to ask. The medical team turned around and left.

# - 20 -

# ANGUS

Doppelgänger
Sunday, October 9, 2033, 8:30 a.m.

Angus turned back to the hospital garden, his palms throbbing. He needed to find someone who had seen the man in the white coat run away. He approached the people close by, hoping that someone had seen the man through the floor-to-ceiling glass windows. The garden was bustling with activity, but despite the intensity of the moment that had just transpired, the surroundings seemed untroubled and indifferent to the recent incident.

Angus considered asking the teenagers playing soccer on the greens, but they were probably too engrossed in their game to have noticed anything. A mother with a crying baby seemed similarly preoccupied, trying to soothe her little one, and a couple pushing a stroller appeared to be focused on their own conversations. Most people seemed to be on the move or too far away to have seen where the man in the white coat had escaped. But Angus remained hopeful that amidst the sea of faces and activities, there might be someone who had seen something. The sun's warmth enveloped him as he moved from one group to another, gently inquiring about the man. Several people had witnessed the chase through the garden, but none of them recalled in which direction the man had disappeared. They had all been distracted by Angus' accident with the soccer ball.

A little girl sat on a bench close to the glass door, playing with a holographic iPhone. She was probably five or six years old, with long brunette braids, a polka dot skirt, and a cast around her left leg. A middle-aged woman, presumably her mother, was sitting beside her, holding two crutches and talking on the phone. Angus approached them. The girl didn't react. The mother looked at his dirty clothes with raised brows and moved a few inches closer to the girl.

"Hello, I'm sorry to intrude," Angus said politely. "Did you see the man in the white coat who just ran into the building?"

The woman lifted the phone a few centimeters away from her ear and looked at him with a disapproving gaze. "Pardon?"

"Did you see a man in a white coat who just ran into the building?" Angus asked again. "Did he turn right or left?"

"Sorry, I cannot help you," the mother said and put her phone back at her ear. "I'm talking with someone." She pointed at her phone and carried on with her conversation.

Angus sighed. It seemed hard to believe that there was no witness at all.

"He ran to the right," the girl said without looking up, typing something on her phone.

"Are you sure?" Angus asked.

"Yeah, he nearly tripped over the puppy over there." She pointed at a young golden retriever, who was running around on the greens.

"Thank you!" Angus said.

The girl continued to type, her gaze glued to the screen. Had she really seen something? Angus opened the glass door. Fifty percent chance to go in the right direction. A cleaning robot beeped a warning signal and drove by. The hospital hallway behind it smelled of soap and disinfectant. A few random people were walking up and down the hallway.

Angus turned right and followed the shiny, freshly waxed linoleum path. If there had been footprints, they were wiped away. The man had probably found a place to hide by now, but Angus wanted to follow his tracks anyway. Important clues could reveal themselves in the most unexpected circumstances.

The hallway was long and narrow, with many sideways taking off to both sides. It seemed impossible to find anyone here. Angus followed the main hallway to a blind end with an elevator. Perhaps the man had taken the elevator to who knew which floor. Or he had taken any of the other hallways that led into other parts of the building. Angus stopped and tried to think. Visitors, patients, and hospital staff rushed by. It seemed as if everybody else had a clear destination except him.

Angus turned around and walked back slowly, past the entrance to the garden and in the opposite direction. This hallway diverged into three smaller paths, resembling a maze of possibilities. Angus' mind was racing, trying to decide which way to go. He couldn't shake the image of the mysterious man in the white coat from his thoughts. He had to find him before he harmed the kidnapped woman.

There was a sign to the ER. He paused, almost convinced he heard a faint voice in the distance. Was it Annya? He couldn't be sure. Perhaps just wishful imagination. But it might be a good idea to talk with her. She was very smart, and she knew the hospital inside out. If anyone could shed light on the man's identity or whereabouts, it was her. There had to be a registry of all physicians in the hospital. Perhaps he could start with that.

As he approached the ER, the sound of Annya's voice became more distinct, confirming that he wasn't just imagining things. Angus picked up his pace, his steps becoming more purposeful as he followed the sound. Annya's voice came from a room with a slanted door midway to the ER entrance. He remembered the room he was heading to—the radiology reading room. He had been there last night. Angus opened the door and stepped in.

There she was, indeed, standing with her back toward him in the dimly lit room amidst the soft glow of computer screens. A different outfit than yesterday—long beige trousers and a white blouse. Her melodic voice and long, silky red hair gave her away. Nobody else had hair like that. Annya looked at a CT scan with radiologist Lili Pham. Their faces were a portrait of concentration as they analyzed the images before them. And—Angus hardly believed his eyes—the man in the white coat stood beside them, following the conversation. Angus jumped to the man and grabbed his arm.

"Why did you run away?" he shouted.

The man looked at the hand on his arm, then at Angus.

"Who are you? What are you talking about?" he asked with an irritated voice, trying to wring his arm out of Angus' grip. Angus didn't let go.

Annya looked at Angus with raised eyebrows. "Angus, what's the matter with you?"

"This man ran away from me in the hospital garden just a few minutes ago," he explained.

"Sorry, Angus. You have the wrong guy," Lili said calmly. "Dr. Queirós Trento was with us in the reading room for the past ten minutes or so. We reviewed imaging studies of two new oncology patients who were admitted overnight."

"Leave me alone," the man barked, trying to wring his arm free from Angus' grip, his voice laced with irritation and defiance.

Angus looked at the man in disbelief. Could he be wrong? The man looked exactly like the man who had run away from him in the hospital garden. He had the same build, the same white coat, and the same facial features. Yes, his face was partially covered by a surgical mask, but the man's hazel eyes and mustache were quite unique. Angus was sure it was the same guy.

"Dr. Queirós Trento was with us here in the reading room for the past ten minutes," Annya confirmed.

Angus looked at her, the man, and Lili. What was going on? Were the two women trying to protect a colleague who had committed a crime?

Lili's eyes flickered toward Angus with an empathetic gaze. "Rogério was reviewing the imaging studies of this teenage girl with us," she said, pointing at the CT scans at her workstation.

Angus looked at the images, confused. What was going on? How could the man run through the hospital garden and review imaging studies in the reading room at the same time?

Lili apparently thought Angus had an interest in the medical images. "The images show a cystic lesion in the right ovary," she explained. "The lesion contains dense calcifications and small hypodense areas of fat. These three components, fluid, calcification, and fat, are indicative of an ovarian dermoid cyst or teratoma. The patient is scheduled for a resection on Tuesday."

"And we had no insurance issues today," Annya added. "The surgery was approved right away."

Angus nodded absentmindedly. He trusted Annya, but he

couldn't put the facts together in a meaningful way. The man in front of him was the man from the garden. He was sure. The same stocky build, same curly brown hair, same eyes, same mustache. Angus had chased him just a few minutes ago. He had seen the sweat soaking the man's white coat when he ran across the lawn. But the white coat of the man in front of him was spotless—dry, starched, and pristine. Perhaps he had changed it? He wore a blue suit underneath, which was equally spotless. His shoes were spotless. No dust or dirt from the garden race. How was that possible? The man evaded his gaze. He *was* hiding something. Angus was sure of it.

"Were you in the hospital garden a few minutes ago?" Angus asked him. He watched him closely. He had a sixth sense for liars and would detect a lie if he was not telling the truth.

"I'm not sure what you're referring to," the man said with a sharp tone. "I was here in the reading room. And before that, I was doing rounds on my patients upstairs. The entire ward can confirm that. Why are you asking?"

"Because I saw you in the hospital garden," Angus insisted.

"Is that a crime?" Lili asked with an innocent grin.

"I told you. I was *not* in the garden," the man said firmly.

Was there a sweat pearl on the man's temple? He brushed it away with the back of his hand. He was not lying, but he was nervous.

"I see." Angus released the man's arm.

"Thank you," the man said with an irritated voice. "I hope you find who you're looking for."

Angus was confused. This man's gaze was straightforward, non-apologetic, and perhaps a little anxious. *No wonder.*

Angus turned to Annya. "Can I talk to you for a second?" he asked, pointing at the door.

"Of course." She flashed her disarming smile.

They stepped into the hallway. "We can talk here." Annya pointed at a door a few meters down the hallway. She opened the door and led him into a small office. The tiny white-painted room had no window, a small cabinet, a desk, and a computer. No personal items, no jacket, no photos.

"Is this your office?" Angus asked.

"Yes and no. It is a shared office," she explained. "Every physician on service can use it."

"I see."

"Angus, why are you acting so strangely?" Annya said with a concerned gaze. "Is Rogério a suspect in your investigation?"

Angus nodded. "I believe he is one of the kidnappers. I recognized him. He saw me in the hospital garden and recognized me as well. Then, he ran away. I tried to catch him but barely missed. He escaped."

Annya shook her head. "Perhaps he resembles somebody else. As I told you, Rogério was reviewing imaging studies with us. I'm absolutely sure he was not in the hospital garden in the last ten minutes or so. He was reviewing cases with us. And when he came to the reading room, he didn't make the impression that he had just escaped an FBI agent. He was not panting, no flushed face, no sweat. He's not your man."

Angus shook his head. "Do you know a physician in this hospital who looks exactly like him? Same height, same weight, same hair, same eyes, same *mustache*?"

"He doesn't have a clone if that's what you're asking," Annya said with a smile. "No, seriously, I'm not aware that he has a doppelganger."

"If it was not him, then there has to be somebody who looks like him."

"Well, I will keep my eyes open and let you know if I see somebody who fits the bill. In the meantime, perhaps consider if your senses are overreacting a little bit?" Annya held his gaze as she pushed her red hair over her shoulder.

"I know what you're hinting at," he said with a smile. "But it's not like that. Nothing can cloud my mind." Angus adored her confidence and her honesty. Most women he met were trying to please him and tell him what he wanted to hear. Not Annya. Her green eyes sparkled when she looked at him just a second too long. She liked him, and she would always speak her mind. Annya was comfortable in her own skin—a woman true to her beliefs and values.

"Thank you for watching this man," he added. "He's hiding

something. I know it."

Annya nodded. "I will keep an eye on him. And I will help watch out for any other suspects."

A thoughtful expression washed over Angus' face. "Could you check the hospital security cameras for me?" he asked. "Just confirm that this man was nowhere near the hospital garden?" He knew that Annya, an undercover CIA operative, had access to the security center in the basement of the hospital.

She nodded. "Of course, I will check the security videos for you."

"Thank you!" Angus paused, looking into her emerald green eyes. He wanted to create an imprint on his brain so that she would always be in his memories.

"Our lunch today is still on, right?" he asked, changing the subject.

She hesitated for a moment, then nodded. "Of course. We said 2 p.m. today. I'm afraid you arrived five hours early," she replied with a touch of playful sarcasm.

Angus chuckled. He was grateful for Annya's ability to handle difficult situations with grace and humor. The tension from their earlier encounter seemed to melt away, replaced by a sense of ease and connection.

"I came to interview the parrot in the garden," he explained. "His feathers matched with a feather that we found in the van of the kidnappers."

"I see. More doppelgangers," she said, her eyes sparkling with a mix of curiosity and amusement.

"How long has the parrot been at the hospital?" Angus asked.

"Perhaps as long as Rogério." Annya laughed. "No, seriously, I'm not sure. I only go through the hospital garden occasionally when I find time for lunch outside. I believe the aviary cage was only been put up recently. It was definitely not here in the wintertime."

Angus nodded. "Thanks. I'm here to find out more."

"I look forward to hearing all about it!" She reached into her pocket for a hair tie, twisted her silky hair into a bun, secured it, and turned around.

Angus wanted to hold the door open for her as they exited the office, but she was too quick for him. She stepped into the hallway, and a whiff of her sweet musk and magnolia perfume wafted over him. She glanced over her shoulder and waved before they parted ways.

Angus' phone rang. He saw on the display that it was Kuruk Ending, Frida's husband. He answered the phone, and Kuruk immediately launched into a barrage of questions.

"Agent Weber, do you have any news for me? Did you find my wife?" he barked. His voice was filled with urgency and anxiety.

Angus leaned into the phone. "We have a lead," he replied, his tone calm and professional. "But I can't share the details just yet."

Kuruk sighed in frustration. "I'm worried sick about her," he said. "Please, tell me anything you can."

Angus hesitated. Everyone in this investigation was a potential suspect, but he also had the impression that Kuruk was genuinely concerned about his wife.

"I promise I'll keep you updated if we find her," he said. "But for now, I need to keep any information confidential."

Kuruk sighed. "I understand," he said. "But please, let me know when you find her."

"Of course," Angus said. "I will."

He hung up the phone and turned his attention back to the case. He knew that he was dealing with dangerous individuals, but he was determined to find Frida and bring her home safely.

# - 21 -

# ANNYA

Surveillance Videos
Sunday, October 9, 2033, 9:00 a.m.

Annya walked back to the Radiology reading room. Lili was reviewing medical imaging studies and dictating reports. Rogério Queirós Trento had stepped away from the workstation, standing close to the door and talking to someone in a low voice on his cell phone.

"Stay in the room and don't go anywhere," he said with a harsh, hushed voice.

Annya looked at him in surprise. His furrowed brow and the tone of his voice were unusual for an interaction with a patient, trainee, or even a family member. Who was he was talking to?

Rogério noticed her probing gaze. "I have to go," he said to the person on the other end of the line. He hung up the phone, placed it in his pocket, and stepped toward her. "Hello, Annya. Thank you for telling the FBI agent that I was reviewing imaging studies here. He scared me. I don't want to be on the watch list of the FBI."

Annya shrugged. "I only told him the truth. You were not running through the garden, Rogério. You and I discussed a case here in the reading room. Angus is a good man. I told him that you were here so that he can find the person he's looking for."

"Thank you! I'm very grateful. Who or what exactly is he looking for? Perhaps I can help?"

"You can ask him yourself if you like. He is still in the hospital garden," Annya responded.

Was there a spark of concern in Rogério's eyes?

"Who were you talking to on the phone?" she asked.

He laughed. "Are you also from the FBI?"

He was quite good at bouncing questions. Annya hadn't noticed that skill before.

"You know that I'm an ER physician," she said with a faint smile. "I just happened to overhear your phone conversation and wondered if one of your patients is not compliant with your instructions. They are supposed to stay in the room, but they are not? That would be important for all of us to know?"

"No, no," Rogério shook his head. "This was not a patient. I would not converse with a patient on my personal cell phone."

"Who was it then?" Annya asked.

Rogério hesitated. "A friend," he finally said, his voice clipped.

"A friend whom you ordered to stay in their room?"

Rogério glared at Annya, his brows furrowed. "This is a friend with a mental health issue," he snapped. "It's a private matter that I don't wish to share."

Annya nodded. "I see. I hope your friend will be alright," she said slowly, holding his gaze.

"I hope so, too," Rogério said curtly. "Now, excuse me. I have a full ward and need to take care of my patients." He stepped around her and left the room.

Annya watched him go, feeling a pang of concern. She regretted that she had disregarded Angus' concerns so easily. There was something fishy about Rogério. He truly cared for his patients, but he was also hiding something. She would keep an eye on him.

She checked her watch. It had been relatively calm in the ER on this early Sunday morning. She could take a quick break.

With a sense of purpose, Annya descended the stairs to the basement, her shoes echoing against the concrete walls. She followed the dimly lit hallway to the security control center, the nerve center of the hospital, where everything was monitored and controlled to ensure the safety of patients, staff, and visitors. She had been here countless times, but each visit brought a rush of excitement.

She approached the double doors and swiped her ID badge. The security system recognized her, and the doors unlocked with a soft electronic hum. She stepped inside the large, windowless room. The walls were lined with monitors, displaying feeds from various surveillance cameras scattered throughout the hospital. The soft glow of the screens illuminated the faces of two security staff, who were observing the ever-changing images before them.

Annya greeted them with a warm smile. "Hello," she said. "I just came by for a routine check."

The security guard closest to her looked up briefly. "Sure, Dr. Segond," he said. "Be my guest." He turned back to the monitor in front of him, where he was eating a bowl of soup.

Annya settled into a chair at one of the workstations. She brought up the security footage for the past twenty-four hours and began to scan.

With her fingers moving deftly across the keyboard, Annya brought up the list of video recordings from the morning. The monitor in front of her came alive with a mosaic of live feeds, each displaying a different area of the hospital. She scanned the feeds, looking for anything unusual.

The hallways showed the usual hustle and bustle of hospital life, with doctors, nurses, and patients moving purposefully through the corridors. Waiting rooms were filled with families and friends, their anxious expressions and hopeful glances revealing the emotional journeys they were undertaking. The clinical exam rooms and patient rooms didn't have cameras for privacy reasons, so she couldn't see what was happening inside them.

Annya looked for Rogério in the hallway that led to the pediatric oncology ward. He had left the Radiology reading room and should be on his way to his patients. But she couldn't see him anywhere. Had he already reached an exam room? That would have been really fast. He didn't strike her as particularly athletic.

She looked around, and to her surprise, she found him in the north wing of the hospital, walking down the hallway on the second floor. That was the hallway that led to the psychiatry ward. What was he doing there?

Annya remembered the strange phone conversation with a so-called friend with a mental health issue. Was he or she hospitalized at SUEC? He hadn't mentioned that.

Rogério went to the entrance of the closed ward, where patients were hospitalized who could be a risk to themselves or others. He rang the bell. A nurse with curly blonde hair opened the door and greeted him cheerfully. This woman wasn't seeing him for the first time. They clearly knew each other. She waved him in and closed the door behind him.

Annya sighed. This was as much information as she could get. There were no cameras beyond this door. She would have to find another way to find out what was going on there.

Annya selected the camera that covered the hallway that led to the hospital garden. The garden itself didn't have any cameras in order to respect patient privacy. The windows of patient rooms in the surrounding buildings faced the garden.

Annya checked her watch. Angus' suspect must have walked down this hallway somewhere between 8:15 and 8:30 a.m. that morning. She selected this time on the display and studied the video.

Indeed, a stocky man with brown curly hair and a white coat rushed into the hallway from the garden around 8:25 a.m. Annya couldn't see the man's face, but his build and movements indeed resembled Rogério a lot.

Annya would have also thought that it was him if she had not known that she herself had spoken with Rogério at the same time in the reading room. It was impossible that Rogério had walked down the hallway and reviewed images with Lili and her in the reading room at the same time.

In addition, the man in the video ran down the hallway in the opposite direction of the ER. At the end, he disappeared in an elevator. Where was he going? Apparently, he was not leaving the hospital. The exit was on the first floor.

Annya systematically checked all other floors. There he was. The man exited on the second floor and—Annya couldn't believe her eyes—walked toward the closed psychiatry ward. He waved an ID at the entrance pad. The door opened, and he disappeared behind it.

Who was he? Whatever was going on here, it had to do with this ward. Annya checked her watch again. Her colleagues in the ER would start to miss her, but she had to find out what this man and Rogério were up to. It would only take a few more minutes.

She left the IT control room and walked up the stairs to the psychiatry ward.

# - 22 -

# FRIDA

The Second Lesson
Sunday, October 9, 2033, 8:45 a.m.

Frida rubbed the diamond of her wedding ring against the restraining belt around her waist, her muscles straining with effort. She had managed to get her flat hand under the belt along her right flank, cutting the fibers of the belt from the inside. This would disguise her work if the nurse would check the belt for some reason.

She made slow progress, and it would likely take hours until she had worked her way all the way through—if she could make it at all. But this was the best plan she had for now. She focused all her energy on the task, ignoring the pain in her fingers and the sweat that beaded on her forehead. She was determined to escape. She had tried to talk to the nurses again, but they wouldn't listen to her. They said that she was delusional and that she needed to stay here for her own safety. Frida knew that she was sane, and she wasn't going to give up until she was free. She didn't belong here, and she was going to find a way to get out.

Frida heard footsteps approaching and quickly placed her arms above the blanket, hands folded with the diamond ring flipped toward her palms. She looked at the closed door, anticipating someone to come in. But the door didn't open. Instead, she heard two male voices arguing.

"Can I not leave you alone for a few minutes," she heard the physician who had brought her here.

"No," the other voice said. "You can't." It sounded familiar as well, but she couldn't quite place it.

The two started arguing back and forth with increasing volume, like the crescendo in an opera play.

Frida held her breath, her heart pounding in her chest. They were arguing about *her*.

"Do you have any idea how much pain she created? I want her dead!" the other barked.

A cold shiver ran down Frida's back. Her life was on the line.

"Shut up. We had a deal," the physician said calmly. "I get my turn. If she does not comply, then you get yours. Either way, you're not a murderer."

"You can spot diabetes, Rogério," the other man said. "But you are completely clueless about human evil. Lies, betrayal, assaults. If you don't shoot first, you will get shot. That's what we are facing here. This bitch will tell you anything you want to save herself, and then she will go to the police and destroy you. Everyone will blame you for taking her. Nobody will thank you for bringing her to a hospital instead of burying her under a pile of dirt where she belongs."

"We had an agreement," the physician said firmly. "I know you are a man of honor."

There was a moment of silence. "Yes, I am," the other man responded.

"You have the key to my office. Take the back stairs and stay there. The FBI agent is still snooping around. He must not see you again."

Frida's heart jumped. The FBI was looking for her. Help was coming. She heard a grumping sound, perhaps some kind of approval. Then, footsteps retreated.

It was calm for a moment. Then, the key in the door rustled, and the door flung open. The man in the white coat entered. Kind eyes. This was the one she could reason with.

"Hello, Frida." He fetched the only chair in the room and sat down beside her bed.

Would she recognize him without the surgical mask? Maybe. "You work here?" she asked.

He nodded. "Yes, I do. I got the position in the oncology ward that you applied for."

Frida felt a lump in her throat. The man with five publications. She had 150.

The man's expression softened as he spoke. "I'm sorry that you didn't get the job." His voice was tinged with sincerity. "It wasn't fair to you. You worked so hard for this. From what I heard from my colleagues, you were an outstanding physician and great scientist."

Frida's head hung low, her expression a mix of frustration and deep hurt. "They looked at me like I was a monster," she whispered, her voice trembling. "They accused me of being power-hungry, self-centered, and lacking empathy. How could they possibly know what I think or feel? I got the highest EQ in my SUEC leadership class, and I cared for my patients day and night!"

"I know," he said softly. "You loved the hospital, and the hospital didn't love you back."

His words hung in the air like a poignant truth, capturing the essence of Frida's pain. SUEC had been a place of dreams and aspirations for her, a haven where she sought to make a difference. But she had been crushed and trampled on.

"And *you*, of all people, came to tell me that?" Her voice quivered as she tried to wipe away these painful memories.

The man's gaze locked with hers, sending a wave of compassion and solidarity. "I'm really sorry how you were treated, Frida. You deserved better. I didn't know any of this until I started and heard stories in the ward. I looked up your file. I think you were being discriminated against. You could have sued."

Frida looked at the man. He was the last person on earth she would have expected to understand. His words created gentle ripples in a pond of hurt and disappointment.

"I was criticized for being too outspoken and impatient, characteristics that would not be criticized in a man. I was advised to be more accommodating and not try to be a leader, which contradicts SUEC's promotion criteria. Yes, this was discrimination. But I couldn't afford a lawyer," she said calmly. "And you know how powerful SUEC is. They would have found a way to make this go away. They were very clever. You're Hispanic, right? I can't really sue for discrimination. The chair hired an underrepresented minority, but he just wanted to hire a division chief who wouldn't be a threat to his position. A man with five publications will stay in that role for a long time. No risk of raising a competitor. A woman with a stellar CV is a different story. They assassinated my career to eliminate a contender. And no one at SUEC stood up for me. No one. That's it. That's the story."

The man nodded. "And so you took things into your own hands. I recognized your name on the health insurance denials. SUEC rejected you. Now, you reject SUEC every day. Did that feel good?"

Frida looked at the man. Did he mock her? He looked back at her with his deep-set brown eyes. Soulful. Waiting.

Frida shrugged, her eyes flashing with barely concealed anger.

"It *is* satisfying. I'm in charge now," she declared, trying to hide the raw emotions churning within. "After all the extra shifts and extra work I did for SUEC, they told me I wasn't accommodating? They labeled me as such. Now they can see what that really means. I'm fighting back the only way I can. I couldn't let them win."

"But you're still angry? You still feel the pain inside?" His eyes were soft and understanding, but there was also a hint of challenge in his voice. Was he trying to goad her? Or was he simply trying to understand her?

Frida hesitated for a moment, unsure how to answer. She didn't want to admit it, but she knew it was true. She was still angry. SUEC had not only denied her promotion, but they had also assassinated her character to justify their actions. After years of working tirelessly for them, her superiors had abused their power to beat her down with fabricated arguments. They had hurt, humiliated, and defamed her. She had cried herself to sleep many nights. They had destroyed her career. They deserved to pay for what they had done to her.

She raised her head and met his gaze, her eyes burning with determination. "Yes, I'm still angry," she said. "And I'm not going to let them get away with it."

He didn't offer platitudes or false comfort. Instead, he held her gaze with unwavering sincerity, acknowledging the depth of her pain.

"You're stuck in your anger," he said. "You're angry at the university, but you're also angry at yourself. You feel like you should have done more to fight back, but you're not sure what else you could have done. You're angry at your husband for not understanding, but you're also angry at yourself for not being able to explain it to him. You're angry at the world, and you don't know how to let go of it."

The weight of his observation settled heavily on her heart. How did he know she was married? Frida palpated the diamond ring in the palm of her hand. Perhaps the man had seen it. The ring felt hard and sharp under her fingertip, a fiber string at the base. A symbol of the past she held onto. Lost love.

"What do you know about my pain?" she asked. "You profited from the whole situation."

The man took a moment to compose himself before speaking again, his voice gentle yet firm. "You know that I was not the reason for your demotion," he said. "If I had not applied, the chair would have chosen someone else. For me, it would have been an honor to work with you. I don't care much about leadership positions. It means much more work for a ridiculously small bonus payment. If I had known all this beforehand, I would have gladly offered the position to you. I only care about the children. They are the real losers here."

Frida made a fist around her diamond ring. "That is too late now," she said calmly, a tear escaping her eye. "Fixing it, I mean."

The man's gaze bore into her, seeing beyond the facade she presented. "You worked an insane number of hours to join an honorable university. Or so you thought. You wanted to step above your humble upbringing and make your family proud. When others watched TV, you were studying. When others went to a grill party, you wrote a research paper. When others celebrated Thanksgiving, you worked extra shifts in the hospital." He spoke with a quiet intensity, recounting her life story as if he had lived it.

"How do you know that?" Frida asked. The man's ability to understand her journey bewildered her.

He smiled faintly. "You're not the only one who worked around the clock and has been stepped on and over," he said, his voice tinged with empathy. "You dedicated your entire life to a noble cause, Frida. And in return, you were disrespected, belittled, and insulted. The honorable organization was not honorable, and you were never a part of it."

Frida's chest tightened as she relived every slight, every instance of being taken for granted despite her unwavering commitment. Nobody had explained the situation so clearly to her thus far. A wave of vulnerability washed over her as she found herself confiding in this unexpected confidant.

"It hurts," she admitted, her voice catching with the unshed tears. "All I ever wanted was to make a difference and to be supported in my aspirations. But it feels like it was all in vain. I lost my purpose."

The man nodded. "Life sucks when you don't know why you're here. The University demoted and insulted you. The insurance company gave you the appreciation and validation you craved. You are good at what you do. And they told you that. Every day. And SUEC got the full force of your revenge. Now *you* are in charge."

Frida nodded. "Yes, I am."

They sat calmly for a while. A hummingbird zipped past the freshly cleaned window, diving into a pink bougainvillea blossom that ranked up the walls.

"Deep down, you know that you're hurting innocent lives, Frida." the man said softly. "Children."

A part of her yearned to release the burden of pain and bitterness that weighed heavily on her shoulders. But another part of her clung to the familiar, the anger that had become a part of her identity. It was a moment suspended in time, a battle between holding on and letting go, between staying trapped in pain and seeking a way to heal.

"I don't make the rules. I'm just doing my work," she said defensively. "The entire healthcare system is on the verge of collapse. Administrative costs, prescription drug costs, and salary payments for doctors and nurses are rising constantly. The system is thoughtless and overpriced. The insurances have to safeguard it because there are no set prices for medical services. Hospitals are free to charge whatever the market may bear. We have to add a moral compass for them. Hospitals must offer financial assistance to those who cannot pay their bills. So, the patients will be taken care of in the end."

The man looked at her, choosing his words carefully. "What about the woman you met this morning? Do you think she and her son were taken care of?"

Frida's voice trembled, her words tinged with frustration. "Well, I'm sorry for what they have gone through. I really am. But the boy will be depressed, no matter what. What about all the women who have undergone a breast amputation? Do they get a free shrink as well? What about psychological assault? Did *I* get a free shrink? Life is hard. There is just not enough money to pay a psychologist for everyone."

"These are children, Frida. Innocent Children." The man sighed and got up. He looked at her with a sad gaze and turned around.

Frida felt an urge to justify herself. "I'm just doing my job," she said to his back with a raised voice. "And why are you lecturing me about moral values? *You* kidnapped me. *You* assaulted me!"

The man looked back at her. Frida palpated her bald head and fought back the tears.

"I'm sorry. This was an accident," he said. "I did *not* shave your head." He walked toward the door.

"Then, get your *accident* under control," she cried after him. "I'm not the criminal here. You will both end up in San Quentin. Or they will send you back to Mexico!"

The man looked over his shoulder once more. "Do you speak Spanish, Frida?"

What a question. Frida took a deep breath. "No, I don't."

"Well, neither do I," he said calmly. He opened the door and passed through. The door closed with a soft thud.

# - 23 -

# TERREL

Caramba
Sunday, October 9, 2033, 9:00 a.m.

Niles and Terrell walked through the hospital garden. The early morning sun cast a warm glow over the neatly trimmed hedges and beds of late-blooming flowers. Niles skipped ahead, his small hand clutching his beloved robot tightly. Terrell smiled, watching his son with pride. Niles was his whole world, and he would do anything to protect him.

They reached the aviary, and Niles stopped short. "Daddy, look!" he cried. "There's a hole in the cage!"

Terrel approached with long strides and inspected the situation. Indeed, the aviary was empty. Seeds, nutshells, and feathers were scattered on the ground. There was a large hole in the mesh on the side of the enclosure. Loose ends of mesh and wire were pointing outward. Somebody had cut the mesh and torn the gap wide open. The parrot was gone.

"Where did he go?" Niles asked, his voice small.

Terrell shook his head. "I don't know," he said. "But someone cut the mesh and let him out."

Terrel looked around. Could a pet parrot fly? Probably. Terrell thought about the woman who had been kidnapped. Could the parrot be connected to her disappearance? He didn't know, but he wasn't going to take any chances. He pulled out his phone and called his boss, Angus.

"Angus," he said, "I think I've found something."

In a flurry of urgency, Terrel relayed the details to Angus over the phone. "Angus, I need you to listen carefully. Niles and I were just at the hospital garden, and the parrot is gone. There's a hole in the aviary, and I don't know if he flew away or if he was killed or kidnapped."

Angus listened intently. "I see," he said. "This is serious. I'm on my way. I'm in the hospital right now. I believe I saw the man who did this. One of the kidnappers was in the garden earlier today. I tried to catch him, but he got away. I thought he looked exactly like the pediatric oncologist, Dr. Rogério Queirós Trento. But Annya assured me that the oncologist had been with her in the ER."

"Dr. Rogério Queirós Trento was in the oncology ward earlier this morning," Terrel confirmed. "I saw him during the rounds. I don't think he is your man."

Angus took a moment to digest the information. "Well, we'll see about that," he said. "There is something fishy about that man. My gut feeling has never been wrong. For now, we need to find the bird. If they went through the trouble of releasing it, the bird must have some crucial information. And I want to know what it is."

"Okay, I will look around. Perhaps it is still somewhere close." Terrel's eyes darted around the hospital garden, scanning for any sign of the missing parrot.

"Parrots are very social creatures," Angus explained. "If he got out of the cage, he's probably scared and confused. He'll likely do what any human would do and fly to a random person or try to find food."

Terrell's curiosity was piqued. "What do parrots eat?"

"Pet parrots eat food pellets. See if you find some in the cage. You can also check for nuts or fresh fruit. Macaws love those."

Terrel looked around the aviary. "I see some food pellets on a tray," he said.

"Good," Angus said. "Get some of those. Then, start looking for the bird. When you find him, don't yell at him. That will only frighten him more and make him fly away. Move slowly and offer him the food. I'm on my way."

Niles observed his father closely. "Will we get the bird back?" he asked with a mixture of concern and unease in his voice.

"Of course," Terrell responded. "We are both detectives now. We will find the parrot and bring him back to his home."

"Yes! I'm a detective!" Niles clapped in excitement.

"We need to get some bird food first." Terrel pointed at the food pellets in the aviary. He tried to squeeze himself through the mesh gape, but it was too small and too high above the ground. He tried to expand the gap with his bare hands. But the wire was sturdy. The hole in the mesh was about two feet in diameter and too high for an adult to climb through it easily.

"Niles, can you get me that bird food?" Terrell asked, pointing at the food tray.

"Sure, Daddy!" Niles' eyes lit up. Terrell lifted him through the hole in the cage, and Niles landed on the floor with a soft thud. His shirt got caught on the broken mesh, ripping a tear in it, but he didn't seem to notice. He walked toward the tray, his shoes and lower pants soiled with dirt and bird droppings. He scooped pellets into his pockets with both hands, then brought a handful to Terrell.

"Good job," Terrell said, lifting Niles out of the cage. Niles giggled and hugged his father tightly.

"Look, there's Mommy!" Niles waved at the building on the opposite side of the garden.

Terrel looked up and saw Imani standing on the balcony in front of their patient room, hands on her hips. When their eyes locked, she beckoned him with her hand. He couldn't see her face well, but her gesture was clear. *Come here immediately*. She was angry.

Best to play innocent. He smiled and waved back enthusiastically. She shouted something, but he couldn't understand. She was too far away. He pointed at his ears and shook his head. He reached for Niles' hand and walked toward the playground to let her cool down. She disappeared in the patient room.

"Can you see the parrot?" he asked his son. "His name is Caramba. He must be somewhere in the garden."

Niles looked up at the sky, scanning nearby trees. "Caramba, I have some treats for you!" he shouted into the air, extending his hand with the bird pellets.

Two kids in a sandbox and a young woman with a stroller turned around, observing Terrel and Niles as they walked toward the trees and called Caramba's name.

Terrel scanned the trees, balconies, edges, and the roof of the hospital building. Nothing.

"I don't see him," Niles said with a shrug. "Perhaps he's gone."

They heard a familiar, deep voice behind them. "These birds usually don't fly far away from their home."

"Hi, Angus!" Niles cried. "Are you searching for Caramba as well?"

"Yes, I am!" Angus said, ruffling Niles' hair. Then, he turned to Terrell. "I have some interesting news."

"What is it?" Terrel asked.

"Guess who the previous owner of the parrot was? Our forensics team just sent me a note."

"I don't know."

"Dr. Julius Philopator Zhang."

"Really? The ER physician?"

"Yes, I just warned Annya. He might be involved in our case."

"That is peculiar," Terrel said. "And how did the parrot get here?"

"Apparently, Dr. Zhang donated the bird to the hospital shortly after he started working here. Our team checked the bird's leg band. He was stolen from a pet store in Las Vegas about six months ago."

"Really?" said Terrel in disbelief. "A parrot thief in an Armani suit? That doesn't make any sense to me."

"I found him!" Niles called in the distance.

Terrel looked around. His son was standing under a pine tree about 200 meters away from them. How had he run away so far so quickly? A beautiful scarlet macaw was sitting on one of the branches, the plumage red, the upper wings yellow, the rump and tail dark blue. Niles approached him slowly, extending his hands with the bird pellets. The bird hopped to a lower tree branch, eying the food in the boy's hand.

"Hi, Caramba, I have a treat for you," Niles said softly, slowly stepping toward the bird. The parrot walked down the branch until he was directly above the boy.

Terrel and Angus had reached the scene. The two kids came running toward them as well, their mother in tow. Another couple with a stroller approached as well.

"Stay back," Angus said with an authoritative voice. "This bird escaped from the aviary, and we need to catch him." He turned to Terrel. "Can you offer your arm to the bird? He needs a place to land. I will catch him from there."

Terrel nodded. He slowly approached Niles and offered his extended arm to the bird, who was approximately half a meter above them. The claws on the birds' feet looked alarmingly large. He was glad he had chosen his leather jacket that morning.

"Hello, Caramba," he said with a calm voice, trying not to move. "You must remember me. We met yesterday."

The bird looked at Terrel and Niles, his head tilted. Then, he eyed Terrel. Did he recognize him from the encounter last night? He hopped onto Terrel's arm. Niles approached slowly, offering the food in the palm of his hand. The beak of the bird was huge. Terrel felt nauseated. Hopefully, he would not bite.

Angus snuck up behind the bird, slowly raising his jacket behind him. He would throw the jacket over him and fetch him.

The bird started to gurgle and trill, transitioning into whistling. He looked at the food pellets, then at Niles and Terrel. Angus tiptoed closer. Suddenly, they heard gunshots.

Niles and Angus jumped backward. Angus' eyes darted around, trying to localize the threat, ready to react if needed. Terrel had recognized the act.

"It is just the bird," he said loudly. "He's imitating sounds." He tried to hold his arm still. He couldn't lose the bird.

The bird led out another round of gunshots. The spectators screamed and ran away from the scene, except one. Imani stomped through the crowd, her face red with anger. She fetched Niles by his free left arm and jerked him back. The pellets dropped to the ground.

"Are you out of your mind?" she screamed at Terrel and Angus.

"Mommy, you hurt my arm," Niles protested.

The parrot spread his wings. Angus tried to throw his jacket over the bird's back, but it slipped off. The bird took off with several squawks, traversing the crown of the tree and disappearing over the roof of the hospital building.

"Do you want to kill our son?" Imani shouted at the two men. "Can I not leave you alone for one hour?"

Angus held up his palms. "I'm sorry, Imani. It was all my fault. The bird is an important witness in a case."

"A *case?*" Imani cried. "You drag our son into an FBI investigation of a bird that imitates gunshots? Which part of *we need our privacy* do you not understand?"

"I'm really sorry, Imani," Angus said. "I didn't mean to cause any harm. I will explain everything to you later. But now, I need to fetch the bird. Please excuse me." He turned around and ran toward the hospital wing where the bird had flown. He approached two security guards at the building entrance and talked with them briefly. Then, the three men disappeared in the building.

Terrel saw his boss disappear. How convenient. He wished he had a similar excuse right now.

Imani turned to her husband, fuming. "Our son is ill, Terrel! Look at him. His shirt is torn, and he is covered in dirt. Who knows what germs he caught from that bird? He has *surgery* tomorrow. If he gets pneumonia or wound infection, it will be *your* fault!"

She was upset, rightfully so. Terrel looked at his feet. "I'm sorry, Imani," he said softly, "I really am. We just came to see the parrot. And then one thing led to another."

"Daddy and I had a lot of fun!" Niles protested.

"Well, we will have a lot more fun on the ward now!" Imani said, with a fake cheerful voice, trying to compose herself. "I wanted to get you so that we can watch the clown on the ward." She reached for her son's hand, and he took it.

Terrel followed them, glancing at his wife from the side. Only he noticed the sharp inhale she took. He felt guilty. He couldn't manage work and family in this difficult time. It amplified the pain. He had to make a clear cut. Imani was right. The bird must have heard gunshots somewhere if it imitated them. The parrot was connected to the kidnappers. He had to keep his family away from the bird.

The three walked toward the hospital wing that housed the children's hospital. Terrell looked up to the pediatric oncology ward on the third floor. There was a man with curly brown hair, a mustache, and a white coat behind the window, watching them. Was that the oncologist, Dr. Queirós Trento? Had he observed the entire encounter with the bird? As their eyes met, the man stepped away from the window into the shadow of the room.

Terrell felt a chill run down his spine. He knew that this was no coincidence. The oncologist had been watching them. He had to be careful. He had to keep his family safe. And he had to find out what the oncologist was up to.

# - 24 -

# ANNYA

Discoveries
Sunday, October 9, 2033, 9:15 a.m.

Annya rushed up the stairs to the second floor when her cell phone announced an incoming text message with a *bling* tone. She looked at the screen. Angus. She opened it.

*The parrot belonged to Dr. Julius Philopator Zhang. Be careful.*

She stopped and texted back. *Always.*

*It was stolen from a pet store,* Angus added.

*Not Julius' style,* Annya responded. Julius had many flaws, including a flexible interpretation of rules and regulations. But he was not a thief. He didn't have to be. His father kept him financially secure at all times. He didn't know what a financial shortfall was. It would never occur to him to steal a pet. If he wanted something, he would just buy it. Perhaps he had bought the parrot from a devious source. That was more like him.

*The parrot escaped.* Angus added. *Let me know if you see him.*

*Will watch out for him.* Annya texted back. Strange request. The bird would hardly stop by in the ER. And who said it was a male bird? Annya needed to work with Angus on some stereotypes. It could as well be a female parrot. But then, who cared? Annya didn't want to complicate the discussion. Her colleagues in the ER were probably already looking for her, and she had to find out where Rogério went.

She continued down the hallway and reached the windowless silver-metal double doors to the psychiatry ward. They were always locked to securely shelter the troubled and the troublesome. Annya rang the bell.

A thirty-something young woman in scrubs with a blonde updo bun and warm, gray eyes opened the door. It was the same woman Annya had seen in the video. She seemed a little irritated.

"Can I help you?" she asked.

Annya held up her hospital ID. She had to improvise. "Hi, my name is Dr. Annya Segond. I'm an emergency physician in the ER on the first floor. We have a pediatric emergency, and I'm trying to get ahold of Dr. Queirós Trento. It seems that his cell phone is not working. He said that he would visit a patient here. Could I speak with him by any chance?"

The nurse looked her up and down. "I'm sorry. We cannot reveal patient details due to privacy regulations," she said. "This includes information about who visits our patients."

"No need to reveal anything," Annya said lightly. "Dr. Queirós Trento already told me that he is here. How would I otherwise know that? We have an emergency in the ER, and I need to speak with him urgently."

The nurse looked at her ID again, contemplating the situation for a moment. Then, she sighed. "Come in." She opened the door and ushered her in.

Annya stepped through the door before the nurse could change her mind. They entered a long, sterile hallway with white tiles, bleached walls, and a single window at the end. The hallway was eerily quiet, and the only sound was the echo of their footsteps. There was less equipment standing around compared to the ER. To the right was the nurse's station, a sterile-looking long desk separated from the rest of the area by a glass barrier. Annya wondered if it was bulletproof. Beyond the glass, she could see another nurse diligently working, her expression focused.

Along the hallway were multiple doors, all with card readers on them. A few stood open, but most were closed. An old man in a hospital gown came toward her, escorted by a male nurse with kind eyes and a stubbled face. They nodded briefly toward Annya and disappeared in one of the rooms.

They reached a door with a sign for Authorized Personnel Only. "Wait here," the nurse said. "This space is for patients requiring extra privacy and monitoring." She swiped her card at the reader in front of one of the rooms. Annya watched carefully. Room 12. The door opened toward a small office-like space with a desk and a mirrored window. An observation room. At the end of the room was another door, probably leading to a private patient room. Annya wondered what might be happening inside those walls, and the presence of an office for the observer added an intriguing element of secrecy.

Rogério was standing in front of the desk, greeting the nurse who was talking to him in a low voice, pointing back at Annya. Rogério looked at her through the ajar door, his face half-hidden by a surgical mask. Why was he wearing a surgical mask? This was not a surgical ward, and there was no infection risk here. Or was there?

It took Annya a few seconds to decipher his expression. His eyes were wide with shock, and he looked terrified. He put his arm around the nurse's shoulder, directed her out of the room, and closed the door behind them. Annya tried to get another glimpse of the room behind him, but she couldn't see anything. Who was in that patient room? She would have to ask Angus to find out. Room 12.

The nurse stepped out of the room, clearly more relaxed than the physician. She was in her element here. Rogério was not. The nurse acknowledged them both with a brief nod, then went back to her duties. Rogério checked the door handle to make sure it was closed. Then, he turned toward Annya.

"Hi, Annya, you have an emergency in the ER? What is it?"

Annya tried to think on her feet. To be believable and disguise whatever shock she'd created, she needed a really good reason to show up here. Rogério was clearly out of his comfort zone.

"Can I talk to you outside?" she asked, mostly to win some time.

"Of course," he turned toward the exit, his hands on the small of her back. Annya suppressed a reflex to assert some physical distance. They passed the nursing station and left the ward. The double doors closed behind them. Annya slightly lifted her elbow, then turned, creating momentum into the front part of her elbow before it struck Rogério's chest.

"Hey, be careful," he said with a snappy tone as he took a step back.

"Sorry," Annya said with an upwards gaze. The hand on her back was gone. "I actually didn't come to see you for a patient," she said with a low voice. "I just learned that the parrot in the garden was stolen from a pet store a few weeks ago. And somebody cut open the aviary and let him loose. He escaped."

She had decided that the best offense was the truth. If Rogério was involved, then she didn't deliver any news. If he didn't know, then there was no harm in sharing this information. Perhaps he could help.

"Really? The parrot from the aviary in the hospital garden is gone?" Rogério seemed genuinely surprised. "And you came all the way here to tell me that? How did you even find me?"

"You mentioned that you had a friend with mental health issues. It was a best guess," Annya lied.

Rogério gave her a suspicious look. "And why is this so urgent? Why do we care about this bird?"

"Well, I just learned that Julius Zhang donated the bird to the hospital," explained Annya. "It was stolen from a pet store. So, he donated a stolen pet to SUEC. I'm his supervisor and have to confront him when he comes for shift change today. But this whole affair does not make sense to me. Julius can buy as many parrots as he wants. Why would he steal one? I wanted to seek your input before I accuse him of a crime he probably didn't commit. You and Julius are friends. What do you think?"

Rogério glanced at her nervously. "Well, I don't know Julius that well. Perhaps he's on a mission to release endangered parrots into the wild. Who knows what is going on in the heads of rich guys like him?"

Annya's mind raced, trying to connect the dots. Her sixth sense told her that Rogério was hiding something. But she couldn't put her finger on what it was.

"I really don't want Julius to get in trouble," she whispered. "If we can find the parrot and return him safely, perhaps we can resolve the whole affair. There could be a good explanation for the *stolen* part. Perhaps Julius bought the bird from a thief."

Rogério observed her closely, scratching the back of his head. Then, he said, "Annya, I want to be frank. I had a little brother who would make up fantasy stories. I have a flashback, like I'm hearing one right now. We are physicians on clinical service at SUEC Hospital. We don't have time for parrots, and even if your story is true, it's none of our business. The police can take care of it. But I have an eerie feeling that you didn't just come by to tell me about some bird. What is *really* going on? Are you okay?"

Had she followed the wrong lead? How embarrassing. Annya pushed the button on her iPhone to create a beeping sound. She used it to get out of difficult situations. She pulled her iPhone from her pocket and pretended to look at a message on her screen.

"Oh, an emergency in the ER," she said. "Sorry, Rogério, I have to leave. I really only wanted to talk about the parrot. I care about Julius, and I don't want to get him in trouble. Please watch out for the bird."

Rogério shook his head. "Of course, if a parrot crosses my path, you'll be the first to know."

"Thank you!" Annya turned around on her heels. The elevator at the end of the hallway opened just in time, giving way to an elderly man with a cane. Annya stepped in. The closing doors ended Rogério's staring gaze like a rescuing steel curtain.

When she exited on the first floor, she sent a text to Angus. *Rogério visited a patient in the psychiatry ward, room 12. IDK if it is related to your case. Perhaps check?*

He responded right away. *Thanks, will do.*

# - 25 -

# ANNYA

The Clue
Sunday, October 9, 2033, 9:30 a.m.


Annya checked her phone. This time, there was a real text message from the ER.

*R U @ cafeteria? Waiting room full. We need you here.*

She texted back, *OMW,* walking toward the ER with long strides. When she passed by the double-glass back entrance door to the parking lot behind the hospital, she spotted Angus. Her eyes traced his familiar contours, his posture a blend of casual repose and poised attentiveness. A rush of emotions surged within her, causing her heart to skip a beat and then dance in her chest like fluttering butterflies brushing against her ribs. He was sitting on a bench beside the back entrance area, leaning toward a large cage in front of him. Was the parrot inside? She was too curious to just walk by. It would just take a minute. Annya approached Angus. Her steps involuntarily quickened, driven by an inexplicable pull.

Indeed, a beautiful red, yellow, and blue macaw parrot was sitting in the cage with a fanned tail, flapping its wings rapidly and biting on the cage bars.

"I see you got him," Annya said as she arrived. Angus' presence breathed new life into the world around her. The colors seemed brighter, the sounds more vibrant. People around them blurred into the background, leaving only the two of them in a space of shared connection.

Angus' face lit up when he saw her. "It took three of us," he explained. "The SUEC security guards lent a hand. We lured him with food pellets and then threw a large towel over him. I held him wrapped while the guards brought a travel cage."

"Do you want to send him away?" she asked. Her gaze lingered on his face, from the square lines of his jaw to the worry lines on his forehead. She felt safe in his presence.

Angus nodded. "I'm waiting for a shuttle. I'll send him to the FBI headquarters. An experienced vet will interrogate him there. And then we'll send him back to the pet store where he was stolen."

The parrot looked at them, head tilted. Then, he squawked loudly, flapping his wings.

"Did he say anything already?" Annya asked.

"I tried to talk with him, but he is too upset at the moment," Angus said, pointing at the bird who was flapping and flailing around the cage, panting. "He needs to calm down and get more comfortable. Hopefully, our vet can help with that."

She found herself drawn to the way his eyes crinkled at the corners when he smiled. A wave of fondness washed over her.

"Did your team check who is in the psychiatry ward in room 12?"

Angus nodded. "Unfortunately, that was a dead end. It is a neighbor of Rogério, who has a long history of depression. She tried to kill herself, and he brought her in."

The parrot sat still on a branch in the cage, glaring at them intently with his bright eyes.

"Rogério saved the patient's life?" Annya asked.

Angus nodded again.

"Rogério Gabriel Queirós Trento," the bird suddenly cried with a wide beak, feathers ruffled.

Angus and Annya looked at the bird in surprise.

"Do you think he knows Rogério?" Angus asked.

"Well, Julius and Rogério seem to be friends," Annya said. "So, I guess it is quite reasonable that the bird met Rogério and learned his name."

"Rogério, Rogério," the bird repeated.

"Caramba, tell us about the kidnapping," Annya asked.

The bird looked at her with a tilted head. A young woman with a dachshund on a leash walked by. The dachshund barked frantically at the bird.

The parrot was not intimidated at all. "Shut up! Shut up!" he shouted at the dog with an authoritative male voice, flapping his wings. The dog winced and rushed by the cage.

A shiny yellow Lamborghini roared into the parking lot, slowly driving to the front row and parking there. The car door opened and

Julius stepped out, walking swiftly toward the back entrance door. He saw Annya and waved. She waved back. He changed his direction and came toward Angus and Annya.

"Hello, Annya. What are you doing here?" he asked as he came closer. "Hello, Angus!"

"I could ask the same," Annya responded.

"Well, I got a call from the hospital. Rogério filed an incident report that he met you in a hallway in the hospital, disoriented, talking nonsense. He was concerned that you were on drugs or had a mental problem or something. The ER couldn't locate you, and so they called me to fill in for you." He smiled at Angus. "I now see what's going on. I didn't buy the drug story. You don't do drugs."

"It's not what you think," Annya interjected, her eyes narrowed in response to the absurdity of the situation. Had Rogério really thought she was compromised? Or was this a move to get her out of the way?

Julius flashed a wide grin. "No worries," he said. "I get it. You had a date. I'm happy for you both. You helped me out a lot last night, so I'm happy to return the favor. Just don't try to pull this on my free weekend. I'm already scheduled to work today, so I'm just coming in a little early. No big deal."

Annya looked at her colleague suspiciously. She had always helped him out, but he had never reciprocated before. And it wasn't like him to volunteer for work. What was going on?

Julius inspected the birdcage. "What is Caramba doing here?" he asked.

"Hello, Daddy. Hello, Daddy," the parrot cried in excitement. He jumped to the cage door, unlatched the cage with his beak, hung off the door, flapped his wings, and landed on Julius' shoulder, nibbling on his right ear.

"How did he do that?" Angus exclaimed. "He needs to get back into the cage!"

"Hi, buddy, great to see you, too," Julius said softly to the bird. He pulled a pistachio from his pocket and offered it to the parrot, who accepted it with an approving squeak. Small nut crumbs landed on Julius' spotless shirt.

"Pistachio!" the bird echoed.

Julius offered him another one.

"No worries," he said to Angus. "As long as I have pistachios, he won't go anywhere. What is Caramba doing in this little cage? Did he commit a crime?"

"It is possible that he witnessed a crime," Angus answered. "This morning, someone created a hole in the aviary and set him loose."

"Really?" Julius looked at the bird. "Is that a case for the FBI? He must have flown around quite a bit. That's why he is so hungry."

"Please put him back in the cage," Angus said with a stern expression. "We don't want to lose him again." He gestured toward the cage.

"No worries. I have plenty of pistachios. I bring a handful for him every day. They're his favorites." Julius offered the bird another pistachio.

"You were his previous owner?" Annya asked in a gentle yet inquisitive tone. "You never mentioned that."

Julius smiled. "Well, we've never talked about our pets," he said. "I got Caramba about three months ago. He was supposed to be a service animal for a sick child, but that didn't work out. Parrots are needy creatures, like children. They're also expensive to care for—large cages, perches, vet visits, special food, and so on."

Annya sensed the importance of this information and leaned in slightly, signaling her empathy and willingness to listen. "And so you took him?" she asked.

Julius nodded, his gaze momentarily flickering to the ground before meeting hers again. "I did. I always loved animals but never had a pet. My father is allergic to cats, I don't have the time to walk a dog, and fish are boring. So, when I heard that Caramba needed a new home, I happily offered to help."

"You adopted the bird?" Annya asked. The image of Julius adopting a pet added a touch of tenderness and compassion to his spotless façade she hadn't expected.

Julius nodded, his voice softening with affection. "Caramba was labeled too needy and too expensive. That struck a chord. I happily accepted the challenge and took him over. The costs were no problem for me, and we have enough personnel at our home to take care of an exotic bird. Caramba is very intelligent, you know. He needs constant stimulation."

"And you thought your service personnel could entertain him?" Annya shook her head. Julius was really living in a parallel universe.

Julius nodded. "That was the plan. I didn't expect Caramba to be so focused on *me*. He would only eat in my presence, and he was very destructive when I was not around. Our house manager called him a chainsaw with wings. Caramba could go through our wooded furniture faster than a tree shredder. Before I donated him to the children's hospital, we had to replace two of our antique chairs in the family room. That was a breaking point for my father. The bird had to leave."

"But you said Caramba was very attached to you? He would not eat without you?" Annya asked.

"Correct," Julius said. "I thought donating him to the Children's hospital might make the transition easier. Rogério and I can visit him every day. He gets a lot of entertainment in the hospital garden, and he will hopefully get used to his new environment with time."

Julius put a nut in the cage in front of them. Caramba hopped to the cage, climbed up the wire, and hung by one toe upside down from the door to reach it. Julius threw another nut deeper into the cage. The bird followed. He closed the cage door and secured it with a band-aid.

"You might want to secure that better," he said to Angus with a chuckle. "Caramba is serial escaper."

"Why would Rogério want to visit the bird?" Angus asked.

Julius looked at him with raised eyebrows. "I thought you were from the FBI? Rogério was Caramba's first owner. I got the bird from him."

Annya exchanged a quick glance with Angus. She could see his thoughts in his stern blue eyes without exchanging a word. Surprise. Doubt. A disguise?

"Can Caramba understand you? Can you ask him a question? Or does he just repeat whatever he picks up?" Angus asked.

Julius shrugged. "He understands words important to him. Cage, shower, kitchen, food, pistachio. He loves to imitate sounds, especially if they stir emotions. He craves interactions and will quickly pick up anything that causes a strong human response. But I don't think you can talk with him like a human if that's what you mean. If you want him to repeat something, just offer him pistachios."

"Angus is searching for a kidnapped woman. Can you ask Caramba if he knows anything about that?" Annya asked. She observed Julius closely. He didn't show any sign of surprise or apprehension.

He laughed. "Sorry, I'm not a bird whisperer. And I cannot imagine that Caramba knows anything about that. He was in the hospital garden for the past few months." He turned to the bird. "Hey Caramba, do you know anything about a kidnapping incident?"

"Caramba was kidnapped," the bird repeated.

"There you go." Julius pointed at the bird. "The only one who has been kidnapped here is the parrot. Now, if you would excuse me, one of us has to get to work."

"I'll come with you," Annya said, getting up from the bench. "I'm really sorry that they called you in. This is a big misunderstanding. I can clear this up."

Julius grinned. "No worries. I owe you. And if that helps, I'm happy to confirm that you're fit for work. But they might do a tox screen on you regardless."

Annya felt a twinge of annoyance, but she was also grateful to Julius for his swift rescue. It had prevented a major disaster. She caught a hint of jealousy in Angus' eyes, and her heart softened. She realized that he might be feeling unsettled by her exchange with Julius. To reassure Angus and reaffirm their bond, she gently embraced him, holding him close for a brief moment.

"See you at 2 p.m.," she whispered, her voice laced with tenderness.

"I'll pick you up at the backdoor to the ER," he whispered back.

Expressing that much affection in public was unusual for Annya, and she was slightly astonished by her own behavior. But she couldn't deny the growing connection between her and Angus. The kidnapping case, their shared moments of honesty, and the trust they had built had forged a spark of something more than friendship. They smiled at each other one last time, and then Annya turned and joined Julius on the way to the hospital.

# - 26 -

# FRIDA

The Escape
Sunday, October 9, 2033, 9:30 a.m.

Frida inspected the restraining belt. She had made a small dent with her diamond ring. But at this pace, it would take her days, if not weeks, to make her way all the way through. She didn't have that much time. She had to change her strategy. The oncologist was an intellectual. He was not a killer. But the other man was. The one who had hit her and whispered into her ear that he would make her pay. Frida shuddered when she thought how violently he had punched her face.

Frida was still puzzled by the resemblance of the intellectual and the violent man. Had she been unable to tell them apart because she had been drugged? Possible. Or was it actually just one man with a split personality? How did an oncologist have such a close connection with the psychiatric ward? Perhaps he was a patient here? A patient with schizophrenia? But if he had been treated for a personality disorder, he would not be able to practice as a physician? Perhaps he was treated for something else, a depression or bipolar disorder, but actually had a more serious issue? Or was she dealing with two men that looked alike? Wouldn't she have noticed some difference between them? Frida tried to remember.

There had been two men in the car. The man who had pulled her into the car was the man she had seen here in the hospital room. She had not seen the face of the driver. It could have been two men that looked alike. Or one schizophrenic psychopath with a hired driver. Either way, the violent man had said that he wanted to kill her. His cruel gaze had been clear. He was only waiting for his turn. And he was impatient. She had to get out of there before he came for her.

Frida rang the patient bell, looking at the closed door, waiting. Nothing. She rang again. It was eerie silence in the hospital room. She could hear her heart pounding against her chest. *Stay calm*, she commanded her deranged self. A bird chirped outside. She rang again. Finally, footsteps approached. Clogs. Hopefully. The door flung open, and the nurse rushed into the room.

"What is it?" she asked with an irritated voice.

"That took long," Frida complained. "I need to use the restroom."

The nurse held up her palms. "I'm sorry. It's Sunday. We are only three people on the ward, and you're not the only patient here. I'll get the bedpan right away."

"I can use the bathroom," Frida said in a calm voice. "I feel much better today."

The nurse looked at her over her shoulder. "You're on restraining order. I'm sorry. I cannot release you."

"Yes, you can," Frida said firmly. "Remember, the bedpan leaked this morning, and you had to change the bed sheets with me in it. That was a lot of work. I just want to make it easier for both of us."

The nurse looked undecided for a moment. Then, she shook her head. But her hands went for the magnet, which was hooked to a cord around her neck. A neck band that also held her hospital ID. She hated the bedpan as much as Frida.

"The restroom is just two meters away." Frida pointed at a door at the rear end of the room. She had seen the nurse emptying the bedpan there.

"I'm sorry. I have my orders," the nurse said with a hint of frustration in her voice. "Believe me, I wish I could do more, but I have to follow the protocols." Her eyebrows furrowed in genuine concern.

Frida raised her bare arms. "Nobody will know. What on earth could happen? Are you afraid of me?" She knew she looked frail with her hospital gown and shaved head.

The nurse slowly closed the patient's door. "Be quick," she said in a low voice. She took the neckband off, removed the blanket, and opened the magnet lock at the restraining belt.

*Some space to breathe.* Frida inhaled deeply. She sat up slowly, dangling her legs off the high bed, then setting her bare feet carefully on the ground. It felt solid. She got up slowly, steadying herself on the bed and extending her arm, pretending to search for support. The nurse offered her left arm. Frida grabbed it with her right hand. She eyed the nurse from the corner of her eyes. She had one shot. Only one. The nurse held the ID card in her right hand and tried to steer her toward the bathroom to the right of the bed. The exit door was on the left.

Frida summoned all her strength. With a quick move, she slammed the nurse against the wall. The woman gave out a surprised cry as her head slammed against the frame of the bathroom door. She slipped to the ground. Her eyes widened in shock. She reached for a dark red stream running down her blonde hair, creating a rapidly growing lake on her right shoulder. Frida leaped forward, grabbed the ID on the floor, turned around, and ran for the door. The nurse grabbed her right foot, pulling her back. Frida responded with a violent kick to her belly. The woman moaned. Frida jumped to the exit door, jerked it open, ran through, and smashed the door shut.

"Stop!" she heard the nurse shouting behind her. "Stop immediately!"

Frida ran through an office-style room into the hallway of the ward. The exit door was on her right, just a few meters away. She leaped toward it and swiped the ID at the exit reader. The door flung open. An old man in street clothes with a cane, presumably a visitor, looked at her in surprise and stepped aside. Frida had not been to the psychiatry ward before, but she knew the hospital by heart. She had worked there for years. She rushed down the hallway toward the elevator. There was a staircase for employees beside them. Frida swiped the ID again and ran down the stairs. Two young women in white coats came up the stairs, engaged in a lively conversation, gesticulating at each other. Frida rushed by. *First floor.* The hospital speakers turned on with a crackling noise. "Code Green! Code Green!" The hospital code for patient elopement. Frida pushed the fire exit door wide open. A cool breeze awaited her. She had made it! She was outside at the back of the hospital.

# - 27 -

# Terrel

The Pact
Sunday, October 9, 2033, 9:45 a.m.

Niles clapped along with the other children in the community room, entertained by the dancing clown. Imani and Terrell sat in the back, holding hands. Terrell had apologized to his wife. His detective instincts had taken over when he discovered the hole in the aviary. He hadn't stopped to think that chasing a bird could put their son in danger. Niles meant the world to him, and Imani knew that.

When they arrived safely on the ward, her anger had slowly dissipated. They were both on edge, going through a terrible time. They vowed to focus on their son now and nothing else. The FBI would have to wait until Niles' surgery was behind them and he was better. To show his commitment, Terrell had turned off his phone and locked it in Niles' room. He felt a twinge of vulnerability when an alarm sounded in the hallway. "Code green, Code green!"

Imani looked alarmed. "What does that mean?" she whispered.

"I don't know," Terrel whispered back. His wife had just recovered from the parrot incident. He dreaded the thought of exposing her to any kind of disturbance again. He glanced around the room. A nurse to his right observed the kids and didn't show any sign of distress. The clown continued the show and didn't seem to be bothered either. Terrel knew that code red was fire, code blue a medical emergency, code yellow a bomb threat and code amber child abduction. So, it was none of these.

"Code green. Does that refer to the garden?" Imani asked.

"Perhaps it has to do with the parrot," Terrel said. "But I really don't know. It could be something entirely different."

"Let me check with the physician. I will be right back." Imani got up from her seat.

"You," the clown pointed at her. "What is your name?"

Imani looked at him in surprise. "Do you mean me?" she responded loudly. "My name is Imani."

"This is my mummy." Niles clapped in excitement.

"Please come to the podium. I need some help opening this box." He pointed at a multicolored box in front of him.

"Go," Terrel whispered. "I will check with the oncologist."

Imani looked from Niles to Terrel. Then, she nodded and went to the front, saluted by a big applause from the audience.

With a determined stride, Terrel got up from his seat. He strode through the playroom and out the door, waving back at the children who waved at him with genuine smiles. Niles' gaze remained focused on his mother on the stage, and Terrel glanced back at them, reassured that they would be okay.

He turned right and walked down the brightly decorated hallway of the pediatric ward, his footsteps echoing against the cheerful paintings on the walls, accompanied by the distant sound of children's laughter. He stopped at Niles' room to retrieve his phone, then continued to the oncologist's office, just a few meters away.

He reached the door and paused, his hand hovering over the knob. With a steady breath, he knocked firmly, the sound reverberating through the empty hallway. There was no answer. He slowly turned the knob and pushed the door open.

Two men in white coats were standing in front of the desk, engaged in a lively conversation. They looked up at Terrel in perfect synchrony. Terrel wiped his eyes. Was there a mirror in the room? No, these were two men who looked exactly alike. Dr. Rogério Queirós Trento, the pediatric oncologist, had a doppelganger. An identical twin. The two men stared at him, eyes widened in shock. One of the men stepped toward Terrel.

"Oh, sorry, wrong door," Terrel said lightly. He closed the door and turned on his heels. If he had just uncovered a secret, then the men would have to silence him. He had to get away—and make sure to lead them away from his family.

Terrel's heart pounded in his chest as he sprinted down the hallway, his eyes fixed on the exit. He knew he had witnessed something he wasn't supposed to see, and the sound of the office door slamming open behind him confirmed his fears. He reached the end of the hallway and burst through the door to the right of the elevator, his only hope the staircase that led to the lobby.

Terrel flung open the door and sprinted down the stairs, two at a time. His heart pounded in his chest, fueled by determination. He could hear the sound of footsteps behind him, and he pushed himself harder.

As he reached the lower levels, cool air rushed against his skin. He burst through the heavy exit door into the extension of the entry hall, hit by intense sunlight that illuminated the entry hall through large arched windows. He shielded his eyes with his hand, momentarily blinded by the sun's glare.

The entry hall was buzzing with activity. Patients of different ages, visitors, and hospital staff were traversing the hall. Some people were resting in plush seating areas; others were standing around the reception area in the middle of the hall. Terrel looked for a place to hide. But the entry hall had an open design, leaving no corners to duck into or secluded areas to find refuge. At least his pursuer would not attack him here in public—if he wanted to stay anonymous and keep his secret. Terrel heard footsteps coming closer.

"Mr. Wright," a male voice behind him called him. "I need to talk with you."

Terrel looked over his shoulder. The oncologist—or his double—was right behind him. "I'm sorry. I'm busy," he said calmly and continued walking. He didn't want to engage with the man.

"It's about the well-being of your son," the man said with a low voice.

Terrel screeched to a halt, a pulse of adrenaline rushing through his veins. He swiveled around, his eyes ablaze. His hand shot out, seizing the man's shirt by the collar. "What about the well-being of my son?" he exclaimed, his voice tinged with fury. The air crackled with tension as he drew the man closer, his grip tightening like a vise.

"Is there a problem?" a man in sweatpants and crumbled shirt intervened. He looked from one man to the other.

"No worries," the oncologist said calmly. "The man is just anxious about an upcoming surgery of his son."

"I can call security?" sweatpants man offered.

Terrel released his grip slowly.

The oncologist straightened his white coat. "No, that won't be necessary," he said with a reassuring smile.

The man shrugged and walked away.

The oncologist waited until the man couldn't hear them anymore. "Listen," he continued with a soothing tone, "I mean no harm. I'm trying to help."

"And you do that by threatening me?" Terrel said in a low voice. *Threatening an FBI agent*, he thought. But the man in front of him didn't know that. Terrel had indicated "government employee" under his profession on the hospital intake form. Imani would surely not share his true profession with anyone. "Dr. Queirós Trento, right?"

The man nodded. "I want to talk with you because you accidentally saw my twin brother," he whispered, the words barely audible above the chaotic hustles around them.

Terrel's eyes narrowed. "I thought you wanted to talk about my son?" he snapped.

The man lowered his voice even further. "Both," he admitted. "Please don't tell anyone you saw my brother here. He may have been involved in getting insurance authorizations for our patients, including the imaging exams and surgery for your son."

Terrel looked at the oncologist with wide-open eyes. This encounter was more complex than he could have ever imagined. "I don't understand. How would your brother help with insurance claims?" he asked.

"I guess he got access to the claim review and approval system," the oncologist said with a wry smile.

The weight of responsibility settled heavily on Terrel's shoulders. This was the clue Angus had waited for. "Your brother hacked insurance claims?" he asked.

The oncologist shrugged. "Maybe? I might be wrong. But if there was so much as a suspicion that a hacker approved the pending claims, then they will all be revoked," he said in a de facto manner. "That would harm our patients—and your son."

"So, your brother is a cyber hacker?" Terrel asked again as he gripped the gravity of the situation.

The oncologist's eyes darted around nervously, scanning the surroundings.

"Please don't say that out loud again," he said calmly.

Terrel's law enforcement persona came through. "If your brother is a cyber hacker, you have to report him to the authorities!" he insisted. "Or I have to report him."

"Think of your son," the oncologist gently reminded him. "Wait for the surgery tomorrow. Then, you can file a report if you like. By that time, my brother will have gone underground."

Terrel stared at the man in front of him, his mind racing. He couldn't be sure if he was talking to the oncologist or his criminal twin brother. The two looked identical. He realized that the fates of the twin brothers and his son, Niles, were intertwined. Time was of the essence for both of them. He had to make a decision—report the man now and risk Niles' surgery being delayed or keep quiet and ensure that his son received the treatment he needed. What would Imani want him to do? Without a doubt, she would want him to do whatever it took to protect their son.

Their eyes locked in a pact of agreement. The path ahead was uncertain, but one thing was crystal clear. Terrel would be a guardian of this enigmatic truth.

# - 28 -

# FRIDA

The Man
Sunday, October 9, 2033, 10:15 a.m.

In a desperate rush, Frida ran down a small path of crunching gravel that snaked away from the hospital building. The fire exit door behind her slammed shut, cutting her off from the facility, but she couldn't afford to hesitate now.

The path beckoned her forward, leading her to a grove guarded by towering eucalyptus and pine trees. She knew she had to disappear within their embrace, away from prying eyes and the danger that lurked within the hospital walls. SUEC was one of the few hospitals in the country with a specialized psychiatric ward, and the gowns worn by patients there were bright green, making them easy for staff to spot. Frida had considered seeking help from a security guard, but she knew they would likely not believe her story and simply return her to the ward, where the injured nurse would seek revenge. Even the residents of the surrounding neighborhood had been warned to call security if they saw a patient in a bright green gown wandering around. It was too risky to simply run through the neighborhood. Frida needed to find a place to hide and change into some ordinary clothes before she could venture out.

Finally reaching the edge of the grove, Frida cautiously slipped beneath the canopy of branches, feeling a palpable sense of relief in the cool shade. Her breaths came in rapid bursts, and her chest heaved with both fear and determination. As the trees grew taller and closer, their dappled shadows danced on her skin, fleeting whispers of hope. The forest's earthy fragrance of eucalyptus mingled with the resinous scent of pine, filling her senses with solace. Her fingers grazed the rough bark of the pines, seeking comfort in the unforgiving world she had been thrust into.

Under the cover of the trees, she carefully walked along the right edge of the parking lot. Perhaps she could find some clothes in one of the cars in the parking lot. Her eyes darted from car to car, searching for any sign of a jacket or sweater. The morning sun bore down with unrelenting intensity, casting blinding reflections off the car windows and making it challenging to peer inside. Frida trudged on, the pine needles now pricking her feet. The cars stood unmoved, their opaque windows offering no clues to their hidden treasures.

A few people rushed to and from the parking lot, not noticing her behind the trees. On the far side of the parking lot, a stunning couple sat on a weathered bench, their vibrant presence in stark contrast to the somber surroundings. The way they looked at each other filled Frida's heart. That was how Kuruk had looked at her before all this nightmare at SUEC had begun.

Before the couple was an intricately designed birdcage with a resplendent multicolored parrot perched inside. It's feathers glimmered like a living rainbow, an exquisite creature that seemed to embody the beauty of the world. What was a parrot doing there? This was not a vet hospital. Frida couldn't help but feel a sense of incredulity. Was she still on drugs, or was this some kind of surreal dream?

The serene scene was interrupted by the deafening roar of a brand-new Lamborghini, which rolled into the parking lot. The car came to a graceful halt, and the scissor doors swung open, revealing a young man in a designer suit and sunglasses who seemed like he had stepped straight out of a fashion magazine. He exuded an aura of confidence, standing tall and handsome with an air of nonchalance that spoke of wealth. Frida crouched behind a cluster of bushes, peering anxiously at the trio through the foliage. These people belonged to a world that was light-years away from her reality of disappointment, fear, and uncertainty. And as long as they were there, she couldn't approach any of the cars.

Frida waited, her heart beating in sync with the slow passage of time. Every minute felt like an eternity. She longed to make a move, to seize the opportunity and explore the cars in front of her for the cover she desperately sought. But the risk of being noticed was too great while the trio lingered nearby.

Finally, the woman and the Lamborghini man left toward the hospital. The third man seemed to focus on the parrot in the cage. This was her chance. The parking lot felt vast and empty. Frida gathered her courage and grabbed a large stone beside her. She emerged from her hiding spot and made her way toward the worn-out metallic blue Toyota in front of her. She peeked inside. Nothing. She checked adjacent cars. Bingo. A jean jacket on the back seat of an old BMW. Frida's heart pounded in her chest as she mustered all her strength and shattered the backseat window. The sound of breaking glass reverberated through the parking lot, sending shivers down her spine. For a moment, she feared someone might have heard the noise, but she couldn't afford to stop now. Quickly, she reached through the broken window, retrieved the jacket, and slipped it on. As she gently caressed the denim jacket, savoring her small triumph, a salve of deafening gunshots erupted. Frida's heart leaped into her throat. *Did the security guards here shoot at car thieves?* She looked up, eyes wide with fear. But there was no security guard. Frida was startled to see a man in a white coat at the far end of the parking lot. It was her captor, standing like a malevolent specter behind the beautiful birdcage. Their eyes locked in a chilling moment of recognition.

# - 29 -

# Angus

The Parrot
Sunday, October 9, 2033, 10:00 a.m.

Angus sat on the bench in front of the hospital, watching Caramba, who eyed him from his cage. Eucalyptus leaves danced in the breeze around them, their silvery undersides gleaming in the sunlight. Angus was determined to personally ensure that the parrot was transferred safely to the FBI headquarters for a professional interrogation by an avian behaviorist. The expert would use positive reinforcement techniques such as treats, toys, or other rewards to encourage the parrot to speak.

While he was waiting for an FBI team to pick up the bird, Angus spoke to the parrot in a soothing voice, attempting to gain Caramba's trust. Perhaps he could get something out of the parrot now. Time was of the essence. Any information that the bird could provide about the kidnapped woman could save her life. Caramba, however, remained cautious, eyeing Angus warily from within his cage while swaying from one leg to the other.

"You're a clever bird, aren't you?" Angus said to him calmly, attempting to play to Caramba's intelligence. "You must have seen and heard a lot of things. Tell me about your previous owner, Rogério. What is Rogério up to?"

Caramba puffed up his feathers and tilted his head, seemingly considering Angus' words.

"Rogério," Angus repeated to remind Caramba of the specific person he was inquiring about.

Caramba's eyes blinked knowingly. But he kept his beak shut.

Angus looked around and found a pistachio on the pavement in front of him. Julius must have dropped it. He picked it up and held it between two fingers in front of the cage, close enough for the bird to see.

"If you tell me about Rogério, I'll give you this."

Caramba tiptoed closer to Angus, peering at the treat with a mix of temptation and caution. Suddenly, with a swift move, the parrot snatched the pistachio through the cage bars and gobbled it up. He fluttered back on a branch in the cage and let out a confident chirp, bobbing his head up and down.

"Now you got your treat. Tell me about Rogério," Angus insisted.

The bird's eyes held a steely determination, unwilling to give in. He let out a salve of high-pitched squawks that sounded eerily like a laugh.

That was annoying. Angus shifted tactics. He leaned in closer to the cage, his expression hardening. "You know, parrot, my friends won't go easy on you like I'm. They might make you uncomfortable. So, think carefully about your next move," he said with a threatening tone.

Suddenly, Angus heard a gunshot. He looked at Caramba. "I won't fall for that again," he declared with a stern and resolute tone. This time, he wouldn't allow himself to be fooled.

The parrot turned around and fluttered his wings, squawking fearfully. Angus looked perplexed at the colorful bird. He had not intended to scare him so badly. Parrots are sensitive creatures, and even small disruptions in their environment could affect their well-being. But Caramba had acted quite boldly when he snatched the treat from his hand. Now, he was intimidated by Angus' voice? That didn't make sense. Had something else caused his sudden mood change?

Angus carefully scanned the area around the cage, searching for any threats that might have triggered Caramba's anxiety. But there were no obvious signs of danger that could explain Caramba's unease. The area around them was quiet and peaceful. Only a handful of people were walking to and from the parking lot. Some of them glanced at Caramba with a brief smile, while others seemed preoccupied and in a hurry. Despite the calm surroundings, Caramba's distress escalated.

His eyes darted from side to side, wide with unease.

"Ronaldo, help! Ronaldo, help!" he screamed, fluttering around.

Suddenly, a salve of gunshots pierced through the air. Angus' head snapped toward the bird, his eyes widening in alarm. This wasn't a mere trick of mimicry. These were real, jarring gunshots. People around them screamed and ran in different directions, creating chaos. Angus remained calm, even though adrenaline coursed through his veins. He glanced around, trying to identify the source of the gunshot.

He looked at Caramba, who ducked down in the cage and screamed again. "Ronaldo, Ronaldo, help!"

Angus felt a puff of wind beside his right ear, followed by a popping sound. Something had hit the cage. Angus' heart skipped a beat as he saw a bullet lodged in the very branch on which the parrot had been perched just moments ago. *They* were under attack. Angus jumped up from the bench and pulled his gun. He grabbed the travel cage and shoved it behind the Lamborghini in front of them. He cowered behind the engine block in the rear and held the cage close, ready to defend the bird.

There was another round of gunshots. A bullet burst the back window with the deafening sound of shattering glass. The chaotic situation around them made it difficult to discern the source of the shots, and Angus couldn't be sure if they were directed at the bird or if the bird was imitating the sounds. Angus' mind raced, trying to process the situation. As he looked around, he caught sight of a man in a white coat running down the walkway toward the small grove at the end of the parking lot. The man had a short, plumpish build and curly brown hair. For a split second, Angus saw his profile as he turned toward the grove. He couldn't believe his eyes. It was the same man he had chased through the hospital garden earlier. Dr. Rogério Queirós Trento. Or was it someone who looked like him? Had he shot at the bird?

Two SUEC security guards arrived at the scene. Angus waved at them to get their attention and directed them toward the grove where the man had disappeared. He explained about the gunshots he had heard and the close call with the bullet in the branch of Caramba's cage. He also mentioned the man in the white coat running toward the grove. The guards pursued the suspect. Angus would have preferred to join the chase, but he knew that it was more important to protect his asset, the parrot. *This is the second assassination attempt*, Angus thought, realizing the gravity of the situation. The parrot must have some crucial information, and Angus was determined to uncover it.

Angus turned to the bird. He was pacing back and forth in his cage, shaking its feathers, bobbing its head, and emitting high-pitched squeaks.

"It's okay, Caramba," Angus said calmly. "I'm here to help. You're safe now."

The parrot watched him with a mix of curiosity and trepidation. Gradually, his squawks softened, and he hopped closer to the edge of the cage, cautiously observing Angus.

"Pistachio?" the bird asked with a tilted head.

The sound of an approaching car cut through the air. Angus felt relieved when he saw a van with an FBI sign pull up. A young man in blue overalls stepped out of the van and introduced himself as the wildlife expert on standby. He removed the band-aid that Julius had placed on the cage, opened the cage door, and offered the bird a hand. Caramba looked at him with a tilted head, breathing heavily. After a while, he decided to hop onto the hand, and the vet examined him carefully from beak to claw. He reassured Angus that Caramba had not experienced any harm and would be interrogated as soon as possible.

With a reassuring nod, the expert lifted the cage into the van and secured it for transport. Metal met metal, a symphony of locks and clasps ensuring that Caramba would have a secure ride. As the expert straightened, his eyes met Angus' once more, a final nod sealing their pact of purpose.

Angus turned on his heels. He had succeeded in delivering Caramba to safety. Perhaps he could help the security guards pursue the suspect now.

The air was still and silent for a moment. People had cleared the area after the gunshots, and the only remaining sound was the gentle rustling of leaves from close by eucalyptus trees.

But all of a sudden, a sharp human cry pierced the air, accompanied by a symphony of fluttering wings. The vet. Angus spun around, his eyes widening in surprise. A whirlwind of colors burst into the sky, and a bird of resplendent plumage cut through the air with an almost supernatural grace. Its wings sliced the air, each beat a whisper of freedom. Time seemed to slow, each heartbeat echoing with the weight of realization. Angus' breath caught in his throat, a bitter tang of recognition mingling with his exhale. They had forgotten to re-attach the band-aid. Caramba had escaped from its cage. As its silhouette dwindled against the canvas of the sky, Angus was left with a mix of emotions—awe, chagrin, and a newfound humility before the capricious nature of fate.

Regret heavy in his voice, the vet apologized. "I should have secured him better," he admitted, a hint of disappointment lacing his tone.

Angus couldn't suppress a wry smile. "No worries," he said, a flicker of lightheartedness cutting through the lingering tension. "He's a bit of a serial escaper, after all."

"Perhaps I can help track him down," the vet said. "I brought some treats." He produced a variety of nuts from his pocket.

"Your help is much appreciated. We captured him before, and we will capture him again," Angus said, his voice ringing with determination.

The driver of the van had witnessed the spectacle. He pulled into a parking slot and got out. With a practical gesture, he offered his assistance.

In the distance, Angus saw the two security guards returning from the grove. He waved at them, and they quickly changed their course and headed toward him. In a matter of moments, they stood face to face with Angus, their faces grim and their expressions etched with a mixture of disappointment and chagrin.

With a heavy sigh, the guard spoke, his voice laced with disappointment. "The man in the white coat managed to escape," he admitted.

*Again*, Angus thought. His gaze met the weary eyes of the security guards.

With a nod of understanding, he sought to rally their spirits. "We have faced setbacks today," he began, his voice steady and reassuring, "but setbacks are just part of the journey. Our determination remains unshaken. We won't give up. We won't back down. We will find the man and the bird."

A glimmer of gratitude danced in the guard's eyes, a silent acknowledgment of Angus' unwavering spirit. Angus knew that anyone could rally behind a winner. It was far more challenging and meaningful to lift those who had stumbled, to motivate them to transform their setbacks into success.

"Thank you," one of the guards said. "We needed to hear that."

"You're welcome," Angus said. "We'll regroup, strategize, and continue the pursuit."

He sent the vet and van driver to search for the bird and asked the security guards to look for the man in the white coat again. The uncertainty of whether the man who had attempted to shoot Caramba was indeed Rogério lingered in the back of his mind. Was he the same man who had kidnapped the woman? Angus was quite sure that it was the same man. He had seen him with his own eyes. It was very unsettling to know that he had a gun. With every passing minute, the chances of rescuing Dr. Frida Ending unharmed dwindled. Caramba had been attacked twice and was now flying around the hospital. How could the vulnerable be shielded from harm? The solution, it seemed, lay in the pursuit of the man himself. If Angus could just be sure about his identity. But was it truly Rogério they sought or a clever impostor?

Perhaps Terrel could help. He could tell him whether he had seen the oncologist on the ward in the past hour or so. Angus pulled out his phone and dialed Terrel's number.

# - 30 -

# FRIDA

The Chase
Sunday, October 9, 2033, 10:15 a.m.

As her captor's piercing gaze fell upon her, Frida spun on her heel and sprinted back toward the grove. The world around her blurred in a haze of adrenaline. Her every move was fueled by the primal instinct to survive. She glanced back over her shoulder, her heart pounding in her chest as she saw her captor's menacing figure silhouetted against the entrance of the grove. He was coming for her, and she knew she had to outrun him.

Frida raced through the trees. Branches scraped her arms, and pine needles pricked her legs, but she didn't dare to slow down. Fear pushed her forward, desperation giving her strength she didn't know she possessed. Behind her, she could hear heavy thuds from footsteps coming closer.

She dashed through the shadows of the trees, the rapid beat of her heart blending with the rustling leaves of the underbrush. She grasped for air but pressed on regardless, sweat beading on her forehead. Her instincts guided her, helping her evade fallen branches and gnarled roots.

Behind her, she could hear the relentless pursuit of her captor, but she wouldn't give in. The man had a gun. She was running for her life. Ahead, the trees thinned, and she could see the edge of the grove, hinting at an escape.

With a final burst of effort, she burst through the tree line and into the open, her heart pounding as she frantically scanned her surroundings for an avenue of escape. But before she could fully comprehend her surroundings, her elation turned to dread as she felt a sudden, strong grip on the jeans jacket she had fought so hard to obtain. Her heart skipped a beat as she was violently jerked back like a puppet ensnared by its master.

The man who had relentlessly pursued her through the grove looked at her with malevolence, his eyes gleaming with chilling determination. He pulled her back into the shadows of the grove, pointing a gun at her.

"Come," he said with a sinister smile. "We have work to do."

Frida felt a shiver running down her spine. Her escape had been in vain. Worse. On the psychiatry ward, she had been protected by the SUEC staff, who falsely believed she was a patient. They had locked her up but otherwise had her well-being in mind. Now, she was at the mercy of a man who hated her—a criminal at best and perhaps a killer.

The man pointed the gun at her and led her deeper into the grove with a firm grip. Under the cover of the trees, they walked to the other side of the parking lot. The man's fingers dug into Frida's arm, a painful reminder of her captivity and his control over her. Frida's heart pounded wildly, drowning out all other sounds around her. The scent of damp earth mingled with the tang of fear.

The man walked with purposeful strides, pulling her along to keep pace, leaving no room for hesitation or resistance. He seemed to navigate the woods with an uncanny familiarity as if he had planned this encounter meticulously.

"You made it easy for me," he answered her unspoken question. "I hadn't made up my mind yet about how to get you out of the hospital. But you just came here by yourself. That must be fate."

Frida didn't say anything. She felt like a pawn in a chilling game. She tried to calm her racing thoughts by acknowledging that if the man truly wanted to end her life, he could have done it already in the shadows of the woods. The fact that she was still alive, though captured, suggested that he had a plan for her, a plan that involved keeping her breathing.

As they approached the end of the grove, the man concealed the gun within the folds of his white coat, a sinister secret hidden from random eyes in the parking lot. He walked casually, adept at maintaining the facade of normalcy.

They exited the grove and walked to a tall, standalone pavilion. Frida's heart skipped a beat as she recognized the familiar contemporary sandstone building, an architectural marvel with arched glass windows that seamlessly blended with the hospital campus. It was the conference building, a place she had visited many times before for academic gatherings and scientific presentations.

The building, usually bustling with activity, now loomed before her, silent and deserted. There were no signs of any ongoing conference, and the absence of people heightened the feeling of isolation. On a Sunday, there was a close to zero chance that anybody would step foot in it—a perfect place to hide a kidnapped woman.

Frida's thoughts raced as she tried to figure out what the man wanted to do with her there. Was he planning to approve more insurance authorizations? Or was he going to kill her? She didn't know, but she knew she had to find a way to escape.

Suddenly, a van with the FBI sign turned around the corner of the nearby street and drove into the parking lot. Frida's heart pounded in her chest as she looked at the van. A glimmer of hope flickered within her, realizing that help might be at hand. However, she also knew that any hasty action could put her life in even greater jeopardy. Jumping in front of the van and crying for help might startle her captor, leading to unpredictable consequences. She had to be careful.

She took a deep breath and tried to calm her racing thoughts. She needed to come up with a plan. She glanced around, looking for an opportunity.

"Don't try anything stupid," the man said with a cold voice as if he had read her mind. "It will be my pleasure to send a bullet through your spine." Under the cover of his white coat, he held the cold metal at her upper back. "You won't die. That would be far too easy," he said calmly. "You will be paralyzed for the rest of your life."

Frida looked over her shoulder into his hateful eyes. "Please don't hurt me," she whispered.

"Do you want to tell that to my little girl?" he snorted. "Keep your mouth shut, or I'll lose my cool. This way."

The mention of his little girl struck a nerve within her, reminding her of the danger she was in. She followed him.

The man led her down a winding path that cut through the perfectly manicured lawn, leading them toward the pavilion. The grass was so green and lush that it looked like it had been freshly mowed. The man's footsteps were the only sound in the air, and Frida could hear her own heart beating in her chest.

He swung the large entrance door open and shoved Frida inside. They entered a spacious, light-infused lobby decorated with the university's logo. The atmosphere was charged with an eerie stillness. There was a reception desk at the center of the lobby, but it was unstaffed. Several comfortable seating areas were scattered throughout the hall, but they were all empty. On the walls to their right were posters and artwork. To their left were the large glass windows, which provided a beautiful view of a small park area and the grove they had just come from.

As Frida's eyes darted through the transparent panes, she could see a SUEC security officer stepping out of the grove, searching the surroundings. A surge of hope washed over her. But she quickly realized that he couldn't see them inside the building. The sunlight reflecting on the tall windows acted as an unwitting shield, concealing their presence from the officer's view. The man turned around and walked back into the grove.

The man beside Frida chuckled. "These guards are so stupid," he said. "Unfit for the real life." Each word dripped with derision, making Frida wonder what he knew that she didn't.

The man shoved Frida toward a small hallway to their right, away from the sign to the auditorium. Frida had been there before. There were several smaller meeting rooms and breakout spaces for small group sessions and workshops. The man opened one of the doors and pushed Frida inside. He closed the door.

They entered a windowless conference room furnished with a rectangular conference table made of rich teakwood. The table was encircled by sleek black leather chairs, each with gleaming aluminum armrests. At the forefront was a computer workstation with a presentation screen mounted on the wall behind it. The only source of light in the room came from a delicate string of neon lights adorning the ceiling, which cast a muted luminance throughout the space. The man pointed to one of the seats beside him. "Sit down," he said.

Frida looked at him with hesitation. She felt a deep sense of unease.

The man pointed the gun at her. "I won't invite you twice," he said coldly.

Frida sat down. The man produced zip ties from his pocket, setting Frida's nerves on fire. She jumped to her feet, her instincts urging her to escape.

With a deft motion, the man reached into his pocket with his free hand, produced a gleaming object, and pressed at the curve of her neck.

The Taser again. Frida's entire body shuddered and froze.

The man caught her and pushed her into the chair. He zipped Frida's wrists to the armrests of the chair. Then he zipped her feet together. Frida stared at him, frozen. She was trapped.

With a contented grunt, he sat down in front of the workstation and placed the gun and Taser casually on the table beside him. From his other pocket, he extracted a pocketknife, opened it, and placed it beside the gun and Taser. He looked back at Frida with a hateful, unyielding gaze.

"Discussions are over," he said coldly.

The wild rhythm of Frida's heart echoed her rising panic. This was a seasoned criminal. Would he harm her? A knot of fear ensnared her throat.

The man turned back to the computer and turned it on with a sharp click. The screen flickered to life, casting an eerie glow on his face and highlighting the sharp contours of his features. His fingers danced effortlessly across the keyboard, demonstrating a fluid and practiced command over the machine before him.

He turned to Frida, his eyes locking onto hers with unwavering intensity. "Let's get started," he said.

# - 31 -

# Terrel

Priorities
Sunday, October 9, 2033, 10:15 a.m.


After the unsettling encounter with the oncologist in the hospital lobby, Terrell nestled himself into a comfortable seat beside a potted palm tree. He needed a moment to process everything that had transpired. He leaned back, closing his eyes briefly while he tried to think. His mind was still reeling from the realization that his son's well-being was intertwined with the case. Amid the hustle and bustle of the passersby, a self-playing piano infused the surroundings with a calming melody. Chopin. Replaying the oncologist's words in his head, Terrel felt somewhat detached from the commotion around him, enveloped in his own world of concerns.

Dr. Rogério Queirós Trento had an identical twin brother who was a cyber hacker. He had approved all insurance claims of children with cancer at SUEC Hospital, including the authorizations for Niles' imaging scans and surgery. This had to be connected to the abduction of the insurance claim agent. The hacker probably needed her to get through the insurance's dual authentication login system, rendering her a critical pawn in his enigmatic scheme.

Terrel couldn't help but contemplate the grim fate that might await the woman once she had fulfilled her role. The criminals would consider her a liability. Would they eliminate her to erase any trace of their operation? Terrel had uncovered critical information for the case, and he knew that time was of the essence to save the woman's life. But he couldn't risk that Niles surgery authorization would be withdrawn. The hacker had authorized his son's surgery. That was why this process had been so fast and easy on a weekend. Niles' life was on the line as well. The doctors had explained clearly that the tumor was very large and on the verge of rupture. Imani was on the brink of a mental and emotional collapse, her composure hanging by a fragile thread.

Terrel's heart ached as he remembered the toll that Niles' tumor diagnosis had taken on his wife. He longed to be a source of strength for her, to alleviate her distress and anxiety. And he remembered the image of his son's gaze, beaming at him with unwavering trust. His squeezing hand reverberated with a whispered promise: *You and me.*

With a determined sigh, Terrel got up from his seat. There was no other way. He was a father first and an FBI agent second. This insurance case had to wait until tomorrow after the surgery.

He strode purposefully through the lobby, making his way to the elevators. He pressed the button and waited, his mind racing. He was worried about his son, and he was also worried about himself and his family.

The elevator doors slid open, and Terrell stepped inside. He selected the floor of the oncology ward, and the elevator began to ascend. As the elevator rose, Terrell's tension mounted. He grappled with a new layer of concern. Angus and Annya were the best federal agents in the country. They would track these criminals down with or without his help. If the oncologist or his brother would become aware of the tightening net closing around them, would they blame *him* and come after his family?

Terrel realized that the escalating danger was poised to erupt into a high-stakes showdown. He had to guard his family closely. With renewed vigilance, he vowed to shield them from threats that might emerge from within or without.

The elevator doors opened with a vibrant chime like a curtain rising on a stage. Terrel walked down the corridor of the ward toward Niles' room, accompanied by muffled sounds of hushed conversations and the intermittent hum of medical machinery. The hallway stretched ahead, a lifeline connecting a myriad of stories and struggles. He passed by Maya's door, Niles new friend who would soon receive MIBG therapy. After that came Grant Smith's room, Jabari Smith's son. Both doors were closed. Terrel scanned his surroundings with a mix of determination and concern. Dr. Queirós Trento's office door was closed, and he didn't spot the oncologist anywhere. Or his imposter.

"Hoopla," a woman's voice chimed, pulling Terrel from his thoughts. Startled, he jolted slightly, his quick reflexes preventing a collision as he had almost run into her. Terrel remembered her hoarse voice and those sad eyes framed by distinct dark rings. It was the woman from the kitchen earlier this morning, the woman from Kansas City. She had a son with a brain tumor.

"Sorry," he murmured. "I wasn't paying attention." He felt embarrassed. Niles' struggles were hard to bear. But there were others who might be grappling with even greater challenges.

The woman offered a small smile, conveying understanding rather than irritation. "No worries," she replied with a reassuring note.

"How are you doing?" Terrel asked with genuine concern.

She glanced at him briefly. "Well, what should I say? My son has brain cancer. I feel awful. But some days are better than others," she responded. "Today, Willis' insurance claims were all approved. A small victory on a journey through hell."

Terrel observed her carefully as she tugged a strand of rebellious hair behind her ear. He felt a profound connection with her struggles.

"How did that happen?" he asked. After the encounter with the oncologist, he had a pretty good idea about what was going on. But he wanted to hear it from her perspective.

"Well, Willi needs brain surgery. But his tumor is too large to safely be removed. Biopsy showed that his tumor has receptors for a targeted drug that can shrink the tumor. If the tumor responds, the surgery can be done. Experts from SUEC and consultants at two additional nationally recognized children's hospitals agreed. But Pleonexia denied the treatment."

Terrel shook his head. "That's unbelievable. Who denies a child with a brain tumor the necessary treatment?" He couldn't fathom the bureaucracy, the heartlessness, that had led to this point.

The woman's gaze bore into Terrel's, her eyes carrying a mixture of anger and frustration. "Yeah, Aziel, the nurse, filed for expedited appeal. But Pleonexia responded that the request was not urgent and sent our case to a regular fourteen-day appeal. Can you imagine how that felt? Knowing the tumor in your son's head is growing every day? Seeing his ability to walk and speak getting worse every day? But the insurance company saw no reason to expedite. What on earth is a reason, then?"

"I'm so sorry." Terrel wished he could erase her pain, but all he could do was listen to her anguish, a fellow traveler on a journey marked by challenges they hadn't asked for.

"Aziel didn't give up and continued to call them," the woman said with a note of admiration. "That man is tough, I can tell you that. Pleonexia finally agreed to expedite and sent our appeal to a third-party company for evaluation. They recommended denial, stating that the drug is not standard of care. Pleonexia took the recommendation and denied the appeal."

"But you didn't give up?" Terrel asked.

A soft sigh escaped the woman's lips. "Dr. Queirós Trento stepped in. He scheduled a 'peer-to-peer' review and found the same person on the call who had denied the prior authorization the last two times. The Pleonexia representative denied the appeal again. We were crushed." Her tone changed. "But this morning, the request was miraculously approved."

"How did that happen?" Terrel asked.

The woman shrugged. "Dr. Queirós Trento blinked at me during the rounds. I know he did something, but he wouldn't tell me what it was. That's okay. I don't need to know. I'm forever grateful, and if I could, I would nominate him for the Presidential Citizens Medal. That man is amazing!" There was a sense of respect in her tone, a recognition of the silent efforts that had led to this point.

"I'm glad it worked out for you," Terrel said politely. "My best wishes to your son!" He chose his words carefully, realizing that he was entangled in a web of illicit activities. The miraculous insurance approval was probably the work of the hacker brother. But he couldn't say anything to the woman. She was so happy, and he didn't want to ruin her moment.

"Thank you!" the woman said. "I heard from your wife that your son's surgery was approved as well. Someone is watching out for us.

We should be very grateful. Good luck tomorrow."

"Thank you!" Terrel watched as she walked away, her words echoing in his mind. The insurance agent had denied the claims and was kidnapped. The kidnapper had authorized the claims. Who was the victim, and who was the villain in this situation? Perhaps the kidnapper had been driven by desperation, seeking a resolution that the conventional system had denied them.

The familiar ringtone of his cell phone broke through his contemplation. He retrieved the device from his pocket. It was Angus.

"Hi, Terrel. Are you in the oncology ward?"

"Yes, I am. What's up?"

"Did you see Dr. Queirós Trento on the ward in the last thirty minutes or so? I just saw a man in front of the hospital who looked just like him. But I confused the oncologist with another man earlier today in the hospital. I'm wondering if the man I saw here could have been the oncologist or if somebody else looks just like him."

"I spoke with the oncologist about fifteen minutes ago in the hospital," Terrel responded. That was a truth, albeit not the entire truth.

"That is perplexing indeed," Angus responded. "I have a feeling that I'm missing an important part of this puzzle. Does the name Ronaldo ring a bell? The parrot mentioned it."

"There is nobody with this name here on the ward, to my knowledge," Terrel responded. Even though the name hadn't immediately sparked recognition, Terrel had a suspicion. But then, Angus hadn't explicitly asked for his theories.

"Okay, please keep your eyes open and let me know if you see anything."

"Of course."

Terrel was glad the conversation was over. He couldn't shake off his unease from withholding information from Angus, his colleague and friend. He pondered the complexities of human communication and the moral dilemmas that could arise from it. Would Angus find out that he had withheld information, and would that impact their relationship? Every choice had consequences. But Terrel remembered his vow. He was a dad first.

# - 32 -

# Annya

The Twin
Sunday, October 9, 2033, 10:30 a.m.

Annya was annoyed. Rogério had indeed filed an incident report, describing that he had found her walking aimlessly through the hospital outside of her usual work area, confused and disoriented. Julius had started his shift early, covering for her, and she had met with a shrink to get clearance for work. To make things more insulting, she had to provide blood and urine samples to prove that she had no drugs in her system.

While she was waiting for the results, Annya went down to the basement to the hospital's security hub. The dimly lit room and rhythmic hum of electronic equipment brought her some solace. She sat down at her desk and stared at the screen on the wall in front of her. It streamed various displays of real-time videos, maps, and charts.

She brooded about Rogério. Something was off about that guy, and it was not because he had written her up. She couldn't quite put her finger on what it was. Rogério had been shocked when he saw her outside of the patient room in the psychiatry ward. Why was that? A sick neighbor with a mental health problem was not a reason to freak out when you met a hospital colleague. Rogério could have shared that with her. Annya sensed that there was something sensitive about that patient. What was it? Was it about her illness? Or Rogério's involvement with her? Perhaps they were romantically involved? But why should that be an issue?

Julius had mentioned that Rogério was Caramba's first owner. But when she had mentioned the parrot to Rogério, he had acted as if he didn't know the bird. Why would he deny this piece of information? It didn't make sense. Annya was sure she was missing something. A crucial piece of information that would bring the pieces of the puzzle together.

Annya looked at the screen in front of her. An intricate network of surveillance cameras documented every nook and cranny of the hospital. Yet, the overwhelming magnitude of the footage was also a challenge. Annya was not sure what she was searching for. Without a clear target, looking for a clue in the videos was like searching for a needle in a haystack.

She opened the computer in front of her. Perhaps she would start with a background check on Dr. Rogério Queirós Trento. Her fingers produced tapping sounds as she explored different online databases. On the luminous screen, a trove of information unfurled before her. The records of the man's academic journey, from medical school to residency training, were meticulously documented. In addition, the SUEC University homepage showcased Rogério's faculty profile, accompanied by a short list of his published works.

It was more interesting what was not there. The realm of social media remained conspicuously absent from Rogério's digital trail. There was no social media account, not a single private photo, no comments, no likes, nothing at all. Annya's suspicion began to grow. The information before her bore an uncanny resemblance to a meticulously crafted persona. The CIA had similar tactics to construct controlled online identities. Rogério's online presence, replete with fundamental professional details yet devoid of any personal nuances, resembled a canvas deliberately kept blank of private information. What was he hiding?

Annya tried to remember the conversation with Rogério in the hospital cafeteria. He had mentioned a girl at his medical school at Stanford, his first true love. What was her name again? Annya leaned back in her seat and tried to remember. The conversation with Rogério was blurry in her mind, like a faded photograph. But the mental haze parted slowly, revealing fleeting glimpses of the information she sought. A smile brushed her lips as she finally retrieved the name from the depths of her memory. Destiny. Her name was Destiny.

With a purposeful exhale, Annya began typing: *Rogério Queirós Trento and Destiny and Stanford Medicine*. She was not really sure what she was looking for. She found the last name of the girl. Destiny Sola. And Bingo. There were old Facebook and Instagram accounts of the girl. They had been deleted due to inactivity, but Meta always kept copies, even for deleted accounts. Usually, a warrant was needed for the police to access such accounts. But Annya had a high-level clearance for emergencies. The life of a kidnapped woman was at stake.

Without a second thought, Annya logged in. She saw that the girl had been pretty active. The photos were a colorful montage of memories, from family vacations to college parties. But it was one particular photo that caught Annya's eye. In the center of the photo was Destiny, beaming in a red dress. Her curly black hair framed her face like a halo. Flanking her were two young men, their faces almost identical. They had stocky builds, untamed chestnut brown hair, and mustaches that seemed out of place on such young faces. The resemblance was uncanny, their features mirroring each other in a striking display of genetic unity. They emanated steadfast unity as if they were two halves of a harmonious whole. Anya's gaze moved from one to the other, her mind beginning to connect the dots. These were two young versions of Rogério. Angus had been right all along. The oncologist had a doppelganger.

Anya pulled her cell phone from her pocket, took a snapshot of the photo, and sent it to Angus with the message. *Rogério has an identical twin.*

His response came right back. *I knew it!*

She typed, *I'm sorry I doubted you,* and pressed the send button, watching as her words disappeared into the digital ether.

A moment later, her phone buzzed with a reply. *No worries,* the message said. *You found the center piece to the puzzle. You're amazing!*

Annya smiled. She was still a little embarrassed about how she had doubted Angus' abilities, but she had learned that he was forgiving and that she could always count on him. She sensed a shift from doubt to empowerment, a trusting partnership.

A SUEC security guard rushed into the room, his face flushed and his forehead glistening with sweat.

"There was a shooting incident in the parking lot," the guard exclaimed. "It is under control now. Nobody was injured. Apparently, a deranged individual tried to shoot a parrot. Our team is trying to find him. But it seems that he got away."

"The man or the parrot?" Annya asked.

"Both."

*Unbelievable.* Annya jumped to her feet, dialing Angus' number.

"Hello?" he answered the phone in his usual calm demeanor.

"Angus, are you okay?" she asked nervously. "I just learned that someone tried to shoot your parrot?"

"I'm fine," Angus said, his voice calm. "I protected him, but he and the shooter both got away. I'll tell you the whole story later."

"Are you sure you're okay?" Annya asked again.

"Of course," Angus said. "Thanks for the photo. It helped me a lot. I've asked my team to send me anything they find on the brother."

"Will you arrest Rogério?"

"On what grounds? If I say that I saw him driving the van, he might say it was his brother. We need to collect more evidence."

"Of course."

"But I got some interesting news as well. Rogério's neighbor, who was believed to have been hospitalized in the psychiatric ward, does indeed possess a documented history of profound depression. Yet, as of now, she is doing well and enjoying a vacation in Hawaii. It was not her in the ward. We checked, and whoever was hospitalized there ran away this morning."

"I'm in the security room," Annya said. "The patient rooms don't have any cameras. But if this patient ran away, I could check the surveillance cameras in the hallway and send you a photo of the patient. When did this happen?"

"Earlier this morning, around 9:30 a.m."

Annya went to the control station, selected the video from the hallway in front of the psychiatry ward, and checked the footage around 9:30 a.m. There she was, a woman in a hospital gown with a shaved head, running down the hallway. Annya selected a frame where the woman looked straight into the camera. She took another snapshot with her iPhone and sent it to Angus.

There was a moment of silence. "That is Frida Ending," he said, his tone a mix of surprise and concern. "Where did she go?"

"Wow," was all Annya could say, encapsulating her astonishment at the revelation. She diligently sifted through the other surveillance cameras. "She took the staff exit to the backstairs and exited through the fire exit door at the backside of the hospital. Angus, this was around the time you were guarding the parrot. If you had turned around, you might have seen her."

"Unbelievable," Angus replied. He took a moment to absorb the information before asking. "Where did she go from there?"

"She disappeared into a small grove beside the parking lot."

"That's where I saw Rogério running—or his brother. He had a gun. We have to find them before it's too late. A SUEC team already checked out the grove but didn't find anyone. I will send a professional team to search the entire premises. They will work undercover so they don't spook the criminals into harming the woman or running away."

"Should I interview the staff on the ward?" Annya asked.

"No, this is not a case for the company," he said with a resolute voice. "We don't know who else is involved. I don't want you to get discredited, harmed, or find yourself in the crossfire. Go back to your ER. We might need you there."

"Let's hope that won't be necessary."

A pause filled the air, the weight of the situation hanging between them. Then, Angus spoke again, his words laced with regret. "Annya, I deeply apologize, but given the unfolding events, I don't believe we'll be able to share our lunch today."

*Of course not.* "Sure, I understand," Annya replied in a composed tone, suppressing her disappointment.

"I do want to take you out as soon as this is over," he added. "I care a lot about you. You know that."

"No problem. We can meet up later," she said with forced

lightness. But in her heart, she knew that there would always be another case. It was probably better to keep this relationship professional.

# - 33 -

# FRIDA

The Transaction
Sunday, October 9, 2033, 10:45 a.m.

The computer screen emitted a soft, muted glow that bathed the conference room in a delicate light. The zip ties around Frida's wrists and ankles bit into her flesh, causing a throbbing pain that seemed to pulse with her racing heartbeat. Her hands and feet were swollen. Were they getting enough blood circulation? Each time she tried to move or shift on her chair, a sharp pang shot up her extremities, making it difficult to concentrate on anything else.

The room seemed to hold its breath as the intimidating figure before her tapped on the keyboard. Frida strained her eyes to decipher the contents of the screen. The man opened a digital window that showed the video feed from the surroundings near the conference center's entrance. The scene came to life, offering a real-time glimpse into a serene world outside the building. The man seamlessly positioned the live video feed in the upper right corner of the screen. Then, he swept open another digital window with a SUEC logo, nestling it in the upper left corner. Frida's curiosity stirred, her brow furrowing as she tried to decipher its purpose. The contents resembled a bank account or something akin to it.

With a swift motion, the man opened a third digital window and enlarged it so that it occupied the majority of the screen. Frida recognized the Pleonexia sign and the homepage of the insurance intranet website. Her heart pounded louder in her chest. The man organized the digital elements with an innate mastery, like a skilled conductor orchestrating a symphony. What was he planning now? He already had access to her claim reviews. As Frida grappled with the puzzle before her, her gaze went to the three weapons on the table—the Taser, the knife, and the gun. A visual testament to the precariousness of her situation.

The man's gaze snapped to Frida, his eyes latching onto hers with a fierce and unyielding intensity. With a pulse of excitement, he said, "Time to dive in, Frida! Let's get this started!"

He grabbed her chair and pulled her closer to the computer screen. The pain from the unforgiving plastic around her wrists and ankles amplified, spreading its tendrils like a vise that tightened its grip. Frida moaned.

"Frida, I'm so grateful that you decided to make a donation!" he said with a cheerful voice.

She looked at him with a mixture of confusion and incomprehension.

He pulled out his cell phone and held it in front of her face. Revelation struck her like lightning. He wanted to gain access to her intranet account through iris identification.

Frida clenched her eyes shut, determined to deny that plan. She felt a familiar cold object at the curve of her neck. The Taser. She wanted to scream, but it was too late.

Frida felt excruciating pain shoot through her body. Then, she started to shake uncontrollably. The skin around the zip ties broke open, oozing blood. Her eyes widened in pain.

Devoid of any visible emotion, the man held the phone in front of her face. The computer window opened with a soft blink. His attention shifted back to the computer, his fingers resuming their purposeful dance across the keyboard.

Frida saw that he had opened the window of the financial department at Pleonexia. Today, Pleonexia would pay out annual bonuses to all employees. This relatively early timing in the fiscal year was chosen to alleviate the administrative burden for account closeouts in December and motivate employees to finish the fiscal year strong. The man entered the intranet site where all bonuses were laid out. He turned around.

"The next time you shut your eyes, I will stab one with my knife," he said coldly.

Frida started to tremble. She didn't dare to close her eyes again. Sweat ran down her temples as the man lifted his cell phone again and held it in front of her. The account on the screen unlocked. He focused on the screen again, typing. A number appeared in the computer window on the left, under the SUEC logo. Then another, and another, creating a mesmerizing procession of data, followed in quick succession, creating a trail of at least fifty numbers.

With a contented grunt, the man pivoted his attention back to Frida. "You're Elena Nurak's right hand, aren't you?" he summarized, his words more a statement than a question.

Frida stared at him. He reached for the Taser. She nodded slowly.

"I need to know her password for her intranet page," he said coldly. "I know you filled in for her earlier this year when she was on medical leave."

Frida looked at the video footage behind him. There was a man and a woman with a SUEC cap walking up and down between the grove and the conference center, each holding a German shepherd on a leash. The dogs had silver SUEC bandanas around their neck. Frida knew the canine therapy team at SUEC by heart. They had visited the pediatric wards often. No German shepherds were included due to their strong protective instincts, which could pose a biting risk. Her heart leaped. Were these people just some SUEC fans, or were they security guards looking for her? The dogs had their noses on the ground, clearly following something.

The man followed her gaze and looked at the screen. Near the conference center, one of the dogs reached a bush, sat beside it, and gazed at the woman. She crouched down, explored the bush, and emerged with something yellow in her fist. Frida's heart sank as she recognized that the woman clutched long strands of blonde hair in her hand. The other dog had led his human to the stairs in front of the conference center. The man emerged, clutching his own discovery of long, blonde strands of hair. The two conversed for a while, then disappeared in the direction of the hospital.

The man beside Frida laughed. "See," he said. "Your hair was cut for a good reason."

Frida looked at him, defeated, tears dwelling in her eyes.

"Where were we?" the man said with a playful tone. "Elena Nurak's password, please." He reached for the gun.

Frida swallowed. She was too afraid to defy him again. She told him what he wanted to know.

With the deliberate shift of his gaze, the man's attention returned to the computer screen. His fingers danced across the keyboard as he entered new commands with purposeful strokes. A new set of numbers appeared on the left upper hand screen. Frida spotted the number. Twenty million dollars. Frida's eyes widened as she realized what he was up to. He was redirecting Elena Nurak's annual bonus payment to a different account. The transaction was scheduled to be initiated at noon, just one hour away.

The man's profile was calm and determined. He hummed a soft melody as he worked, his movements in perfect harmony with the hum of the computer. Frida understood that he was a skilled hacker. What would he do with her when he was done with his transaction?

# - 34 -

# Annya

The Connection
Sunday, October 9, 2033, 11:00 a.m.

Annya went back to the emergency room and was greeted enthusiastically by the charge nurse.

"Annya, it's great to have you back!" she exclaimed with a tone that mingled urgency and expectation. "Julius needs you in suite 2."

*Of course, he did.* Annya suppressed a sigh while reminding herself to be grateful that her junior colleague had come to her rescue. She walked down the freshly bleached hallway and entered a compact, rectangular patient room with pristine white walls. At the heart of the room, a stretcher cradled a teenager. He looked vulnerable and distressed, his eyes wide with fear. Beside him sat a middle-aged woman with blonde-dyed hair. Her worried expression spoke volumes about her relationship to the teenager—she was clearly his mother.

Julius was sitting at a small desk beside them, entering something on a computer. He looked up when Annya entered the room. Relief illuminated his expression like a beacon in the storm. The tension that had etched his features seemed to ease in her presence. Turning to the distressed mother by his side, Julius' voice carried a note of assurance.

"This is the expert I was talking about," he said, his words a testament to the trust he placed in Annya's capabilities—and his lack of confidence in his own.

Annya greeted the family and strode to the computer station. With practiced ease, she accessed the system and began to review the comprehensive array of lab tests and imaging studies that Julius had conducted. Her dedication to detail guided her as she meticulously scanned the information before her.

She turned to the family and explained the diagnosis. The patient almost certainly had an osteosarcoma, a malignant bone tumor. The diagnosis had to be confirmed by a biopsy. Additional tests would be needed to check for metastases elsewhere in the body. The results would be used to create a treatment plan.

It was a lot to take in. The mother immediately grasped the gravity of the situation. A malignant bone tumor. Annya's gaze shifted between her and the teenager, realizing the emotional weight her words carried. But her role as a healthcare provider meant delivering the truth, no matter how challenging. Both of them welled up with tears—a reflection of the shock and despair that had washed over their lives. The next steps were clear: consulting a pediatric oncologist, discussing treatment options, and navigating the path forward.

Throughout the weighty conversation, Julius had remained silent. However, as the prospect of consulting with the pediatric oncologist emerged, a spark of determination ignited within him.

"I can bring the family to the oncology ward," he offered, his voice carrying a sense of purpose.

Annya's gaze shifted to him, her curiosity piqued. She understood that his intention was probably well-meaning, but his enthusiasm for taking on a staff-like role raised questions. Why was he so eager to go to the oncology ward? Was it simply a way for him to feel like he was helping, or was there something more sinister at play? While her instincts stirred with suspicion, her training urged her to tread carefully. She didn't want to make any assumptions without evidence, but she couldn't help but wonder if Julius was somehow involved in the kidnapping scheme.

Annya's thoughts were interrupted by the mother's response. "Thank you, Dr. Zhang. That would be much appreciated," she said, her voice filled with gratitude and appreciation.

Annya nodded in agreement. As she glanced at the patient's file, a detail caught her attention. Julius had already taken the initiative to inform the oncology team and obtain clearance for the patient's admission in the ward. Was that unusually proactive for Julius? Regardless of the reasons behind it, his initiative had streamlined the process and eased the transition for the family.

With a final gesture of connection and reassurance, Annya extended her hand to both the patient and his mother. As they departed the patient room, Annya's gaze lingered on Julius, who accompanied them. Something about him didn't sit right with her. She couldn't put her finger on it, but she had a strong gut feeling that he was hiding something.

Annya pulled out her cell phone and dialed Terrel's number. It went straight to voicemail. She sent a text message. *Julius coming to oncology. Pls check for anything unusual.*

A moment later, her phone chimed with a reply. *Sure.*

Why did Terrel not pick up? Of course, there could be a million reasons. He was with a sick child. Annya reasoned that she could always review security camera footage later if necessary.

# - 35 -

# Terrel

### The Loss
### Sunday, October 9, 2033, 11:00 a.m.

Terrel retraced his steps to the children's playroom in the oncology ward. When he left during the clown show, the room had been a canvas of colorful chaos and laughter. Now, it had returned to a tranquil stillness. The clown was gone. The show was over. A glance around the room revealed that Imani and Niles were not there anymore either. The words of the oncologist echoed in Terrel's mind like a haunting refrain, creating a knot of worry in his chest. In a burst of anxiety, Terrel rushed to the patient room.

He swung open the door with a loud bang, startling Imani and Niles. Niles' eyes twinkled with residual mirth, as if to say, "You missed quite the spectacle!" Imani, her cheeks flushed, greeted Terrel with a knowing nod. She explained that Niles' new friend Maya had felt a bit yucky after the show and went to her room for a nap. Imani had decided to take a break as well.

Terrel looked at his wife. She was tired, but her complexion was still radiant. Her paler hue was a testament to the emotional and physical energy she had expended, but there was a grace about her, a quiet strength that spoke of her ability to weather storms with unwavering resolve. Terrel marveled at her resilience.

Niles, on the other hand, had his usual energy. He played with his robot on the floor, a bundle of perpetual motion, pretending to be in an imaginary universe, weaving stories only he could fathom. Terrel watched his son with a mixture of amazement and fondness, his heart warmed by the boy's unyielding zest for life.

Nile's eyes sparkled when he looked up at his dad. "Hello, Dad. Where have you been?" he asked.

Terrel couldn't help but smile at his son's genuine enthusiasm. He crouched down to Niles' level, their eyes meeting in a shared moment of connection. "I was just checking around, making sure everything's okay," he replied, his tone gentle and reassuring.

Niles continued to gaze at him with wonder and delight.

With a chuckle, Terrel extended his arms, inviting his son into an embrace. As they wrapped their arms around each other, the room seemed to brighten with an intangible warmth, a reflection of the unwavering bond that held them together.

"Did you find out what code green means?" Imani asked.

Terrel nodded. "Yes, it meant patient elopement. Apparently, a patient ran away from a closed psychiatric ward."

Imani's eyes widened in surprise, her hand instinctively moving to cover her mouth. "Oh my goodness," she exclaimed. "Is he dangerous? I hope we are safe here."

Terrel reached out and gently clasped her hand with a reassuring squeeze. "No worries," he said softly. "The hospital staff is trained to handle situations like this. They're focused on keeping us safe."

Imani nodded slowly. "Of course they are." Her eyes held a subdued glimmer that spoke of fatigue. She had been giving endlessly—to her son, to the challenges of the hospital environment, and to the emotional rollercoaster they were all riding.

Terrel embraced her tenderly. "I can take Niles for a walk," he offered. "Then, you can take a nap."

Imani looked at him, her gaze a reflection of her internal deliberation. The offer was a lifeline, a chance to catch her breath and recharge. After a moment of contemplation, she nodded slowly, a hesitant smile forming on her lips.

"Just be careful," she said, her voice tinged with a mixture of concern and humor. "Please avoid eloped patients, FBI agents, and shooting parrots."

Terrel chuckled. "I promise to steer clear of all those potential hazards," he replied with a wink. Their journey was marked by challenges, but it was also illuminated by the small moments of connection that they shared. Imani reached for a blanket and settled onto the sleeping couch at the back of the room.

Terrel reached for Niles' small hand. "Hey, buddy," he said, his tone gentle and inviting, "would you like to explore the area around the hospital?"

Niles' eyes lit up like twin stars, his energy reignited by the prospect of a new adventure. He tugged his robot under his arm and nodded vigorously, his excitement bubbling over.

"Yes, Dad! Let's go explore!" he exclaimed.

Terrel's heart swelled with pride and joy. Hand in hand, they left the room and embarked on their adventure, their steps echoing with the promise of exploration.

Willis's mother, the boy with the brain tumor, was still standing in the hallway, this time engaged in a conversation with Jabari Smith. As sunlight filtered through the nearby windows, it bathed them in a soft, golden glow. Like angels. Or archangels.

"Hello, Niles and Terrel," Jabari greeted them. "What are you up to?"

"Hello, Jabari," Niles' bubbled with enthusiasm, his eyes bright with anticipation. "We're going for a walk. Are you and Grant up for joining us?"

"Ah, man, I wish we could, but we're knee-deep in crafting a breaking newspaper article," Jabari responded, more to Terrel than to Niles. "Big news—the oncology program's scoring a major donation!"

"That sounds very exciting," Terrel responded. "What is the donation for?"

"Oh, you'll get all the juicy details tomorrow morning," the woman chimed in. "We cannot share more before it is published. But it's good news. Very good. It's all about our children."

Terrel's gaze shifted between them. Could this be somehow tied to the case? Was he meant to relay this information to Angus? But a newspaper article couldn't hold much harm. With a nonchalant shrug, he decided, "Well, I guess we'll catch you later."

He squeezed Niles' hand, and his son offered a casual wave. Then, they continued their stroll down the hallway.

Terrel decided to stay clear of the hospital garden. He didn't want any more distraction or drama. He led Niles down the stairs toward the back exit of the hospital. He had noticed a grove with tall trees there and a small park between the parking lot and the conference center. That's where they would go.

They exited the hospital and strolled along the parking lot. Niles spotted a sleek and luxurious sports car parked close to the sidewalk. Its glamour was marred by a shattered back window, a stark contrast to the car's polished exterior. Terrell's instincts as a detective kicked in. He scanned the area for any signs of trouble, but it seemed deserted. Still, he couldn't help but feel uneasy. He tugged his son's hand tighter, guiding him with a determined swiftness. The grove, a tranquil escape from the bustling backdrop of the hospital, beckoned like a sanctuary.

As they stepped into the grove, cool air embraced them, carrying the sound of rustling leaves and the distant songs of birds. Niles' eyes widened as he took in the new surroundings. The towering trees around them formed a cathedral-like canopy overhead, their interlocking branches weaving a tapestry of sunlight and shadow that danced upon the ground. They stepped onto a verdant path blanketed with fallen leaves and moss-covered logs. Small creatures darted in and out of the underbrush. With an exuberant burst of energy, Niles broke free from his father's grasp and bounded forward, his steps alive with the thrill of exploration. His keen eyes spotted a salamander cloaked in shades of earth and moss. With a soft click, he took a photo with the camera in his robot.

"Hey, Dad," Niles said, his voice carrying a mixture of enthusiasm and wonder. "Look what I just took a picture of." His thumb swiped across the screen of the robot, bringing up the image of the salamander against the backdrop of the vibrant underbrush.

Terrel took in the intricate details of the creature Niles had captured. "Wow, Niles, that's incredible," he exclaimed, his voice carrying genuine admiration. "You got a great photo there."

They continued along the path, and Niles took a few more photos. They could share them with Imani later. Terrel relished the serenity and beauty of this serene place.

The path meandered through the grove like a silver ribbon, leading them to a clearing at the other end. On their left, an imposing conference center stood as a modern counterpart to the wilderness behind them. To their right, a small park emerged, adorned with the vibrant colors of flowers and the gentle melody of trickling water.

"Dad, look!" Niles exclaimed, his finger pointing toward a water fountain in the distance. "Can we go over there?"

Terrel caught Niles' hand again and squeezed it gently. "Of course, buddy," he replied. "Let's go see it."

Hand in hand, they ventured into the park. Two souls connected by the magic of a shared adventure. They approached the fountain, and a refreshing mist enveloped them, cool and invigorating against their skin. The fountain was composed of a central ellipsoid stainless steel sculpture, which was surrounded by a pool of water in a polished white granite basin. At the pinnacle of the fountain, a delicate cascade of water emerged, descending gracefully down the central steel sculpture in slender streams, its crystalline droplets reflecting the sunlight like a thousand miniature prisms. Around them, modern granite benches embraced by vibrant blooms invited visitors to pause and soak in the tranquility that radiated from the water sculpture.

Unable to contain his excitement, Niles ran to the fountain, his fingers brushing lightly against the cool, moss-kissed stone. He cupped his hands and dipped them into the fountain, relishing the sensation of the cool liquid trickling through his fingers. He took some photos with his robot.

"Make sure he doesn't get wet," Terrel reminded him. "I doubt that he's waterproof."

Niles nodded and continued to explore the fountain, his robot tucked under his arm.

Terrel closed his eyes for a moment, allowing the tranquil sounds of flowing water to wash over him.

The cheerful voice of his son ended his daydreams. "Hello, Uncle Weber!"

Terrel blinked in surprise. Indeed, there he was. His colleague whom he had promised to avoid today. Angus emerged among tall rhododendron bushes on the other end of the park, walking toward them. Niles waved at him enthusiastically, and Angus waved back. Then, Niles turned his attention back to the water fountain while

Angus approached Terrel.

"Unexpected run-ins, huh?" Angus quipped softly, his tone carrying a mix of amusement and understanding.

Terrel looked around. Hopefully, nobody would see them. "Hello, Angus. What are you doing here?" he greeted Angus, masking his underlying tension. "Did you catch the parrot?"

"I did. But he escaped again."

Terrel's pulse quickened slightly. He couldn't help but worry that Imani would see them here, or the oncologist, or even his criminal twin. He glanced around, but the area was deserted. *No need to get freaked out for nothing*, he told himself.

"Sorry to hear that the bird got away again," he said. "What about the kidnapped woman? Any leads on her?"

Angus let out a sigh. His gaze focused on the park behind them, where two men with dogs on leashes were slowly meandering. "We are still on the search but made some progress. It turns out that Dr. Rogério Queirós Trento has an identical twin. His name is Ronaldo Queirós Trento, and he is a warranted cyber hacker."

"Is that right?" Terrel replied, his tone carefully modulated to feign surprise.

Angus nodded. "Apparently, Ronaldo has quite the reputation in the underground hacking world. It's intriguing to think that two brothers could lead such divergent lives, one an acclaimed physician, the other a warranted criminal."

Terrel's mind became a whirlpool of contemplation. Were they that different? Both twin brothers helped children with cancer, though through very different means. "Nature versus nurture," he mused aloud. "Two brothers of the same blood. Do you know what led them on different paths? Character, choices, environment?"

"Well, our FBI team has been diligently piecing together their backgrounds over the past few hours. Both brothers hail from a modest immigrant family in New York City. Rogério, it seems, was determined to rise above his circumstances. He managed to secure scholarships early on, which served as stepping stones for his journey from one prestigious school to another."

Terrel leaned in slightly, engrossed in the unfolding narrative.

"On the other hand," Angus continued, "Ronaldo, the twin, found himself pulled in a different direction. Early on, he showed an uncanny aptitude for technology, but instead of pursuing legitimate avenues, he chose a darker path, delving into the world of cyber hacking."

"Different life choices?" Terrel asked.

"Well, it's not that easy," Angus explained. "Rogério's path led him to the West Coast for his training as a physician. But as fate would have it, their aging parents needed assistance managing their family restaurant back in New York, and that's where Ronaldo's trajectory took a different turn. He stepped in to help with the restaurant's operations."

"Life has a way of redirecting our paths," Terrel mused, his voice carrying a mixture of contemplation and empathy.

Angus nodded in agreement. "Indeed. And in Ronaldo's case, life at the local college wasn't easy either. He faced discrimination and bullying because of his sexual orientation. That led him to seek refuge at home, where he channeled his technological prowess into the realm of cyber hacking."

Terrel's eyes widened, recognizing the deeper layers at play. "So, his involvement in hacking was a response to the challenges he faced?"

Angus nodded. "I guess it became a means for him to regain a sense of power and control, a way to navigate a world that had shown him its uglier side. By pursuing a career as a hacker, he could avoid the bullies, work from home, and help his parents with the restaurant."

Terrel's thoughts raced as he pieced together the puzzle. The choices people made weren't solely driven by ambition or character; they were also a response to the circumstances that life had presented.

"What cyber hacking crimes did he commit?" Terrel inquired, his focus narrowing on Ronaldo's actions.

Angus sighed, his expression growing somber. "Ronaldo's activities in the cyber world were quite extensive. He's been involved in cases of data breaches, financial fraud, and even hacking into government systems. Our investigation has uncovered a web of illegal activities that spanned across various sectors."

Terrel looked at Angus, absorbing the gravity of the situation.

One thing was clear. He couldn't get involved.

Angus proceeded to explain the situation further, his tone carrying a sense of urgency. "The FBI has obtained a search warrant for Ronaldo. Over the past few years, he's managed to live in the shadows, evading capture. If we were to apprehend him here, it would be a significant breakthrough."

Terrel's inner resolve strengthened. He reminded himself of the boundaries he needed to maintain. Every word, every decision, could have far-reaching consequences. The water fountain's gentle sound seemed to echo his thoughts, a reminder that life was full of twists and turns, but his primary concern at the moment was Niles. Amidst the intricacies of the investigation and the weight of his professional responsibilities, Terrel knew that he had a fundamental duty to focus on his son's well-being. He was a father first, FBI agent second—FBI agent on family leave to be precise.

As Terrel's eyes settled on the fountain, he felt a sudden pang of unease. He glanced around, his heart racing. Niles was nowhere to be seen. The spot where his son had stood just moments ago was empty.

# - 36 -

# Annya

The Confession
Sunday, October 9, 2033, 11:30 a.m.

The ER clock ticked away, its movements matching the pulse of the hospital. Annya navigated the ER corridors, her white coat billowing behind her. In one alcove, a patient with a forearm fracture awaited her, her face a mixture of pain and hope. Annya's gloved hands moved with precision as she tended to the injury.

In the next room, a heart attack patient lay on a hospital bed amidst beeping monitors. Annya stood at the patient's side, directing the medical team with a calm and reassuring voice.

She continued to work tirelessly, touching the lives of many people, each diagnosis a testament to her commitment to her calling.

She almost missed Julius as she passed by the physician's office. He sat at the desk, his head in his hands, his shoulders slumped. His posture made her stop in her tracks. She stepped into the office to check on him.

As he looked up at her, she noticed that his eyes were red and swollen. They were filled with a mix of emotions: frustration, weariness, and perhaps even a hint of surrender. Annya's heart ached at the sight of his vulnerability. She approached him with gentle steps, her eyes holding his gaze.

"Hey Julius, what's going on?" she asked calmly.

"I can't say," he responded with a hoarse voice.

Annya closed the door softly behind her with a faint click. With a grace that mirrored her empathetic nature, she settled into a chair that faced him.

"I'm a secret keeper," she said softly.

Julius' gaze wavered, torn between the impulse to remain silent and the desire to release the thoughts that bound him.

Annya just sat there, waiting. The room seemed to hold its breath—an intimate interlude suspended in time.

Finally, with a sigh that carried the weight of his emotions, he began to speak. "I'm so confused," he admitted, his voice heavy with frustration. "Rogério and I had an affair for the past two months." He looked at Annya to gauge her reaction.

She remained impassive, her eyes fixed on his face, her gaze a steady anchor in the midst of his emotional maelstrom. "And?" she asked.

"Well," he continued, his voice a fragile thread, "most of the time when I met him in the hospital, he acted like he didn't know me."

Annya allowed his confession to linger, to breathe in the space between them. "It sounds like you're grappling with a complex situation," she began. "The emotions you're feeling, the confusion you're experiencing—they're all valid. It's not uncommon for individuals to show different sides of themselves in different contexts. The private moments you share with Rogério might reveal one facet of his personality, while the demands and pressures of a public setting like the hospital could lead to a different demeanor."

Julius nodded. "I would understand if it were that easy. But it's not," he said, his voice carrying the weight of frustration and yearning. "Yesterday, I met him on the stairway in the hospital," he recounted. "He pulled me into a corner and kissed me so passionately that *I* got uncomfortable." Julius' gaze flickered to Annya, a fleeting glance that sought to decipher the nuances of her response.

Annya smiled at him with a mix of empathy and encouragement.

"But today, I met him on the ward," he continued, his voice tinged with frustration. "I asked him if he wanted to go out tonight. He looked at me as if he didn't know me at all and told me that I should not contact him again." Julius' words carried the sting of rejection. "We were together for two months. Did he just break up with me? I'm so confused!" he exclaimed.

Annya's heart went out to Julius. She understood the emotions that were churning within him. He was feeling confused, hurt, and betrayed. She wanted to help him, but that would mean revealing classified information. Julius had probably dated Rogério's twin brother, who was pursued by Angus right now—not Rogério himself. If she told Julius the truth, it could jeopardize Angus' operation. Annya was torn. How could she help Julius without putting Angus in danger?

"Could there be a rationale behind his actions?" she proposed.

Julius looked at her. "What rationale could explain this erratic behavior?" he asked.

Annya's eyes locked onto his. If she divulged the truth, he could inadvertently expose the secret to the very brothers they were trying to outwit. Duty took precedence. She could tell him later.

"Maybe he's found a new love," Julius' voice trembled with a hint of sorrow.

A thought struck Annya. Perhaps Julius could help crack the case.

"If you're open to it, I could swing by his apartment tonight," she suggested, "and see whether he's alone or not."

"Would you really do that for me?" Julius' eyes searched hers for reassurance.

"Sure, I owe you for taking over my shift yesterday," she said lightly. "I'll stop by his place if it isn't too far. Could you give me the address?"

Julius looked at her, uncertainty in his gaze.

"I'll come up with a plausible reason to have a conversation with him," Annya said with a reassuring smile.

"Perhaps it is a good idea," Julius said slowly. "The uncertainty is killing me." He grabbed a sticky note from the desk, hastily jotted down the address, and handed it to her. "A million thanks!"

"No problem." Annya glanced at the note and recognized the street. It was just two blocks away. "Alright, we should have more clarity later today," she affirmed. "If he's alone, I'll have a candid conversation with him to uncover the truth. But for now, let's get back to our tasks."

Julius thanked her once more and rose from his seat with renewed vigor.

They both left the physician's office and stepped out into the bustling hallway. The charge nurse caught sight of them and waved toward the patient exam rooms with a furrowed brow. Julius instinctively followed her down the corridor.

Pausing briefly, Annya pulled out her phone and swiftly composed a text message to Angus.

*I've got Rogério's brother's address*, she typed, attaching a photo of the scribbled sticky note.

Almost immediately, her phone chimed with a response. *Unbelievable. You're a genius*, Angus' message read.

A triumphant feeling of progress surged through her veins as she resumed her stride beside Julius.

# - 37 -

# Frida

The Witch
Sunday, October 9, 2033, 11:30 a.m.

The man focused on the computer screen. His eyes narrowed as if he were peering into a world of hidden intricacies. Frida looked over his shoulder, trying to decipher what he was up to.

Lines of code flowed on the screen like ink from a master calligrapher's brush. The man's brows furrowed with the weight of contemplation, his lips moving as he silently calculated the trajectory of each action. Every command he entered seemed to be a brushstroke in a digital masterpiece.

As he delved deeper into his work, he existed as both creator and conductor, his thoughts materializing in the electronic tapestry he wove. Pleonexia was the target of this covert operation, and the hacker had devised a meticulous scheme to siphon away millions of dollars. The intricate dance of digital infiltration reached its climax. Frida glanced at the clock in right upper corner of the screen. Time was running out, with only half an hour left before the transaction would be executed.

A cadence of keystrokes reverberated through the air like the fading notes of a piano's last chord. Frida's intuition told her that the hacking was almost over. As the man neared his goal, Frida knew that her own fate hung in the balance. She was tied up and restrained, and each passing moment made her feel more vulnerable. Would he let her go or would he kill her?

The man's gaze migrated toward the upper right corner of his computer screen. There, a live feed from the surveillance camera captured his attention, framing the area in front of the conference building. A multi-colored parrot, resplendent in its plumage, landed gracefully upon the base of the stairs in front of the main entrance area. Its feathers shimmered in the sunlight, a living canvas of greens, blues, reds, and yellows. A young boy, a robot toy tugged under his arm, approached the parrot with a mixture of wonder and excitement. With an air of delicate curiosity, the parrot cocked its head to the side, its intelligent gaze fixed upon the boy and the gleaming toy.

In the distance, two men were engaged in a lively conversation. Frida's captor zoomed in. A man of seasoned years and commanding presence stood in a perfectly tailored gray suit in front of a younger black man in a leather jacket and jeans. The video displayed their exchange of words and gestures. The elder man's hands moved with the elegance of a maestro while the younger man's animated expressions painted the air with the vivid strokes of his emotions. They were clearly discussing some kind of serious subject.

The hacker swore loudly, then shot to his feet, knocking the chair over. His face was twisted in a mixture of shock and anger. He refocused the live feed to the stairs in front of the conference center. The boy extended his free hand to the parrot, offering a food pellet from his pocket. The bird's gaze flickered between the outstretched hand and the boy's earnest face as if engaged in a silent conversation. With a graceful bound, the parrot hopped from the first onto the second step, a gesture both playful and calculated. The boy's eyes lit up, his laughter carrying the joy of connection. A curious duet unfolded between the boy and the parrot. The bird leaped upward, and the boy, in turn, followed without hesitation. Together, they scaled the stairs until they arrived at the grand entrance of the building.

The hacker reached for the gun, Taser, and knife, stuffing them into the pockets of his white coat. Then he turned to Frida.

"You won't say a word, now or when I come back," he said with a stern expression. "One word out of your filthy mouth, and I will shoot you. Is that clear?"

Frida felt a shiver running down her spine. She nodded slowly.

The man leaped across the conference room, his shadow stretching across the wall like a dark stain. He grasped the door handle and turned it, the door swinging open on well-oiled hinges.

The corridor beyond was bathed in a pale light, and the man stepped through, leaving the room's stillness and the hum of the computer behind.

Frida stared at the open door, her heart pounding in her chest. She was still tied to the chair, her wrists and ankles bound with ziplines. She pulled at the restraints, but they were too tight. There was no way she would be able to free herself. She didn't dare scream for help, either. The hacker was probably not far away. She had to find a way to escape, but how? She looked around the room, searching for anything that could help her. There was nothing, just the chair she was tied to, the conference table, the computer, and the blank walls. She was trapped.

On the video display in front of her, Frida saw the man stepping onto the front porch. The boy looked up, his expression a mixture of astonishment and curiosity. The man held out his arm to the bird. Miraculously, the parrot hopped onto his proffered arm, traversing the distance to his shoulder with an air of familiarity. The boy laughed. The man smiled and opened the front door, gesturing for the boy to come inside. The boy hesitated for a moment, then took a step forward. The man closed the door behind them, and the two of them disappeared from view. Frida continued to watch the empty screen for a moment, her thoughts racing. What did he want from the little boy?

Frida looked toward the empty hallway. Would they come here? Time seemed to stretch as the doorframe remained empty for a few minutes. Then, the figures of the boy and the man materialized, enveloped in animated conversation. The parrot perched on the man's shoulder chattered livelily, its vibrant plumage a riot of colors against the subdued backdrop.

"His name is Caramba," the man explained.

"Rolando, Rolando!" the parrot squawked jubilantly, its feathers rustling against the man's shirt.

Curiosity gleaming in his eyes, the boy turned to the man, his words tentative. "Who is Rolando?"

A smile danced on the man's lips as he responded. "That's Caramba's previous owner."

He softly closed the door and turned the key, sealing the world outside. He extended a bag of nuts to the boy. "Would you like to feed him?"

The boy's face lit up, accepting the gift with excitement. "Thank you, Dr. Trento," he said.

Frida's heart raced as she realized that the boy had mistaken the man for the pediatric oncologist, Dr. Rogério Queirós Trento. That was why he'd followed him so willingly.

The parrot, ever watchful, observed the exchange, its eyes gleaming with intelligence.

The boy had spotted Frida. His gaze lingered on her, a mix of wonder and confusion. He misinterpreted her stare and extended his hand with the bag of nuts.

"We got those from the vending machine," he explained.

Her gaze went from the boy to the man. The hacker put his hand in his pocket so that she could see the handle of the gun. He pointed the hidden barrel toward her.

Frida said nothing.

"Are you Maya's sister?" the boy asked.

Frida didn't respond.

The innocence woven into the boy's questions seemed to soften the sharp edges of the man's features. "Did you meet Maya on the ward?" he asked.

The boy nodded. "Maya is my friend. She does not have any hair on her head, just like her." He pointed at Frida. "Why does she not speak?" he asked.

"She is a witch. She walks around at night, hurting little children like you and Maya," the man replied, a smile curving his lips. "That's why I had to tie her down."

"Really?" the little boy asked, looking at Frida with wide-open eyes. "Is she dangerous now?" He studied Frida with meticulous attention, his gaze unwavering and inquisitive.

Frida couldn't shake off the feeling of being unsettled by the boy's perception. His gaze had a way of peeling back layers of herself she might not have fully acknowledged. The questions lingered in her mind. Did he see her real self? Was she evil after all?

"As long as her hands are tied, we're safe," the man explained. "But we have to make sure she can't clap her hands. Every time she does, a child on the ward doesn't get their treatment and their tumor grows bigger."

The boy nodded as if he understood. "Why does she not speak?" he asked.

"Because I forbid it," the man said. "Remember, she is a witch. She can destroy little children with a curse. For example, Caramba here was once a beautiful young girl. The witch cursed the girl, and now she is a parrot."

"Wow." Niles' gaze shifted between Frida and the vibrant parrot.

Frida saw how the man waved a sign at the bird.

"Help, I'm not a parrot!" he squeaked.

Niles looked at him with wide-open eyes. The man burst into laughter.

"Can you please feed me," the parrot added.

The man pointed at the bag with nuts in Niles' hand. "Should I help you open it?" he asked.

"Yes, please." Niles handed him the bag.

The man undid the bag containing the nuts, grasping each side firmly and parting them with a tug. He pointed at the table.

"Caramba, come here," he said.

The parrot climbed down his extended arm and stepped onto the polished conference table.

The man pointed at a chair at the conference table, about a meter away from Frida. "Can you sit down here?" he asked Niles politely.

Niles responded with an eager nod, promptly settling into the designated chair.

"Can you please feed me," the parrot said again, casting a hopeful glance and walking toward Niles.

The man handed him the bag with the nuts. "Remember, one at a time," he said.

The parrot eyed the bag in the boy's hand and came closer. Niles extended his flat hand to the bird, offering the nut. The parrot plucked it from his palm.

The man leaned against the edge of the table, a contented smile gracing his lips.

"I wish Maya had played with him like that," he said. "But unfortunately, she was afraid of him."

Niles looked at the man. "I can show Maya how to feed him," he said.

"I would love that," whispered the man.

As Niles maintained the gentle rhythm of feeding the parrot, his focus unwavering, the man strode purposefully over to the computer. With a deft motion, he roused the screen from its slumber, the computer's display flickering to life. Frida looked over his shoulder. Almost 12:00 p.m. His scheme was almost done.

# - 38 -

# Terrel

The Robot
Sunday, October 9, 2033, 11:45 a.m.

Just a few minutes ago, Niles had stood before the fountain, his form outlined against the backdrop of flowing water. Then, in the blink of an eye, he had vanished. Terrel frantically circled the fountain, calling out for his son, his words echoing off the surrounding stone.

"Niles, where are you? Come back!" Terrel's shouts carried desperation and fear, his voice cracking as he strained to locate any sign of his missing son. Had he run away, or had someone taken him? With each hurried step around the fountain's perimeter, his heart pounded more in his chest, a crescendo of worry and determination. Terrel felt dizzy. If he didn't find his son in the next few minutes, his chest might as well explode.

The waters of the fountain continued to dance and sparkle, their tranquil surface a stark contrast to the turmoil within Terrel's heart. He cast his gaze in every direction. Every moment that passed felt like an eternity, each second an eternity of uncertainty. Terrel's voice grew hoarse from his repeated calls, his shouts a poignant expression of a father's love and anguish.

Angus observed Terrel's frantic search for a few minutes. Then, he swiftly approached Terrel as he circled the fountain.

"Terrel," Angus called him out, his voice steady yet laced with empathy. "I'm here to help you. Let's work together to find your son."

Terrel's wild eyes met Agent Weber's reassuring gaze.

"You don't understand. The very fact that I talked with you might be the reason why Niles is in danger now," he shouted.

Angus' calm demeanor provided a stabilizing presence amidst the chaos of the moment. "Then, whoever intimidated you has messed with the wrong guy. We are the FBI, Terrel. We will find your son. Tell me everything you remember," he instructed, guiding Terrel to a bench nearby.

Terrel let out a sigh, tears welling up in his eyes. "I'm sorry, Angus, I should have come to you right away. I'm scared for my little boy. Please help me."

He looked at Angus with hesitation. Then, he shared the events from the ward as concisely as possible. The twin brothers in the oncologist's office, Rogério and Ronaldo, the chase through the hospital lobby, the revelation that Ronaldo had hacked the insurance company and approved all pending claims of children with cancer, and the threat to undo his son's surgery authorization.

Angus shook his head. "I don't understand. If he approved all claims already, why did he pressure you to stay silent? If Ronaldo abducted your son, why would he do it now, after the job is done?"

Terrell's eyes were filled with tears. "I have no idea," he said. "But we have to find him, Angus. Every minute counts. I can't lose my son. I can't lose him."

Angus put a hand on Terrell's shoulder. "We'll find him," he said calmly. "I promise."

Terrel's phone burst into a lively melody, demanding his immediate attention. He swiftly retrieved it from his pocket, the caller ID revealing Imani's name. Apprehension surged within him as he answered the call. "Hello, Imani, what's up?"

"Hello, Terrel!" Imani's voice carried a burst of energy. "Thank you so much for looking after Niles. I can't even express how much better I feel now. I was utterly exhausted, but now I'm like a new person. Should we meet in the hospital cafeteria for lunch?"

"Meeting in the hospital cafeteria?" Terrel's eyes darted to Angus, who responded with animated gestures of disagreement.

What should he do? Angus, gesticulating fervently, signaled him to withhold information.

With a cheerful tone, Terrel responded, "Absolutely, I'm all in for lunch! How about in an hour?"

Imani's voice revealed her surprise. "An hour? Well, the ultrasound is a big deal this afternoon. We need to be on the ward so we don't miss the call for it. Where are you guys? I can come over?"

Thinking quickly, Terrel aimed for a balance between truth and convenience. "No need to join us first," he replied smoothly. "Actually, we're just around the corner from the cafeteria. We'll be there in about half an hour."

Imani's tone shifted to contemplation. "Okay, then," she said, her words measured. "See you soon, I guess."

Terrel concluded the call, his attention briefly snagged by the display of his phone. There, among the notifications, was a fresh text message. He hadn't noticed it previously. When had it arrived? Perhaps during his conversation with Imani?

Curiosity piqued, he opened the message. It revealed a snapshot of the parrot they had pursued earlier in the day, perched on a conference table, delicately grasping a cashew nut.

Angus peered over his shoulder. "Ah, that's Caramba, the parrot!" he declared, recognition lighting up his face.

A rush of astonishment surged through Terrel. The image was a part of the same text thread that contained the photos from their morning stroll through the grove. A connection sparked in his mind— it had been taken using Niles' robot. "Niles must have taken this photo," he realized aloud.

Angus regarded him with surprise and curiosity, clearly eager for an explanation.

Terrel continued, his excitement palpable. "Remember, Niles got that toy robot from the clinic?" he said. "It's equipped to capture images—plus, it's got GPS capabilities!"

Terrel's heart raced, his mind racing even faster. Swiftly, he downloaded the photo to his photo app and activated the map function. There, on the digital map, a flag was planted on the campus behind the hospital, mere meters away from their current position.

Angus, ever observant, extended his finger toward the flag on the map. "The conference center!" he exclaimed, his eyes widening in realization. "That's where they are."

Terrel's immediate instinct was to dash toward the conference center, his concern for Niles propelling him forward. But Angus, the voice of reason, intervened, holding him back with a determined grip.

"Wait," Angus urged, his tone measured. "Let's not rush blindly. We need to consider how Niles could have entered that building on his own. And where did he get those nuts? There might be more to this situation than meets the eye. It's possible that whoever is responsible for this might be with him—perhaps the same person we suspect is behind this whole affair."

Terrel's emotions swirled. "I have to rescue my son," he exclaimed.

Angus provided the necessary restraint. "You will," he assured, his voice firm. "But charging in without a plan won't help anyone. We need a strategy."

Taking a deep breath, Angus began outlining their approach. "First," he said, his voice steady, "we need more information. We should discreetly approach the conference center to find out who might be with Niles—and if they are armed. There was a shooting incident in the parking lot earlier today."

Terrel's heart raced, fueled by worry and regret. "I hope Niles is okay," he lamented. "I should have been more vigilant. I can't bear the thought of anything happening to him."

Angus attempted to provide some reassurance. "Remember, he managed to send those photos with his robot," he said. "That's a positive sign. At least we know he's not restrained, and he's capable of operating the robot."

Terrel nodded, tears in his eyes. "You're right. If he could send those photos, he must be okay. But I can't directly communicate with him through the robot."

"Can you send a photo back?" Angus asked. "Maybe that's a way to signal that you're nearby and waiting for him."

Terrel nodded in agreement. "Yes, I can do that. Let's try it."

With determination, Terrel took a selfie, extending his hand as though he were inviting the viewer to join him. He hoped that Niles would interpret the gesture as an invitation to meet up with him. He quickly sent the photo to the robot.

Both men stared at the phone display, a tense silence settling around them. The seconds stretched on, each one laden with expectation. But there was no immediate response from Niles.

Angus' voice broke the silence, his tone gentle yet reassuring. "Give it time, Terrel. Niles might not see the message right away. Or he might need a moment to process it and decide what to do."

Terrel nodded, his emotions a mix of hope and apprehension. They continued to watch, their eyes fixed on the phone display, waiting for any sign of a response from Niles.

Nothing.

Terrel's determination surged, propelling him into action. With a swift, purposeful stride, he moved toward the conference center, his heart pounding with a mix of urgency and resolve.

"I'm getting him out of there now," he declared, his voice laced with fierce determination.

"Wait, be patient," Angus advised, his voice a plea for reason.

But Terrel was already on his way. His mind was set on rescuing his son, and he wouldn't let anything stand in his way.

His steps quickened as he closed the distance to the conference center, his emotions a whirlwind of worry and determination. Every second felt like an eternity, his thoughts consumed by the image of Niles and the unknown man inside that building. The urgency of the situation had ignited a fire within him—a fire that refused to be extinguished until Niles was safe in his arms.

Suddenly, a diminutive figure descended the stairs of the conference center in a flurry of motion.

Although his appearance had changed—his clothes and even his body movements seemed different—his profile was unmistakable. It was Niles.

"Niles!" Terrel cried out, his voice a mixture of relief and astonishment.

For an instant, Niles glanced in their direction, his eyes meeting Terrel's before he sped off toward the grove with a surprising burst of speed.

Angus, sensing something amiss, halted abruptly and studied the fleeing figure. There was an oddity to the child, something that stirred his intuition, though he couldn't quite put a finger on it. The boy's uncanny velocity for someone so small was only part of it. There was something else that eluded his understanding.

"Wait!" Angus exclaimed, his voice edged with concern. He lunged into motion, racing after Terrel and the child.

Their pursuit led them into the woods, their feet pounding against the earth. As they ventured into the grove, the boy vanished from sight, leaving behind an echoing sense of mystery.

Terrel raced around frantically, calling for his son. But his calls went unanswered, the forest absorbing his pleas.

"Niles!" Terrel's voice cracked with desperation, reverberating through the tranquil woods. "Niles, where are you?"

Terrel' gaze swept over the surroundings, his mind whirling with disbelief. What had just transpired? It was as if a veil had been lifted, revealing a reality that defied logic.

Together, Terrel and Angus embarked on a frantic search, their determination unwavering. With every step, they grappled with the bizarre turn of events, driven by a shared purpose—to find Niles.

# - 39 -

# Annya

The Revelation
Sunday, October 9, 2033, 12:00 noon.

The chaotic scene in the emergency room had settled down, giving Annya a chance to catch her breath. But her thoughts were still on Angus. The security guard had mentioned a shooting scene in the parking lot, where they had met earlier that morning. The shooter was still on the loose. Angus had told her that he was fine, but she wasn't convinced. She knew Angus well enough by now. He was the type to put his duty above everything, even his safety. That was what made him so good at his job.

Annya decided to head to the security center in the basement and check discretely on Angus through the surveillance system. She didn't want to appear clingy by bombarding him with messages. She just wanted to make sure he was okay.

With measured steps, Annya descended the staircase to the security center. The ID badge dangling from her neck caught the scanner's gaze, and the door opened to grant her swift passage. As she entered the large room, a security guard looked up from the screens in front of him and greeted her politely. The hum of computers and the chatter of voices filled the air.

Annya made her way to the large screen at the end of the room, which covered a mosaic of live feeds from the hospital's security cameras. She scanned the videos of different parts of the hospital, the lobby, the waiting rooms, and the area around the hospital, looking for Angus. She saw doctors and nurses moving through the halls, visitors waiting in the waiting room, and an air taxi landing on the landing pod behind the hospital.

Her eyes caught a strange commotion behind the parking lot, between the conference center and a nearby grove. It looked like Terrel's kid, Niles, was running from the building toward the grove. Annya rushed to the computer and zoomed in to confirm. Yes, it was definitely Niles. But why was he heading into the woods? What was going on?

Annya zoomed in more. It was strange. The child was sharp for a few seconds and then seemed to transcend like a ghost. There was Angus and Terrel, waving and shouting. The two men ran after the child. Why would Niles not turn around to his father? Why did he run into the woods instead? That made no sense.

The silhouette of the child flickered and then disappeared. Annya wiped her eyes. It was not that the child had disappeared in the woods. It had dissolved in plain air like a puff of smoke. What was that? Angus was just as baffled. He stopped and stared at the spot where Niles had been moments ago, clearly confused. Terrel wasn't giving up. He charged into the woods, and after a hesitation, Angus followed.

Annya hit the pause button on the video, then rewound it, her gaze fixed on the child in the scene. Niles' form, seemingly palpable yet transparent, exhibited an uncanny mix of tangibility and intangibility. The contours of his body shimmered with a surreal luminescence while he was running away from the conference center, but then gradually dissipated as he neared the edge of the woods.

Bit by bit, Annya realized what she was witnessing here—a vologram, a hologram captured on video. Probably the best one she had ever seen. Niles wasn't physically there; it was a projection of him, a holographic image.

With this revelation in mind, Annya redirected her focus toward the conference center, the place where this odd projection had originated. To dig deeper, she needed a different camera angle. She selected another camera to scrutinize the building's entrance. And just like that, her investigative efforts paid off. There it was, confirming her suspicions—a projector discreetly mounted beneath the roof, positioned right above the entrance. The pieces of the puzzle were falling into place. Had someone created the vologram of the boy to lead the FBI agents away from the building? What was going on inside?

Annya's curiosity deepened as she accessed the surveillance cameras inside the conference facilities. What she saw was unsettling. All the camera screens were black, as if they had been turned off or disconnected. This raised suspicions in her mind. Should she text Angus about it? But he was busy chasing the child, and checking messages might not be a priority.

Time was ticking, and Annya felt a sense of urgency. She decided to take matters into her own hands. After all, she was trained for this. With a purposeful stride, she left the security center, ascended the stairs, exited the hospital, and crossed the parking lot toward the conference center. Each step carried her closer to the heart of the mystery she was determined to solve.

# - 40 -

# Frida

The Third Lesson
Sunday, October 9, 2033, 12:00 noon.

Shutting down all computer screens, the man rose from his desk chair. Frida held her breath. A veil of suspense hung in the air. Concealing his actions from the boy's view, he pivoted, discreetly retrieving the gun from his pocket. He turned toward the wall so that Frida couldn't see what he was doing either. What was he up to? He was fiddling with the gun. Frida's senses were heightened, her pulse matching the drumbeat of her anxiety. Would he kill them now?

The boy remained focused on the parrot in front of him. He carefully extracted the final nut from the bag, his eyes a blend of wonder and delight. Extending his offering to the parrot, he watched as the colorful bird accepted the morsel, emitting a satisfied chirp in response. The parrot's keen gaze was fixated on the boy. Its feathers, a tapestry of scarlet red, emerald green, and vivid blue, shimmered in the ambient light, each iridescent hue reflecting a myriad of shades as it shifted.

The boy murmured with a twinge of sympathy, "Sorry, that's all of them."

The parrot looked at him for another moment, its eyes twinkling with understanding before it fluttered back to its original perch on the man's arm.

The man smiled and stroked the parrot's feathers. "Welcome back, Caramba," he said. "I've missed you."

The parrot squawked in reply and nuzzled the man's cheek. "Rolando, Rolando," it said, its voice a sing-song melody.

"Dr. Trento, he thinks your name is Rolando," the boy said. "But it's Rogério, right?"

The man nodded. "That's okay. I don't mind."

They shared a hearty laugh, the parrot's chime-like squawk joining in. With deliberate steps, the man approached the boy. He slowly put the gun on the desk in front of the boy. The boy looked from the man to the gun with wide-open eyes.

"Do you know what that is?" the man asked.

Niles nodded. "My daddy has a gun as well," he said. "But I'm not supposed to touch it."

"Well, you're allowed to touch this one," the man said.

Niles' gaze oscillated between the gun and the man, torn between curiosity and uncertainty, his innocent mind trying to navigate the complexity of the moment.

"Caramba ate a lot of nuts. Now he's thirsty," the man continued. "I need to step out for a moment and fetch him some water." He pointed at Frida. " But we have to make sure the witch does not curse us in the meantime."

"I can come with you," the boy said with a quiver in his voice, his scared gaze shifting from the man to Frida.

Frida's heart clenched as she caught sight of the fear lingering in the boy's eyes, his wide, innocent eyes fixed upon her. The weight of his apprehension and vulnerability touched her deeply. This was all a big misunderstanding. She was not the monster here. But she didn't dare to speak. The gun was on the table.

"You have to watch her so that she cannot curse anyone," the man repeated. "You are a big detective, aren't you?"

"Yes, I am," the boy declared, nervously looking at the man for reassurance. "But what if she wants to hurt me when you're gone?"

"That's why I'll leave the gun with you," the man said.

The boy looked at the polished pistol on the table. Frida held her breath. The boy reached out and took it. A shiver went down her spine. How could he manipulate a child like this?

"It's heavy," the boy said, intrigued by the unfamiliar object.

"Yes, it is." The man chuckled. "Now, point at the witch."

The boy followed the command.

Frida's eyes widened in fear. Would the child shoot her now?

"No need to shoot her if she doesn't move," the man said calmly. "This is only to protect yourself, understood? You only shoot if she says something."

The boy nodded eagerly.

"I'll be back in just a minute," the man reassured him with a soothing tone.

"I want to call my daddy," Niles said with a hint of urgency.

"Absolutely, we'll call your daddy as soon as I return. It won't take long, just a minute," the man promised.

Niles forced a smile and nodded bravely. The man's shadow loomed on the wall as he approached the door. The parrot on his shoulder squawked and flapped its wings. The man unlocked the door, stepped through, and closed it behind him. The sound of his footsteps and the parrot's chatter faded into the distance, leaving behind a vacuum of quiet, an emptiness that held the weight of the unknown.

The boy's nervous gaze remained locked on Frida, his hands gripping the gun with a fervent intensity. Seeking reassurance, his eyes flicked to the toy robot beside him.

"We do this together," he uttered. His words a delicate declaration of camaraderie.

Frida, keenly aware of the boy's scrutiny, felt a longing to communicate her truth, to express her own side of the story. Yet, the fear in the boy's eyes held her back. She had worked with children in the hospital long enough to know that reasoning with an adult was a different endeavor from engaging with a frightened child. A surge of frustration welled within her as the urge to defend herself clashed with the realization that any movement or sound could yield unpredictable consequences.

The awareness that the boy saw her as a threat struck Frida with a profound sense of unease. For the first time, she was compelled to see herself through the eyes of another. The weight of the boy's apprehension became a mirror that reflected the consequences of her actions in a way she hadn't fully grasped before. As her empathy stirred, she began to grapple with the implications of her past—her work as an insurance claim agent who denied medical care to children.

A stark parallel to the witch's curse she had been likened to, both seemingly causing harm to innocent lives. As she looked into the frightened eyes of the boy, Frida began to see the interconnectedness of her choices with the lives of those she had affected. The barriers she had erected to safeguard her own interests started to crumble, revealing the far-reaching consequences of her decisions on others. In this moment, Frida recognized the gravity of her past actions and how they intertwined with the situation at hand.

A sharp bang reverberated as the door swung open, its suddenness commanding attention. A woman in a white coat and a long red ponytail entered with a determined stride, her gaze sweeping the room in a practiced assessment of potential threats. Her surprise was palpable as her eyes fell upon the boy.

"Niles, what on earth are you doing? Put the gun down."

Niles responded with a vehement shake of his head, his grip on the gun unyielding. "Hello, Annya. I have to guard the witch," he said with a determined note, the conviction in his voice belying his young age.

Annya exhaled, her patience and understanding evident. "Niles, listen to me. This is not a witch," she began, her voice gentle yet firm. She pointed at Frida, her sweat-soaked figure a stark contrast to the notion of a malevolent crook. "This is a woman who is bound to a chair. Can you see that?"

Niles hesitated, his gaze shifting between Annya and Frida. His voice held a hint of explanation as he defended his stance. "She is a witch, and we have to guard her so that she does not curse anyone."

Annya closed the distance between herself and Niles with cautious movements. With a soft tone, she addressed the boy's concerns. "Okay, Niles, I understand," she began, her voice a soothing balm. "We want to make sure the witch does not curse anyone." She paused, letting her words sink in before continuing. "We can guard her together. I'll help you."

The boy's gaze shifted between Annya and the woman on the chair, his inner struggle evident in his eyes.

Annya's voice wove through the tension, a reassuring thread of shared experiences. "Remember when you had your ultrasound scan?"

she asked gently. "You were scared as well. But we did it together, and it wasn't that bad."

Niles' memory stirred at her words. "I remember that," he acknowledged, a glimmer of recognition crossing his features.

"We do this together as well," Annya emphasized, slowly coming closer, bridging the gap.

He looked at her, torn between his own doubts and the trust that her words were building. Yet, before he could respond, Annya lunged forward and took the gun from his grasp.

"Hey, I need to hold it," Niles protested, his voice a mixture of surprise and protest.

Annya paused, her breath steadying as she tugged the gun under her belt. Her eyes met Niles', a mixture of understanding and firmness in her gaze.

"I take care of it from here," she said calmly.

They heard the echo of footsteps coming closer. Annya pulled the gun and positioned herself in front of the door. Two men appeared at the doorway: a middle-aged white man in a gray suit and a younger black man in a leather jacket and jeans.

"Daddy!" The joy in Niles' voice was unmistakable as he rushed into the arms of the younger man, his father. Their embrace was a mix of relief and affection.

Terrel held his son tightly. "Are you okay, Niles?" he asked with a blend of concern and care.

Niles eagerly recounted his recent adventure, his words spilling out like a waterfall. "Yeah, Dad! I helped Dr. Trento catch the witch. He let me feed his parrot. I had to make sure the witch didn't curse anyone!"

Terrel crouched down to Niles' eye level, his voice gentle yet cautious. "Sweetie, I think there might be a misunderstanding. Witches aren't real—they're only in stories."

Niles responded with a mix of certainty and enthusiasm, "Well, this one is real, Dad!"

The room seemed to hold its breath, a moment suspended between a child's imagination and an adult's logic. Terrel's gaze softened as he looked at his son, realizing that sometimes, youthful belief can reveal truths beyond what grown-ups comprehend.

"Well, I'm relieved you watched her," he said with a smile. "Your mother is already in the cafeteria. How about we go and have lunch with her?"

"Yes, I'm hungry!" Niles replied eagerly. He reached out for his father's hand while clutching his robot toy with the other. Terrel exchanged a quick glance with Angus, silently communicating, *Can you handle things from here?* Angus nodded in response.

"I'm so relieved you're safe," Terrel said to Frida with a warm smile. He waved goodbye and, hand in hand with Niles, left the room. The hallway echoed with their footsteps, a father and son moving forward together.

Frida looked at Annya, relief flooding through her. "Thank you for rescuing me," she said. "I remember you from the ER."

"Of course," Annya responded. "I'm glad we came in time. You were very lucky. Most kidnappings don't end like this."

"I know," Frida whispered. "I'm glad to be alive."

"Do you have a knife or something that can cut these?" Annya asked Angus, pointing at Frida's wrists and ankles, which were still bound by zip ties.

Angus shook his head. "I don't have a knife, but I know a way to break them." He stepped closer to Frida, examining the zip ties that held her captive. His focus was on the small plastic locking mechanism at the end of each tie. Using his fingernail, he carefully held back the plastic lip in the lock head that secured the tie's tracks. With a deliberate motion, he disrupted the mechanism, causing the zip tie to loosen. He repeated the process for the remaining ties, gradually freeing Frida from her restraints.

"Thank you!" she whispered. "Are you from the police?"

"FBI," he said shortly.

Her composure wavered as the weight of the moment and the flood of emotions converged. She could no longer hold back the tears that had been welling up inside of her. They streamed down her cheeks, each droplet a testament to the overwhelming release of pent-up feelings. The weight that had settled upon her shoulders seemed to ease, and she released a sigh of liberation. In that moment, as Frida allowed herself to cry, she finally let go of the pain she had been carrying for so long.

She felt foolish for having been drawn in by the allure of recognition and glory. Her cheeks flushed with embarrassment as she realized that her actions had mirrored those of an evil witch in a fairytale. She had been so blinded by her own ambition that she had lost sight of what was truly important—life. A profound journey marked by the spectrum of human emotions, ranging from the exhilarating highs of joy and love to the contemplative depths of sorrow and introspection. The intricate tapestry of relationships formed with family, friends, and even strangers, intertwined with the captivating beauty of the natural world, where acts of kindness and compassion illuminated the intricate mosaic of human existence.

Frida was relieved and ready to be alive. She had almost died today, but a second chance had been handed to her. She held it with both hands, treasuring the promise it held. She realized that she was ready to let go of the past and open the door to a new beginning.

Annya looked at Angus with a worried expression. "Where should we start looking for the kidnapper?" she asked. "Do you think he'll return?"

Angus shook his head. "I'm afraid not," he said in a somber tone. "Ronaldo managed to escape. The SUEC search team is already on the scene, scouring the building and its surroundings, but I haven't received any updates suggesting they've located him. We got sidetracked by a hologram, and my hunch is that he used that diversion to slip away unnoticed."

Annya sighed. "I understand," she said, nodding. She wasn't sure if she was disappointed or relieved. Ronaldo had kidnapped a woman, but he had not harmed her, apart from a few bruises. He had helped children with cancer by approving their insurance claims and stealing money from a corrupt insurance company. Was he a modern Robin Hood?

# - 41 -

# Angus

The Foundation
Monday, October 10, 2033, 2 p.m.

Angus stepped into the patient room, a bouquet of flowers in his hand. Niles lay in his hospital bed, his breathing slow and steady, though his forehead glistened with beads of sweat. He seemed drained from the ordeal he had undergone. Various intravenous tubes snaked their way into his arm, each delivering a different substance. A drainage bag peeked out from under the sheets, serving its purpose.

Terrel sat by Niles' bedside, his eyes glued to his son. Angus' entrance prompted him to look up. Weariness mingled with a flicker of relief in his eyes.

Angus offered a gentle smile. "I heard the surgery went well?"

Terrel nodded a mixture of gratitude and fatigue evident in his expression. "Yes, they managed to remove the tumor in one piece. Thank you for coming by." His gaze went to the flowers in Angus' hand. "And thank you for the flowers."

Angus handed them over, keeping the rose he wanted to take to the ER. Terrel didn't seem to notice. He got up and put the bouquet in a vase on the windowsill.

"I wanted to apologize to Imani for adding to her stress in these already tough times," Angus said. "Where is she?"

"She went home briefly to freshen up, fetch some clean clothes, and grab necessities," Terrel explained. "She'll be back soon."

"How did she react to the hostage incident?" Angus asked.

A warm smile touched Terrel's lips. "Actually, she doesn't know about it. When we met in the cafeteria yesterday, Niles shared his story about a parrot and a witch. Needless to say, she thought he was weaving tales. With the surgery looming ahead, I decided not to burden her further. She was already quite tense with Niles' upcoming procedure. We had the ultrasound and anesthesia preparations in the afternoon, followed by the surgery this morning. There simply wasn't a right time to delve into anything else."

"Given the circumstances, that's understandable," Angus said. He looked at his colleague. Niles' surgery, it seemed, had etched its mark on Terrel's features, leaving behind traces of weariness and strain.

"Will he make a full recovery?" Angus asked.

"Yes, everything looks good so far," Terrel said. "He still needs to go through chemotherapy. But Dr. Queirós Trento explained to us that this could be mostly done on an outpatient basis. I'll take a family leave for the next few weeks. My family needs me now."

Angus nodded. "Of course. Take as much time as you need."

Angus and Terrel shared a quiet vigil. The rhythmic rise and fall of Niles' chest and the steady cadence of his breath created a soothing atmosphere.

"Did you see the *New York Times* article?" Terrel broke the silence.

Angus was glad that Terrel brought it up. He had not been sure how to raise the subject. "Yes, it's quite an astounding piece," he responded. "The speed at which it made the news is remarkable. I wondered if this was orchestrated."

Terrel nodded. "One of the parents here happens to be a *New York Times* reporter. I bumped into him in the hallway, and he mentioned that he received a tip from an anonymous source. He couldn't reach the donors on a Sunday, and he verified the story with the oncologist before publishing it this morning."

Terrel reached over to the table beside him and picked up an iPad. He navigated to the *New York Times* website, where the headline beckoned: "Employees of Pleonexia Make $35 Million Donation to Children's Cancer Foundation." He began to read aloud, "Employees of Pleonexia, led by their CEO, have generously donated their annual bonuses to establish a groundbreaking foundation dedicated to children battling cancer. The CEO of Pleonexia has become a role model by contributing $20 million to the cause."

Angus nodded, his mind tracing the intricacies of the situation. "They're being praised as modern-day angels—interviews, press coverage, the whole nine yards. Nobody mentioned that a hacker orchestrated the transaction."

"They're not asking for their money back?" Terrel asked.

Angus shook his head. "They were outraged at first. But after much deliberation, the CEO has chosen to play along, basking in the adoration. They're in too deep now to reveal it was a hack, let alone ask for the money back. And that's not all. The example set by the insurance agents has triggered a wave of additional donations to the new foundation. It seems that everyone wants to be a part of this spectacle."

"Do you know what the money will be used for?" Terrel asked.

"As far as I've heard, the foundation is focused on research, treatment, and providing necessary resources for these young patients."

"That's a good cause," Terrel said.

Angus nodded. "I guess so."

"So, you won't arrest Dr. Queirós Trento?"

Angus shook his head. "Rogério? No, we don't have any hard evidence that he was involved. He stated that he received an email from the CEO of Pleonexia, informing him about the new foundation. That, of course, was a fake email. The CEO never wrote to him. Rogério probably knew that his brother wrote the note, but we can't prove it. It was written from the CEO's account. Rogério forwarded the note to hospital administration, and they processed it from here. Frida Ending testified that she was kidnapped by his brother Ronaldo only. A man with calloused hands, which Rogério does not have. Someone must have driven the van, and we suspect that it was Rogério. But we can't prove it."

"What about Ronaldo?" Terrel asked. "If the insurance staff claims that they made a donation voluntarily, does that mean no crime was committed?"

Angus shook his head. "Let's start with the facts. We're aware that Ronaldo breached the insurance accounts. The CEO raised a major fuss until the *New York Times* piece was published. And there's more to it than just the hacking. He kidnapped a young woman and a child—your child," he emphasized, his gaze locking onto Terrel's. "He assaulted the woman and handed your son a gun. Think about the possible consequences if Annya hadn't intervened."

"Annya said that the gun wasn't loaded," Terrel noted. "Don't get me wrong, Angus. I want Ronaldo to face the consequences of his actions. But it's worth considering that his moves weren't irrational. In fact, they were quite calculated and strategic."

Angus nodded in understanding. "You're right. His actions were meticulously planned and executed. He's shown a remarkable level of cunning and foresight. However, that doesn't absolve him of the law's grasp. Justice will be served for crimes committed."

"Best of luck," Terrel said with a shrug. "It seems he's vanished into the shadows once again. Tracking him down won't be easy."

Angus nodded. "I know. I will at least try." He looked at Niles, who was still sleeping in his hospital bed. "I'm glad your son is doing okay, all circumstances considered."

Terrel gave him a grateful nod.

Angus turned around and quietly left the ward, the weight of their conversation and the mysteries it held still echoing in his mind.

He headed toward the emergency room, a route he knew all too well by now. He held the beautiful rose in his hand that he had found in Ronaldo's apartment. He felt a bit awkward holding it without any wrapping, but he didn't have time to conceal it. He approached the reception desk of the ER, a hub of activity in the otherwise controlled chaos, and inquired about Julius.

The receptionist, a paragon of professionalism, directed him to a waiting area with a practiced gesture, as she probably had countless times before. Taking a seat, Angus settled in, caught between resolve and unease. Just when restlessness began to claw at his composure, Julius emerged from the labyrinthine corridors. His features briefly lit up as he saw Angus, a curious smile tugging at the corners of his mouth.

"Hello, Agent Weber," he said. "Congratulations for rescuing the kidnapped woman. Everyone is talking about it. How can I help you? Were you looking for Annya?"

Angus met Julius' gaze head-on. "Thanks, and no, I'm not here for Annya today. I'm here for you."

Julius' gaze went to the rose. "I have to admit, I'm not exactly in the market for whatever intentions you might be holding." His smile flickered with amusement.

Angus held Julius' gaze. "Don't be silly, Julius. I'm merely a messenger. We searched Ronaldo Queirós Trento's apartment, unearthing this." He lifted the rose, a relic of clandestine discovery. "It has an attached message for you, and I wondered if you could tell me what it means."

Julius' brows knitted with confusion. "I'm sorry, but I'm not familiar with anyone named Ronaldo Queirós Trento," he said, his voice tinged with uncertainty. "Is he related to Rogério, perhaps?"

"Actually, he's Rogério's identical twin brother."

A flicker of disbelief traced its way across Julius' features, the mental puzzle slowly resolving. His chin dropped slightly, the weight of realization settling in. "You mean there's a twin brother?" His voice wavered with astonishment.

Caught in the midst of this intriguing exchange, an elderly lady nearby cast a curious glance at the unfolding conversation.

Sensing the need for privacy, Angus gestured toward the back exit. "Perhaps we should step somewhere quieter?" he suggested.

Julius nodded, his expression a mix of anticipation and apprehension. "Definitely."

As they emerged into the open air, Angus resumed the conversation, his tone measured. "Julius, just to make sure we're on the same page, it appears that you had a romantic involvement with Ronaldo Queirós Trento, who happens to be Rogério's twin brother."

Julius looked at him in shock, mouth open, whispering, "Oh my god..."

Angus continued gently, "Yes, indeed. And it appears that he left this rose for you."

"For me? Why wouldn't he give it to me himself? Is he not feeling well?" Julius inquired, his voice tinged with concern.

"I'm afraid he's involved in a complex situation," Angus explained. "He manipulated Pleonexia's health insurance system, approving pending claims for children with cancer."

A mix of awe and admiration colored Julius' voice. "Wow, like a modern-day Robin Hood! Why did he do that?"

"He has a daughter who was denied cancer treatment."

"He has a daughter?"

"Yes, his marriage ended due to repeated affairs with men, but he remained devoted to his daughter. He consistently sends financial support to his family, and he manages to visit his daughter regularly, even as a wanted hacker. And now, he's executed his grandest scheme yet. He approved not only his daughter's pending insurance claims but those of the entire ward. Illegally, he siphoned off millions of dollars into a newly established foundation for children with cancer."

Julius smiled. "He truly is one-of-a-kind."

Angus shook his head. "I'm afraid what he did is illegal, Julius. He embezzled millions of dollars and vanished without a trace. We believe this rose, along with its message, might be his attempt to reach out to you." He handed the rose to Julius.

Julius accepted it as if cradling a precious gem. Its deep red petals held a quiet beauty, its significance amplified by the delicate note attached to its stem. With careful fingers, he unrolled the paper and read the message: "For Julius: hhs brx lq frfrd, pdohahvh."

Julius looked up at Angus, a mixture of curiosity and puzzlement in his eyes. "Do you have any idea what this means?"

Angus nodded with a knowing smile. "Of course, I'm the FBI, Julius. It's a simple Caesar cipher with a shift of 3."

"What does that mean?"

"It's a basic form of encryption where each letter in the original message is replaced by the letter that is three positions down the alphabet. So, 'hhs brx lq frfrd, pdohahvh' deciphers to 'see you in Cocoa, Maldives'."

Julius' face lit up like a Christmas tree. "Wow," he exclaimed once more, a blend of surprise and excitement in his voice. "I thought he broke up with me, but he didn't."

Angus let out a small, frustrated sigh. It seemed that his point hadn't come across as intended. "I don't think he actually means for you to meet him in the Maldives," he clarified. "My suspicion is that 'Cocoa' might refer to a place you're familiar with. And he hasn't provided any specific date or time, so it's possible you have a routine or some context that makes this message meaningful."

Julius tilted his head slightly, his gaze upward. "I'm sorry, but I honestly have no clue what you're talking about," he replied with a cheerful tone. "Agent Weber, I appreciate your efforts in bringing me the rose. It means a lot to me."

Angus studied Julius' demeanor, his instincts nagging at him. There was something beneath the surface, a hidden truth that Julius was unwilling to reveal. He kept his expression neutral, although inside, he was growing more convinced that surveillance might be necessary.

Julius beamed with innocence, offering a warm smile. "Is there anything else you need to ask, Agent Weber?"

Angus gave a reluctant nod. "I suppose we're done for now."

"Thank you!" Julius turned around, the rose cradled in his hand. He strolled away with a spring in his steps, a carefree tune escaping his lips. Angus' gaze lingered on him until he disappeared through the emergency room entrance.

# - 42 -

# Annya

Closure
Saturday, October 15, 2033, 4:00 p.m.

It was a warm afternoon in San Francisco, with the sun casting a golden glow over the city. Annya stood on the porch of the charming Victorian residence, admiring the view. The two-story building was nestled into a quiet corner of the Marina District. The light blue painted house featured white shuttered windows and an elegant staircase crafted from polished white wood, which was adorned with intricately carved banisters. The porch offered a view of a blossoming garden, filling the air with a delicate floral scent.

Annya pressed the doorbell. Kuruk Ending, Frida's husband, opened the door and greeted her. He was a tall, handsome man with sun-kissed blond hair and hazel eyes that twinkled with a warm smile. He was dressed casually in jeans and a t-shirt, but there was an air of refinement about him.

"Welcome, Annya," he said, shaking her hand. "I'm Kuruk. Please, come in."

He ushered her through a slender corridor with meticulously painted wood panels, which exuded an ornate elegance that was both beautiful and inviting. They entered a spacious living room with floral-patterned wallpaper, tall French windows, and opulent brocade curtains. Frida sat on a grand velvet chair close to the window, wrapped in a blanket, with a pot of tea and cookies resting on a polished mahogany coffee table beside her. Her bald head was a stark reminder of her recent assault, but delicate patches of new hair offered hope for recovery.

"Hello, Annya," she greeted softly. "It's so nice of you to come over. Please take a seat."

"Thank you," Annya replied, settling onto the generous coral velvet sofa.

"I'll leave you to chat." Kuruk offered a warm smile before departing the room.

"I see you've moved back in," Annya observed, more a statement than a question.

"Yes, we're back together," Frida affirmed, smiling. "We realized how much we need each other. Sometimes, a life crisis can help you see what's truly important. Can I get you some tea?"

"Yes, please."

Frida poured tea into an empty cup. Annya accepted it, along with a cookie. Their eyes met, sharing an unspoken understanding.

Annya ventured, "So, how have you been holding up?"

"I resigned from my position at Pleonexia," Frida explained. "It was a mistake to work there. I let my anger get the best of me. You know how sometimes victims become perpetrators themselves? I shouldn't have taken my frustration out on others, especially Rogério. It wasn't his fault. He's a good guy."

Annya raised her eyebrows. "Even after he kidnapped you?"

Frida smiled at her. "Well, we don't have any evidence that he was involved, right? His brother was the driving force. His little girl needed treatment, and he didn't know where to turn. No one should resort to crime to save their child, but I understand that his situation was complicated."

Annya gazed at her, attempting to grasp the situation. "Have you found peace of mind after the recent assault?" she asked.

Frida met her gaze. "I'm seeing a therapist, if that's what you mean. I'm grateful to be alive. I thought I was going to die. But honestly, the physical assault was easier to come to terms with than the professional assault I endured at SUEC. Ronaldo was fighting for his little girl. While his actions were wrong, I can understand his motives. Yet, the SUEC leaders who sabotaged my career walked away without consequences. Their actions set off this whole ordeal."

"When you were denied a promotion to chief position?"

Frida nodded. "With the explanation that I'm a self-serving monster who's only after power. I wanted a promotion. No man would be criticized for that. But I was destroyed by character assassination. My chair couldn't deny my outstanding productivity, which was beyond dispute. So, he portrayed me as an aggressive woman that nobody wanted to work with. After that, everyone thought it was okay to treat me poorly. It was hell."

Annya nodded. "I understand."

Frida glanced at her with a hint of amusement in her eyes. "I'm not sure you understand how much damage they've done. The leaders at SUEC are still at it, undermining and sidelining other women who threaten their egos. You know my husband works at SUEC too. Often, you're the last to know about new political ploys that affect you. Did you know that *your* department chair was trying to demote you, too? He wanted to promote Julius to ER chief, pushing you aside."

Annya looked at her in disbelief. "That can't be true." Her work was her identity.

Frida confirmed with a solemn nod. "It's not just about the title. It's what comes after that when people treat you like something's wrong with you. The pitying looks, the second-guessing of everything you say, your subordinates not following your lead. That's where the real dread lies."

"I haven't heard anything about this," Annya said, a touch of frustration in her voice.

"Well, here's the kicker. Julius turned down the offer," Frida revealed. "He said you're the most experienced physician in the ER division, maybe even the whole department. You save lives every day, and you deserve to be the chief. He even said that if he ever ended up as a patient in the ER, he'd want you to take care of him."

"Wow!" Annya was deeply moved. Julius hadn't said a word. "That is more than kind of him."

Annya had always been annoyed by Julius' lack of medical knowledge and his spoiled behavior. He was the son of one of the richest men in Silicon Valley, after all. But the last few days had shown her that he was a young man of extraordinary character.

Julius had saved her twice, once from an alleged intoxication and once from the machinations of her department chair. He had stood up for her, even when she wasn't there. He had told her chair that she deserved to be the ER chief, even though it meant that he would not get the promotion himself. She had misjudged and underestimated him. He was a decent and caring person with a strong sense of justice.

Frida interrupted Annya's thoughts. "Absolutely, the world needs more people like Julius. But the real challenge is addressing the problem of power-hungry and greedy leaders. Not just at SUEC, but at businesses like Pleonexia too."

Annya met Frida's gaze, curious about her thoughts. "What would you propose?"

Frida's voice grew firm. "There need to be personal consequences for leaders who exploit and destroy others for their own benefit. If we let them act without consequences, they'll keep doing it. We can't have a just culture if we allow unacceptable behavior to go unchecked."

"How would you ensure accountability?" Annya inquired.

Frida's response was thoughtful. "Well, we need more people like you, Julius, and Rogério."

Annya looked at her in disbelief. "The man who kidnapped you?"

Frida smiled faintly. "We discussed this before. We have no indication that Rogério was involved. He received an email from Pleonexia about the new foundation for children with cancer. Did you know whom he suggested as the CEO of the foundation?"

Annya shook her head.

Frida's smile broadened. "It's me. I'm the new CEO of the SUEC foundation for children with cancer."

Annya stared at her. What a scheme. That was how the brothers had won her over. Was this a good ending to her story?

"Congratulations!" she managed to say. She couldn't help but wonder if this was the fitting resolution to her story.

"Thank you!" Frida responded with a genuine smile.

Annya looked at Frida, trying to understand. Frida's revenge against SUEC, fueled by anger and frustration, sparked a chain of crimes. The twin brothers kidnapped her, they intercepted wrongful insurance denials, and Ronaldo stole from Pleonexia. But Frida and the twins redeemed themselves by creating a foundation for children with cancer. They took matters into their own hands. After all, aren't we all responsible for what happens around us and have the power to make a difference?

"How will you handle the new foundation?" Annya asked.

Frida's expression radiated a strong sense of purpose. "Due to the attention generated by the *New York Times* article, we received an additional five million dollars in donations from people across the country who donated their annual bonus payments as well. SUEC contributed another 5 million. So, our starting budget is now 50 million. My plan is to invest it thoughtfully, generating dividends that will sustain us for years to come. I intend to allocate 10 million to provide legal support for parents, 10 million for enhancing resources in the oncology clinic, and 20 million for research initiatives."

"That is quite a program." Annya was impressed. "It adds up to 40 million, but you have 50 million?"

Frida nodded. "You're absolutely right. We're investing the remaining 10 million in endowed professorships for emerging leaders chosen by the community. Parents and ward staff will vote for someone on the front lines who deserves a leadership role. This empowers the community to select their leaders based on merit, not political schemes. It's about giving the power back to the people, just like Julius did for you."

Annya's eyes sparkled with appreciation. "That's truly remarkable!"

"Yes, *that* brings me peace of mind," Frida replied with a warm smile.

The doorbell rang.

Annya rose from her seat. "Is someone else coming over? Maybe I should head out."

Frida smiled mischievously. "No need to worry. It's for Kuruk."

Annya looked at her cell phone. 3:30 p.m. If she wanted to change for the dinner with Angus, she had to get going.

"It was really nice to talk with you!" she said. "I'm glad things have taken a good turn for you."

"It was nice to talk with you as well," Frida said. "And it's reassuring to see capable women making strides at SUEC!"

As they shook hands, Annya felt a sense of camaraderie and connection that had blossomed between them. It was a feeling of shared understanding and the potential for positive change.

Annya went through the beautiful hallway to the door. Kuruk had just opened it.

In the frame stood Julius. His perfectly pressed white shirt, impeccably tailored trousers, and polished leather shoes a picture of sophistication.

He looked at Annya in surprise. "Hi, Annya. I didn't expect to see you here."

Meeting his gaze, Annya greeted him with a smile. "Same here. Did you get your car fixed?"

"Yes, fortunately, only the glass was broken. It was an easy fix. And Caramba returned. He flew back to his aviary in the hospital garden. The guards located him there and sealed up the gap in the mesh. So, now I can visit him again every day."

Annya looked at her colleague. She had learned so much about him in the last few days. It felt like she saw an entirely new person in front of her.

"I'm relieved that you got your parrot back," she said. "And I've also just learned that you stood up for me without mentioning a word."

Julius chuckled. "Ah, the perplexed chair, I see. Doesn't seem like he knows who's really running the show in the ER."

She felt bad that she hadn't told him about the twin lover. But Angus had. Everything had to happen at its designated time.

"I didn't know that you knew Kuruk?"

Frida's husband smiled. "Oh, we have regular virtual community gatherings via Zoom. They are named after islands. Today, we are meeting on the beautiful island of Cocoa, Maldives. Virtually, of course. Access is provided through a secure network to preserve everyone's privacy. I will show Julius how to join."

"Cocoa, Maldives?" Annya repeated, turning her gaze to Julius.

He shifted awkwardly from one foot to another. "I'd appreciate it if you didn't mention that to Angus."

"What if I work for the FBI as well?" Annya said playfully. Of course, she couldn't tell Julius that she was working for the CIA.

He looked at her nervously. "Well, if that is the case, I would appreciate if you wouldn't mention it either."

Annya looked at them, contemplating. She hadn't been officially assigned to this case, nor had she received any instructions to gather intelligence on it. Everything had to happen at its designated time.

"Well, it is the weekend, isn't it?" she said slowly. "I might need to share this information on Monday."

Julius nodded. "That sounds reasonable."

Annya's gaze shifted from Julius to Kuruk, her thoughts swirling. Had Julius been part of this scheme after all? The twin brothers, he, the parents, Kuruk, and ultimately Frida all joined into a common scheme to seek justice where the system had failed them.

Kuruk met her gaze with a subtle, knowing smile. He gave her a slight nod as if acknowledging a shared understanding and then waved her goodbye.

# - 43 -

# Annya

### The Date
### Saturday, October 15, 2033, 6:00 p.m.

Annya had been reluctant to go on another date with Angus. Their first two dates had been canceled due to unforeseen circumstances. How could two workaholics have a future? Wouldn't there always be something getting in their way?

But in the end, Angus had convinced her to give it another try. To make the evening a success, they had agreed on a few ground rules for their date. They would both commit to start the date punctually, a small gesture to show mutual respect to each other. Additionally, they had decided to put in the effort to look their best, leaving behind their work attire. And perhaps the most important rule was to power off their cell phones, preventing any calls, texts, or emails from intruding upon their time together. They were determined to make the most of this rare opportunity to simply be present with each other.

They had chosen a secluded spot away from the bustling city to enjoy each other's company. Luna Blu in Tiburon fit the bill perfectly with its intimate Italian charm set against the waterfront. As they walked through the restaurant and stepped onto the deck, they saw the San Francisco skyline looming in the distance. Its spires and towers were embraced by the afternoon fog like a blanket that put the stress of the day to sleep.

Heads turned as the waiter walked them to their table. Angus wore a finely tailored charcoal-gray suit, which was impeccably cut to fit his broad shoulders and lean physique. Beneath the jacket, he wore a crisp white dress shirt that accentuated his strong jawline. Annya had chosen her favorite navy blue dress, a sleek silk fabric that draped gracefully over her figure and complemented her fiery red hair.

As they sat at their table, they could see the sailboats gently swaying in the harbor in front of them, their sails catching the breeze. The sun was setting, casting a golden glow over the water. The warm light reflected off the sails, creating a shimmering effect. It was a truly magical sight.

The evening air was cool, and the waiter thoughtfully turned on the heaters on the deck. The gentle warmth wrapped around them, making them feel cozy and content. They ordered a bottle of wine and savored the moment, enjoying each other's company and the beauty of their surroundings.

Annya couldn't help but glance at Angus. It wasn't so much his looks. She felt comfortable and safe in his presence. She was drawn to his gentle smile and the way his brow furrowed in concentration as he perused the menu. Her eyes found their way to him without conscious effort.

Suddenly, Angus looked up, and their souls met. Annya felt a jolt of electricity course through her as they held each other's gaze.

He leaned in and whispered, "You look beautiful."

"Thank you," she whispered back, her smile blossoming.

The waiter approached to take their order.

Grilled zucchini. Cioppino times two.

The waiter nodded and left their table.

Annya and Angus couldn't take their eyes off each other, their smiles growing wider with each passing moment, deepening the connection between them. The atmosphere around them seemed charged as they both grappled with their feelings.

"I'm glad I came," she said, brushing her fire-red hair behind her ear.

"I had hoped you would say that," he responded with a content smile.

The initial awkwardness of meeting her colleague for a date slowly dissipated. Annya felt an unusual ease with Angus. He had unlocked a hidden part of her, one that had long been concealed beneath layers of reserve. She found herself opening up in ways she hadn't with anyone else, and it was both liberating and exhilarating. She shared her experiences about her late husband, a Russian spy who had tried to kill her, and how she had joined the company and tried to restart a new life as an emergency physician at SUEC.

Angus, in turn, spoke of his adventures traveling the world, the people he had met, and the lessons he had learned along the way. They continued to talk for hours, sharing stories and getting to know each other better.

The waiter brought the bill. As the night drew to a close, Annya and Angus looked at each other with disappointment that their time together had come to an end. They both rarely got to indulge in personal time like this. Annya, an emergency physician and undercover CIA agent, and Angus, an FBI director, constantly put their personal lives on hold in the name of duty, ensuring the safety of others.

As they leaned in close, Annya sighed. "We both chose these paths because we wanted to make a difference, but it can be exhausting."

Angus nodded. "The more responsibility you shoulder, the more they expect from you."

"It's not just about the long hours or missed personal moments," Anya continued. "It's also the emotional toll of knowing we can't save everyone but feeling responsible for trying."

Angus gently touched Annya's hand. "You're right. We can't save the world, but we can make a difference in the lives we touch. Maybe that's enough."

A sharp crack pierced the evening air, and a majestic bird soared into view. Its colorful form and wings glistened in the fading light, its tail plumage a canvas of ruby red, vivid yellow, hyacinth blue, and emerald green. It descended gracefully and alighted on the railing of the deck, right beside Angus and Annya's table.

They stared at the resplendent bird, which basked in the warm glow of the deck heaters. Its radiant plumage seemed to come alive, casting an enchanting spell over the scene.

"Caramba," the bird chirped melodiously. "Pistachio, please."

Angus jumped to his feet, his eyes darting around the serene surroundings. The presence of the parrot was perplexing. It seemed to have either escaped from captivity once more or had been released intentionally. Regardless, its owners, Julius, Rogério, or Rolando, had to be in close proximity.

They saw a seaplane a few hundred meters away, bobbing gently on the tranquil bay waters. Someone in the pilot's seat vigorously waved toward them. Was it Julius?

Annya waved back instinctively.

Julius let out a sharp whistle. The colorful parrot, responding to his call, gracefully took off and soared toward the waiting seaplane. With precision, the bird entered the open window, disappearing inside.

There was another passenger in the plane, a man with curled hair and a mustache.

Angus' fingers hastily powered on his phone, speed-dialing the FBI headquarters. "I've located the suspect in a seaplane at the Corinthian Yacht Club in Tiburon," he blurted out. "I don't believe seaplanes are permitted to take off from here. Can you track it?"

A rapid exchange of information took place over the phone.

Annya, watching Angus with concern, spoke up, "Thanks for the wonderful evening, Angus." She knew he was preoccupied and gently added, "I can see you're busy. I'll let myself out. It was truly a delightful night."

Annya got up from her seat.

"Just a moment," Angus said to the voice on the other end. He kept a hand over the phone's microphone and looked at Annya. "Annya, please wait," he asked.

"No worries. I understand." Annya gave him a nod.

Angus looked at her, hesitating for a moment. Then, he continued his phone conversation.

She turned around and left the restaurant.

The parking lot was across the street, bathed in the feeble glow of geriatric streetlamps. Annya made her way toward her car. She checked the time on her iPhone. 9:30 p.m. Time had flown by, and the sparsely occupied, dimly lit lot only contained a handful of vehicles. Her car stood alone under a looming tree. As she approached her vehicle, her thoughts drifted to Frida. Hopefully, she would heal from the trauma of her abduction.

Suddenly, a tapping sound, like approaching footsteps, echoed behind her. *Tap, tap, tap*—it drew nearer with each passing second, undeniably directed toward her. Annya's instincts surged into alert mode. In certain situations, mere seconds could determine life or death. The footsteps were now uncomfortably close, right behind her. Annya reacted swiftly, coming to an abrupt halt, and snapping her head backward with force, a self-defense maneuver ingrained in her during her CIA training.

But her pursuer was equally quick and agile, swiftly retreating. Annya lost her balance, stumbling backward. Her arms instinctively flailed backward to cushion the fall against the pavement, but someone intercepted her. She pivoted her elbows to fend off the intruder, but they elegantly sidestepped her efforts.

With a graceful twist, she found herself face-to-face with Angus. "Hello, Annya," he whispered. "I was wondering if you'd mind spending a little more time with me. Would that be alright?"

Annya couldn't help but smile warmly. "Angus, you might want to work on your stealth skills," she teased. "Following a woman in a dimly lit parking lot like this, especially one trained in self-defense, could have ended differently."

Angus chuckled. "No worries. I can keep up with strong women," he replied, flashing a playful grin. "I just wanted to let you know that I had an absolutely wonderful time tonight."

Annya couldn't suppress her smile. "There it is again," she said, her eyes sparkling. "I think you might need some serious lessons."

He leaned in and planted a soft kiss on her lips. Annya wrapped her arms around his neck and kissed him back. She closed her eyes, and they melted into a lingering kiss. The world around them seemed to blur as the perfect ending to a perfect night unfolded.

# ACKNOWLEDGMENTS

I would like to express my deepest gratitude to the people who played a role in bringing this novel to life.

To my colleagues, students, and friends who shared their thoughts on positive and negative experiences in the academic world, your insights were invaluable.

To my wonderful husband, Dr. Thomas Link, who was with me every step of the way, thank you for your unwavering support. Your insights and feedback on suspense-building techniques were essential to this book's success.

To the Pegasus Medical Writing Group at Stanford, thank you for your feedback on early drafts of the book. Your help in refining the plot and developing the characters was extremely helpful.

To Lauren Schoenthaler, thank you for your advice on the legal aspects of writing a detective story set in a medical setting.

To Elisabeth Daldrup, Berthold Schroeter, and Hendrik Daldrup, thank you for your feedback on the final draft of the book and for creating the book's website and connecting our team with readers. Hendrik, your dedication and hard work have been essential to the success of this project.

To my editor, Jen Boles, thank you for your exceptional work editing my novel. Your meticulous copy editing and suggestions were invaluable, while still preserving the original tone of the story.

To Kostya from GetCovers.com, thank you for designing the stunning cover art. Your creative vision and eye for detail have captured the mood and tone of the mystery perfectly.

And finally, to you, the reader, thank you for picking up this book. I hope that the experiences shared within its pages will give you the strength to face challenges in the academic world and stand up to any adversity you encounter, no matter how big or small. Your engagement with the themes of identity and ethics in medicine is important to me. If this story can change even one person's life for the better, then the long hours of writing it were worth it.

# ABOUT THE AUTHOR

Elisabeth Link, MD, is a Professor of Radiology at Stanford University and a member of the Pegasus Physician Writers at Stanford, a group of physicians who write creatively. She lives in San Francisco, California, with her husband Thomas Link, MD.

Dr. Link began writing creatively as a child to entertain her grandmother in Germany. Later, as a college student, she published reflections about life and experiences with her dog Bobby in local newsletters. After medical school, Dr. Link moved to the United States, where she found a supportive community of writers at the Pegasus Physician Writers group at Stanford. Her curiosity about human interactions and power dynamics in academic settings led her to write detective stories that capture readers' attention while also making them reflect on important themes such as identity and social justice.

Dr. Link is a passionate advocate for women in STEM (Science, Technology, Engineering, and Mathematics/Medicine). She is widely known for her powerful reflections and opinion pieces, such as "The Fermi Paradox in STEM - Where Are the Women Leaders?" (https://doi.org/10.1007/s11307-017-1124-4). Her novels feature strong female protagonists who conquer major obstacles in the academic world and inspire others—female, male, and non-binary—to stand up for themselves and face their own challenges

Dr. Link has received more than fifty honors and awards for her creative works over the past three decades, but the feedback from her students is most rewarding to her. One mentee wrote:

*"I'm aware that I cannot control the barriers that enter my life, but, like water, I will never be broken. Medicine is an intellectual journey, and I'm determined to reach my goal of becoming the best doctor my patients will ever encounter."*

# A NOTE FOR THE READER

Thank you for reading an authorized copy of this book. Monasteria Press LLC is an independent publisher, and we rely on the support of our readers to continue publishing new books. By purchasing our publications, you are directly supporting our authors and enabling us to continue doing what we love.

If you enjoyed this book, please consider leaving a review on Amazon, Barnes & Noble, Powell's, Goodreads, or Twitter. Reviews are essential for helping us to spread the word about great books and can make a real difference in an author's life. Our authors invest significant time, effort, and heart into their writing, and knowing that their words have had a positive impact can be a great source of encouragement. Additionally, your review can provide valuable feedback for both authors and other readers. Many readers rely on the opinions of their peers when deciding what to read, making reviews a powerful tool for spreading the word about great books.

Please keep in mind that other readers may appreciate the element of surprise, so please refrain from giving away the entire plot in your review.

Thank you for being part of our community! To explore more titles from Monasteria Press, please visit our website: monasteria-press.com. We look forward to welcoming you back soon!

The Monasteria Press Team

# BOOKS BY ELISABETH LINK

**Who Killed Nia Johnes?**
Elisabeth Link, MD
Monasteria Press 2023


Her lifeless body was found lying in her wrecked car, with a bullet hole in her head. Dr. Nia Johnes, a young researcher at Silicon Valley University of Evolutionary Computation (SUEC) had been murdered in cold blood. CIA Agent Dr. Annya Segond, SUEC's radiologist Dr. Lili Pham, and FBI Agent Terrel Wright believe her research work on infectious diseases could have been the reason for her murder. Before they could make anything out of the few leads they had on the case, another researcher at SUEC narrowly escapes a shooting attack. Are the unexplained infections plaguing the campus somehow connected? What are the unsettling research activities that the SUEC leaders would prefer to keep quiet? With an assassin on the loose and not knowing who to trust, Agent Wright, together with doctors Segond and Pham, must fight to save their lives and their careers as they race to prevent further deaths and to uncover the shocking truth behind who killed Nia Johnes.

Lovers of mystery murder novels won't get enough of Elisabeth Links' *Who Killed Nia Johnes?* With an intriguing plot, the author bases the storyline on a tale of scientists, medical research, a hitman, sleuths, betrayal, blackmail, deceit, and espionage. Amidst the whirlwind of pursuits and inquiries, Dr. Link skillfully incorporates the breathtaking scenery and architectural beauty of Northern California. There is suspense, thrills, and adventure.

Paperback ISBN: 978-1-958277-04-1
Hardback ISBN: 978-1-958277-00-3
eBook ISBN: 978-1-958277-03-4
Library of Congress Control Number (LCCN) 2022921262

# BOOKS BY ELISABETH LINK

**The Stolen Brain Chip**
Elisabeth Link, MD
Monasteria Press 2021

A fast-paced mystery novel with an educational twist. The story revolves around a fictional university in the hills above Redwood City, CA, known as Silicon Valley University of Evolutionary Computation (SUEC). Newly developed brain chips, designed to amplify cognitive abilities, are stolen. Thus begins a string of events that leaves fifteen people injured, five hospitalized, and four dead. Dr. Lili Pham, Dr. Annya Segond, FBI Agent Terrel Wright and FBI Agent Angus Weber start a race against time to rescue a young student from a ruthless killer, retrieve the brain chips and prevent a bomb explosion.

To find the killer before he strikes again, it will take more than traditional on-the-scene evidence. The clues about the murderer revolve around various types of bone fractures that characters in the novel suffer—pathological details that new medical students and radiologists often have a hard time remembering. Some of the fractures provide clues to the mysteries of who the killer is and who stole the brain chips. The book also includes x-ray images showing what those different fractures look like. This is a great read for anyone interested in medicine and medical education.

The novel has a strong female protagonist and conveys the concept that we are all heroes-in-waiting. The time will come when each one of us will get a chance to step up and be the hero.

Paperback ISBN 978-1-7372582-3-0
Hardback ISBN 978-1-7372582-5-4
eBook ISBN 978-1-7372582-4-7
Library of Congress Control Number (LCCN) 2021950975